Clowns and Cowboys
(A Miranda and Parker Mystery)
Mystery)
Book 3

Linsey Lanier

Edited by

Editing for You

Donna Rich

Gilly Wright
www.gillywright.com

ISBN: 194119107X
ISBN-13: 978-1-941191-07-1

CLOWNS AND COWBOYS

The popular Miranda Steele stories from Linsey Lanier continue in a new series!

Fulfilling your destiny…one killer at a time

When PI Miranda Steele gets a call from an old "friend" in Dallas, Texas and decides to take his case, her boss and husband Wade Parker is none too pleased. Especially when she insists he stay home due to his recent injuries. No way, Jose.
But when Southeastern sophisticated meets Southwestern country, tempers blaze hotter than Texas chili sauce, sending Miranda into turmoil. How can she solve this case with the clash between her past "friend" and her present husband raging? She needs to figure it out soon.
The murder of a circus clown is about to lead her to something not even Parker could have predicted.

THE MIRANDA'S RIGHTS
MYSTERY SERIES

Someone Else's Daughter
Delicious Torment
Forever Mine
Fire Dancer
Thin Ice

THE MIRANDA AND PARKER
MYSTERY SERIES

All Eyes on Me
Heart Wounds
Clowns and Cowboys
The Watcher
Zero Dark Chocolate
Trial by Fire
Smoke Screen
The Boy
Snakebit
Mind Bender
Roses from My Killer
The Stolen Girl
Vanishing Act
Predator
Retribution
Most Likely to Die
(more to come)

MAGGIE DELANEY POLICE THRILLER SERIES
Chicago Cop
Good Cop Bad Cop

THE PRASALA ROMANCES
The Crown Prince's Heart
The King's Love Song
The Count's Baby

For more information visit www.linseylanier.com

Linsey Lanier

"Death values a prince no more than a clown."
Miguel de Cervantes Saavedra

CHAPTER ONE

"I'll see what I can do."

In her cube at the Parker Agency where she was now a Level Three investigator, Miranda Steele hung up the phone and stared blankly at her computer. The text on the screen—data from the super boring worker's comp case she'd been piddling over—blurred before her eyes.

Soft typing and voices floated over the fabric-covered walls, but all she could hear was her heart pounding in her ears. She was shivering all over, like she was coming down with the flu.

But it wasn't the flu. It was that phone call.

Her old pal Yosemite Sam, as everyone used to call him on the work site, was in trouble. She hadn't seen him in, what? Ten or eleven years? Not since they'd been in Phoenix together. She smiled at the memory playing in her head. Cruising down a dusty Arizona highway with Sam on a pair of motorcycles.

He'd taught her how to ride.

Talk about a blast from the past.

Then her smile faded. Sam was in Texas now, outside of Dallas—where there had been a murder.

He needed her help.

Her mind buzzing, she tapped her fingers on the smooth gray surface of her desk. What in the world was she going to say to Parker?

She and her sexy husband had just come back from a case overseas and he'd wanted to take a break. He needed it, so she'd agreed. He'd been beaten up pretty bad and wasn't fully recovered yet.

But this call from Sam?

She couldn't ignore it. Even though she had a feeling Parker wasn't going to go for it. Well, she'd just have to face Parker head on.

Straightening her shoulders, she rose, picked up the notepad she'd scribbled some data on, and headed for her boss's corner office. Double time.

1

At the end of a row of cubes near the coffee maker, Miranda barreled around the corner—and nearly collided with someone who should have been watching where he was going.

She looked up and saw her buddy Dave Becker.

"Oh! Steele. I—I'm so sorry," Becker stammered in his typically nervous way. He'd had his big nose buried in the e-pad thingy he was carrying and hadn't been watching where he was going.

She took in his jeans and T-shirt and noticed his hair was growing over his ears. Plus his eyebrows looked bushier than she remembered. She realized she hadn't seen him in quite a while.

She pointed at his outfit. "Out of uniform today?"

Not that she relished the dress code herself or policed her coworkers. It just seemed odd for Becker not to be in the required suit and tie.

He blinked at her as if he'd just woken up. "I guess you haven't heard, what with you and the boss being out of town so much. I've moved to Digital Forensics. I've been working with Jenkins in the lab."

"Digital Forensics?"

"Yeah. You know. Cyberstalking, hacking, data recovery. We just closed a missing persons case tracking the guy's emails. He was alive, in a hotel down town. Not kidnapped, as his wife feared. Marriage is in trouble, though. He'd been emailing a hooker, seeing her on the side. Was at the hotel with her, if you get my drift."

"Yeah, I get it." The scumbag. But Miranda was impressed. She'd never thought of her old buddy Becker as a techno-nerd.

She waved a hand at the tablet. "You're really turning into a geek there, huh?"

He blushed shyly. "I think I've found my passion."

That was cool. Everybody needed a passion. But Becker seemed out of place by himself. "Where's Holloway?" The two used to be inseparable and were her first buds at the agency when she started.

"In the field."

So Holloway hadn't followed in his sidekick's geeky footsteps.

"With Wesson," he added staring at his screen.

"Wesson? Really?" Definitely not one of Miranda's favorite people. She wondered how Holloway had gotten teamed up with that bitch.

"Yeah. Oh, Joan wanted me to ask you something."

"O…kay." Miranda poked at the carpet with the toe of her shoe. She hadn't talked to her best friend in a long while and Fanuzzi was probably pissed about it.

"Let's see. What was it, again?" He stared down at his e-pad, gave something a swipe.

Yep, Becker was getting to be a real absentminded professor.

Something came to him and he brightened. "Oh, I remember. About the party."

She folded her arms defensively. "What party?"

His eyes grew round. "I wasn't supposed to tell you. Or maybe they decided it wasn't going to be a surprise. No, that's right. They couldn't make it a surprise since you and the boss are travelling so much nowadays."

She folded her arms tighter. "What the hell are you talking about, Becker?"

"Your anniversary. Joan wants to throw you a party. She wants to set a date for it and start planning. She wants you to call her."

"Anniversary?"

"Yeah. You know, wedding anniversary? Ours is coming up, too. Right around the corner. But we might postpone our celebration..." His voice drifted off as he stared at his pad again.

Miranda blinked at him.

Had it really been a year since her friend and Becker had tied the knot? Since she'd walked down the aisle in that awful gown? And...wait. Her friends wanted to throw a party? Hadn't the wedding itself been enough?

"Uh, it's not necessary. I'm sure Parker will have something planned."

The corners of Becker's lips turned down and he suddenly looked like a lost puppy. "Really? Joan is going to be so disappointed."

Oh, good grief.

When she'd first met Fanuzzi—Miranda couldn't shake the habit of calling her by her maiden name—they'd been on a road crew together. Joan Fanuzzi was the Dump Person and had directed the heavy machinery. She was one tough broad. The last thing Miranda had expected was for Fanuzzi to drop the crew, go into catering, and live for putting together fancy parties.

But she couldn't disappoint the woman. Fanuzzi had been loyal to her when she didn't deserve it. Besides Miranda wasn't good at making friends and didn't have many. She didn't want to lose her best one.

"Okay. Tell her to call me sometime."

"How about now?"

Miranda curled a lip. Since when did Becker get so pushy?

She glanced down at the pad in her hand. The paper one. Not possible. Sam needed her help. "Can't right now, I'm on my way to see Parker."

Becker's face faded from a scowl into that schoolboy awe he used to wear when they were in training whenever she'd mentioned the top investigator he fairly worshiped. "Got another case?"

Couldn't talk about this one. "Maybe. We'll see."

And she stepped around him, leaving him staring at his tablet for an answer.

CHAPTER TWO

Miranda found Parker's door ajar and knocked on it gently.

"Come in," he said from within.

Gathering her nerves, she stepped into the big corner office with a smile plastered on her face. With its tall windows, its glossy glass furnishings, its sedate blue-and-gray tones Parker's work domain both soothed and intimidated clients at the same time.

Kind of like she felt right now.

She caught the scent of coffee and saw he had his classy gold monogrammed mug on his desk. He had on a deep charcoal silk suit and a gray-blue tie that would have gone well with his eyes. If it weren't for the streak of purplish red under one of them.

His face was still heart-stopping enough to kill for, even with the mark. And the thought of the hard muscled body beneath that fancy suit made her stomach quiver. That and the knowledge that he loved her. She'd never get used to it. Never get over her surprise at that simple fact.

And she loved him right back.

With not one of his styled salt-and-pepper hairs out of place, he focused on his computer screen, though he knew she was there. He could always sense her, just the way she could him.

Still she cleared her throat to draw his attention. "Got a minute?"

He turned his gaze toward her, fixed her with those wonderful, sexy eyes. "I always have time for you, my love." His voice was low and throaty and laced with that wealthy, sophisticated Southern accent that was unique to him.

Enough to make any woman drool.

"I need to talk to you about something."

His expression grew serious. "Of course."

She took a seat in one of the cushy pale blue guest chairs and tapped a pen on her notepad. How was she going to say this?

Carefully, she decided.

"I, uh, just got a call from a friend."

4

His brow wrinkled and he suppressed a wince. Facial movements still hurt. "A friend?"

"Someone I knew a bunch of years ago. We used to work together." No need to tell him any more than that. Still she could see the curiosity on his face. She'd always told him she had no friends before she came to Atlanta. That was basically true.

"What did your friend want?"

She shifted her weight in her chair. "There's been a murder. The local cops think it was natural causes."

"And it wasn't?"

"My friend thinks somebody killed this guy."

Parker sat back in his chair. "I see."

"And so, we've got another case." She gave him a pert grin.

Parker put a finger against the lip that was no longer swollen and studied his wife. Her dark hair was full and wild as usual, and he couldn't keep from imagining the feel of it in his hands.

It had been too long since he had been able to make love to her.

She had on a lightweight tweed ensemble in one of the dark shades she preferred, with form-fitting slacks and a belted jacket that hugged her narrow waist. He eyed her lean, fit body, now almost fully recovered from injuries she'd suffered several months ago. Desire grew inside him as he watched her cross her legs this way and that.

Her anxiety, whatever its cause, amused him. She wasn't the anxious type. He knew her. Even better now. When he looked at Miranda Steele he saw even more of what he'd always seen in her. Unstoppable strength, raw determination, amazing courage. She'd saved his life with those qualities.

It pleased him that she wore his mother's sapphire-and-diamond ring along with its match. Her wedding ring. Though she refused to wear it on assignments for fear of losing it. It pleased him, too, that she worried about losing it.

And this past week, after his own injuries, she'd been taking care of him, mothering him, showing more of a domestic side than he knew she possessed.

He wanted her now, just as he had at so many other impractical times. He loved her with all his being. But he also noted she had slid her pen behind her ear and was twisting her rings around her finger. A gesture that told him she was hiding something. It wasn't difficult to deduce what it was.

"What's your friend's name?" he said as if making idle conversation.

Miranda pursed her lips back and forth and looked down at her hands. She stopped twisting her rings and pulled her pen from behind her ear. Why had she thought for even a minute she could keep this from Parker? He'd seen right through her.

"Sam," she told him.

"Sam is short for Samantha, I presume?" There was so much snide irony in his tone, the air was instantly thick with it.

Miranda rolled her eyes. "Okay, smartie. It's a guy."

His brows rose. "Oh, really?"

What an actor. He'd known that as soon as she mentioned him. She caved. "His name's Sam Keegan. Like I said, we worked together back in Phoenix some years ago. He wants my help. There's been a murder."

Idly Parker opened a folder on his desk, scanned its contents. "Has he been arrested?" Another snide remark, since she'd just told him the police thought the guy died from natural causes.

"No…the vic was Sam's best friend. His name was…" She consulted her notes. "Tupper Magnuson. He was a clown."

Eyes still on the folder Parker frowned. "Not a very respectful way to speak of the dead."

"No. A real clown. You know, white face, floppy shoes? Sam's in the circus now."

He closed the file and looked up at her. "Interesting. Where?"

"Texas. East side of Dallas." Not her favorite place in the world, but that didn't matter. She waved her notepad. "I've got to go help him, Parker. He's an old pal."

Parker leaned back in his chair and rocked a bit, his sexy gray eyes narrowing into analytical mode. "Why did he call you?"

She let out a scoff. "He saw me on TV when we were in Vegas."

"Did he?"

Was that so hard to believe? "Maybe he thinks I'm a damn good detective."

"I know you're a damn good detective. But are you sure that's what he really wants?"

She'd known she was going to have trouble, but she didn't think he'd take this angle. "What are you saying? You think he made the case up? Why would he do that?"

"Any number of reasons. How long has it been since you saw him?"

"About ten years."

"And have you heard from him at all during the intervening time?"

She shook her head.

He nodded as if he'd won an argument. "Have you done a background check on him?"

"A background check?" she sputtered as she shot to her feet.

"It's not unusual to run one on a potential client you barely know."

She tromped to the window and stuffed her hands under her arms. She hated to admit it, but Parker had a point. She hardly knew Sam any more, no matter how sharp her memory of him was.

He was a wild guy when they'd worked together. A real risk-taker. And a drifter like she'd been. Sounded like he still was. This could be…some kind of ruse. Hell, if his friend was murdered, he might be the killer and he might just want her to find a way to get him off when the police figured it out. No, that wasn't Sam.

Still, a background check might not be a bad idea.

Calmer now, she turned around to face her husband. "Okay. I'll run him. And if he checks out, I'll go to Texas."

Now it was Parker's turn to jump to his feet, though there was a grimace of pain on his handsome face as well as a good splash of shock. She saw him almost grab his side. Those bruised ribs of his were a bitch.

"You? As in alone?"

"Of course." She waved her notebook at him. "You can't go. You're still convalescing. I'll take some vacation time. Do it on my own time. Pro bono, if I have to." Sam probably couldn't afford a third of their hefty fee.

Parker let out a dark, wry laugh. "This venture is a partnership, Miranda."

"Right, like our marriage. We take care of each other, watch each other's back. And if one of us isn't up to a job, the other fills in and takes up the slack." She stepped to him, about to give him a quick kiss on the lips.

Before she could, he grabbed her arms and held her in a firm grip. "We're Parker and Steele Consulting. Either we both go or neither of us does." His eyes flashed cold.

She'd seen him angry plenty of times, but she'd never seen quite that hard steel look in them before. She met his gaze and wrestled with the anger rupturing inside her.

Now she had to choose between helping Sam and risking Parker getting reinjured? What did he think he was doing? Why was he making this so hard? Or didn't he think she could handle a case by herself? That thought infuriated her even more.

She considered having it out with him right here in his office during business hours. But that would only make it worse. And waste time. Instead, she decided to make a deal.

She pulled out of his grip. "Okay, Parker. If you want to put your health at risk, I can't stop you. So how about this? We go, but if I think you're overdoing it, you have to go back to the hotel and rest."

He drew in a slow breath, his expression softening. "And if I refuse to go?"

With a smug grin, she shrugged. "You can't refuse. It's my turn to be in charge."

His eyes almost twinkled as a corner of his lip turned up just a bit. "We'll see." He settled back into his chair, pretending not to feel any pain.

He played with the folder again, picked up a pen, put it back down. He'd almost succeeded in making her scream with frustration when at last he nodded slowly. "Very well, Miranda. We'll both go to Dallas."

She let out a breath. "You won't be sorry. Sam's a good guy."

"I'm sure he's a fine, upstanding citizen." He turned back to face the computer screen. "And since you're in charge, you can book the reservations."

That made her blink. "Oh, really?"

Now he gave her a full smile. A smile dripping with quiet victory. "After you get me the results of that background check."

CHAPTER THREE

It took the rest of the afternoon to get the background results, and when Sam's record came back clean, Miranda had to work with Gen to book the hotel and plane tickets.

What a joy that was.

Parker's daughter had softened a lot toward her after everything they'd all been through, but working with Gen was still about as much fun as pouring acid over your own head.

And Parker wasn't impressed at all with Sam's background.

It was a lot like hers had been when she first met Parker. Bouncing around from job to job, a night in jail here and there after a bar fight. Like her, he was the antsy, restless type. He'd joined Under the Big Top, Inc. three years ago, and the travels of his new employer now satisfied his wanderlust, she supposed, so there'd been a semblance of stability since then.

But a deal was a deal, so they went home, had some dinner, and Parker reluctantly packed a suitcase before they headed off to the airport.

The flight was non-stop, a little over two hours, and they landed in Dallas Fort Worth International just before 11 PM.

Miranda had tried to catch some shuteye on the plane, but it hadn't worked out. Her mind had been too consumed with how to keep Parker from overdoing it and how to keep him from finding out...well, that didn't really matter now. Did it?

As they stepped off the ramp and into the boarding area, Miranda thought Parker looked weary. They'd get a good night's sleep at the hotel and get started on the investigation in the morning, she decided.

About to tell him the plan, she took a step toward the exit—and stopped dead in her tracks.

Her gaze swept over the form leaning casually against the short wall separating the waiting area from the corridor.

Thick blond waves under a mocha colored Stetson. Rugged blue work shirt, rolled up at the sleeves. Worn jeans tight enough to reveal equally rugged muscles. Cowboy boots and a pair of teasing, forest green eyes. He looked good. Aged a bit, but so had she.

Those eyes drank her in, one lip turned up in the smile of a genuine flirt. "Hey, babe," he crooned in that familiar southwestern accent.

Miranda didn't know what to think. She'd left him a text message saying when they were coming and the flight number, but she hadn't expected him to be here.

She sauntered over to him. "Well, well, well. If it isn't ole Yosemite Sam."

"If it isn't ole Kick-Ass Steele." Before she could stop him, he took her in his arms, spun her around, and planted a kiss on her lips that took her breath.

Mostly because it was so unexpected.

"Put me down before I have to kick *your* ass," she laughed.

"Yes, ma'am." He did so, took off his cowboy hat and made a low bow as he tucked the Stetson under his arm.

He might have recently joined the circus, but he'd always been a performer.

Miranda glanced back at Parker.

He stood quietly observing in investigator mode, a look of strained amusement on his face. He was trying to seem pleasant and unperturbed, but she could tell he wasn't happy at all with this greeting.

She pretended to straighten her hair. "Uh, Sam. This is Wade Parker. He's my partner."

"Partner?" Sam said in his lazy drawl.

"We consult together. We'll both be working your case." They'd made a deal not to tell clients they were a married couple and she didn't intend to change that now. She was an investigator in her own right and didn't need to ride on Parker's coattails.

"I didn't realize I was getting a two-for-one deal." Sam chuckled.

"He's also my boss. Owns the agency where I work."

"I'm impressed." Sam stretched out a hand. "Glad to meet you, Mr. Parker."

"The pleasure is all mine," Parker said in a rich, aristocratic southeastern tone that perfectly hid his sarcasm from anyone but Miranda's ears. "I hope we'll be able to bring you some resolution very soon."

Yeah, the sooner the better as far as Parker was concerned, she thought as she watched the men eye each other like two bulls at a rodeo sizing up the competition.

"Well," Sam grinned. "I'm your ride. Had to park in the back forty, so it'll be a ways."

Parker shot her a quick *didn't-you-book-a-rental-car?* look.

She shrugged in reply. "Can't turn down the local hospitality, can we?"

"Of course not." Parker forced another smile for Sam. "Then we'd better get going."

9

CHAPTER FOUR

Back forty was right.

Before they got outside they had to plod through what seemed like acres of shiny corridors filled with ads, signs welcoming them to the Lone Star State, and souvenir shops flaunting embossed leather boots and western ties and cattle figurines. Then they had to take a shuttle to the far parking lot.

By the time they reached Sam's vehicle, which turned out to be a beat-up, cherry red pickup truck with a rusty grill, Miranda was worried about Parker's condition. But she thought it would only make things worse if she said anything in front of their new client.

After Sam put the luggage in the back of the bed, the three of them piled into the front seat with Miranda in the middle.

Sam took off and they bumped along TX-161, enduring the pickup's poor shocks. The brightly lit, steel-and-glass city loomed ahead of them, while miles of prairie stretched into the night on either side.

Along with decent shocks, the truck lacked an A/C so they had to ride with the windows down. The country air blowing through her hair brought back memories. As Miranda recalled, Texas was a lot like Atlanta. Only bigger, flatter, hotter, and more permeated with the scent of cow.

Dallas, she knew, had started out as a cattle town, had turned into a rail town, and finally into a tech town. The place was now home to the corporate headquarters of a boatload of technology and telecom companies.

But her memories of the place weren't so flashy.

About five years ago she'd made her way back out west when she'd heard of a job on an oil rig outside Denton. The work had been hard and the harassment from the male coworkers had been brutal. She'd had to put a few of them in their place with the Maui Thai moves she'd worked up over the years.

She'd never really liked it here. Less now that she knew this was where Leon had picked up her scent so to speak—despite the bovine odor in the air. She didn't want to think about him.

She glanced over at Parker.

His posture erect, he stared out the windshield wearing a stoic look. His jaw was tight. He had to be in pain. She could almost feel it herself. Or maybe that was her conscience. She should have fought harder to come here by herself. But as much as she hated that he was suffering, deep down she was glad he was here.

She didn't want to be alone with Sam Keegan.

She took a deep breath and broke the awkward silence. Time to get down to business. "So, Sam. Tell us about your friend, Tupper Magnuson."

Hands on the wheel, Sam's face went tender. "Good old Tup. I'm really going to miss him."

"How long have you known him?"

"Since we were kids, really."

"That long?"

"We went to grammar school together." Sam shook his head. "That Tupper. What a card. He was the class clown. You know, always joking around, making all the kids laugh, getting them in trouble? But he always manned up and took the blame when the teacher came down on somebody else."

"Like you?"

He nodded. "A bunch of times. And not just when it was his fault. He was a real friend."

Sounded like a standup guy. "Guess it wasn't much of a stretch for him to become a real clown as an adult."

"He was a natural. His family moved and I lost touch with him after the sixth grade."

"And you met up with him again after you joined Under the Big Top?"

"Close. A little over three years ago The Big Top came to Phoenix and I heard they were looking for new acts. Thought I'd try out as a lark. Didn't expect anything to happen. But when I auditioned, there was ole Tup. We didn't even recognize each other at first." He laughed softly and wiped a finger under his nose.

"What happened?"

"Somebody watching the auditions told him my name. He came over and we squinted at each other for a few minutes, scratched our heads. Then it dawned on us and we figured out who we were. After that it was all hugs and backslaps. To this day, I think he was the reason I got hired. He must have put in a good word for me."

Interesting. Miranda glanced over at Parker. He was silent but taking it all in.

"So what was it like working with him?" she asked.

"Oh, great. We weren't in the same act, of course."

"What is your act, anyway?" Miranda felt Parker twist around at the way the words had come out. "I mean, you didn't tell me on the phone what you do in the circus."

A big sly smile spread over Sam's face. "I ride a motorcycle."

"That's a circus act?" She always thought motorcycles were just for fun.

He chuckled. "Me and six other guys ride around in a big, round steel cage."

Miranda sat up, her blood surging with a sudden rush of excitement. "Really? Upside down and everything?"

"Uh huh. And colored lights are flashing and the music's going. It's pretty dramatic."

"Sounds like it. Very cool."

He grinned with modesty. "Tup taught me how to work the crowd. He gave me a lot of tips when I first started." His voice grew soft. "But he was always friendly to everybody. Everyone in the show loved him. The audience, too. Especially the kids. Tup used to visit the local children's hospitals wherever we were and did a modified version of his act. You know, magic tricks? Pulling balloons or paper flowers out of his jacket. The kids adored him."

Sam was quiet for a long while and Miranda thought she caught the glisten of tears in his eyes.

"I just don't know why anybody would want to kill him."

"That's what we're here to find out."

He nodded, swiped a finger under his nose again. "Do you want me to take you straight to the hotel? Or would you...?" He glanced at the clock on the dash that amazingly wasn't broken. "Jeez, it's awful late."

Yeah, it was. And Parker was shifting in discomfort beside her. "I think we'd better turn in and get started in the morning."

"Sure thing. I just thought..."

"What?"

"Maybe you'd like to see Tup's trailer. It's where he...where it happened."

"He was killed in his own place?" Sam hadn't given her a lot of details on the phone.

Grimly Sam nodded.

Miranda turned to Parker. "You up for that?"

He replied with a stiff nod. "The sooner we get started the better."

And the sooner they could finish and leave. She was with Parker on that one, but she wished he'd get some rest first. It was supposed to be her call whether he went to the hotel to rest or not, but it probably wasn't a good idea to mention that in front of Sam.

Parker leaned forward and peered around her. "Mr. Keegan, are you sure the police don't have the residence cordoned off?"

"Please, call me Sam. No. They think it was natural causes right now."

So they wouldn't have used the yellow tape. Pretty quick decision, though.

Parker gave him a short nod. "Then we shouldn't have any trouble gaining access."

CHAPTER FIVE

Sam drove them down I-30 and through the city. Traffic was light, except for the eighteen wheelers and the occasional cluster of late-night revelers, and after another half-hour, they turned onto a narrow dirt road about a mile or two past the Cotton Bowl stadium.

Miranda peered out the window at a large grassy area filled with campers and trailers parked in long rows six or seven deep. In the distance she could make out the shape of the big tent where the performances went on.

So this was where circus folk lived.

Sam's truck rattled down the path until they reached a nice looking Winnebago nearer the tent. He pulled along the side of the road and stopped.

Miranda squinted at the shiny white vehicle under a nearby light. "That it?"

"Yep. Tup rated a nice RV since he's a headliner. A few of the other top performers have them as well." He gestured to the various sized mobile homes scattered around the lot. "The rest of us are in the rattier ones down the way." He made a gesture indicating the space farther back.

Floodlights twinkled in nearby trees. Lights came from the windows of a few of the trailers, but no one was outside. Everything seemed still as a morgue. No doubt they were all mourning the loss of a fellow performer.

Sam got out of the truck while Parker opened the passenger door and helped Miranda down. She made sure she didn't put her weight on him, but she wasn't going to refuse the gallant gesture in front of the client. Especially another male. Especially this male. Too much raw testosterone floating around in the air.

Sam headed toward a small hand-built set of steps in front of the RV door and reached into his pocket. "I've got a key. Tup always let me make myself at home here."

Just as he put a boot on the first stair, Parker blocked him with an arm. "Don't, Sam."

Sam squinted at him, as if he were being challenged. "What's the matter?"

Miranda wanted to know, too.

She watched Parker pull two thin pairs of flesh-colored plastic gloves out of his coat pocket. How come he was always so well prepared? He handed one to her. "In case the police aren't finished here."

"I see," Sam said thoughtfully. "Guess you do know your business."

"Yes, we do." Parker slipped on the gloves, took the key from Sam as if he were their real estate agent turning over the property and trotted up the steps.

Miranda didn't see a wince on his face, but she knew he was holding it in.

He unlocked the door and switched on a light.

She followed him inside while Sam trailed behind her.

As soon as she crossed the threshold Miranda felt her clothes start to fill with sweat. The A/C had been cut off and the place was downright sweltering. It smelled relatively clean, except for the lingering odor of recent death.

But they had a job to do. She looked around.

It was a nice, cozy place. The typical cramped living quarters of a house on wheels. Tiny kitchen, small stove and fridge, probably propane, a fold out dining table. Living room with a couch that doubled as a bed, teeny bathroom in the back. But everything looked new.

"Tup just got this place about a month ago." Sam explained. "His old RV was pretty nice, but the owner thought he deserved an upgrade."

Miranda nodded her acknowledgment and stepped across the living room to the bathroom. She opened the door and peeked inside. Small shower and sink. Relatively clean linoleum floor. Linens, soap, after shave. Typical guy's bath. She closed the door and only needed two steps to be back in the main area.

The décor here was a blend of cowboy rustic and modern, nothing too expensive. Faux wood paneling and faux wood flooring. A big screen TV on the back wall. Under it stood a narrow credenza holding video equipment and some books. Paperback Westerns and some hard covers. She read a few of the titles. Biotechnology, Genetics, Cloning. That was weird.

"Was Magnuson into science?"

Planted between the small living room and the kitchen, Sam shrugged. "He was into a lot of things." His voice had a faraway sound to it.

Miranda eyed the navy blue velour couch in the middle of the room. It looked almost new. Except for a dark stain in the middle of it she'd seen when she'd passed it. She had a pretty good idea what that was. It was what Sam was gazing at now.

Pretending not to notice the couch, Parker opened cupboards in the kitchen. "You say this was where your friend expired?"

"Expired? Oh, yes. I found him right there on the couch last night." Staring at the piece of furniture, Sam let out a low guttural moan.

Miranda took a step toward him. "Are you all right, Sam?"

"It's just that…when we walked in here just now…just for minute I was thinking, 'Tup's probably in the john.'" He gave a short, painful laugh. "I still can't believe he's really gone. How could somebody do this to him?" He sank down into a nearby chair and put his head in his hands.

Miranda wanted to give him a comforting hug. "We'll find out who did this," she told him. And she meant it.

Then she looked up and saw Parker had paused in his search, a cabinet door open in his hand. He gave her a long, steady look. Did he think Sam was about to confess something? Or had he decided the police were right about the natural causes?

When Sam didn't say anything else, Miranda decided to prod a little. "What time did you find Tupper?"

"Last night about ten. We finished the evening performance around nine and we were going to go out for pizza together. One of the guys in my troupe, Danny, was driving. We waited for Tup in Danny's trailer half an hour. When he didn't show, I came over here to see what was up. And there he was…Oh, God."

"What did you do?"

Sam raised his gaze to the ceiling. "I was so stupid. I told him I was hungry and to quit playing possum. We always kidded around with each other. He was such a practical joker. I—I thought he'd open his eyes and laugh at me. But he didn't move. I went over to him, gave him a shake. He didn't respond. I thought, wow. He's really getting me good this time. And then I—I smelled that awful smell."

The smell that had made the stain on the cushion.

"I knew something awful had happened. I pulled out my cell and called 911. They took forever to get here. The whole time I waited, I tried to revive him. I slapped at his wrists, his face. Nothing." Sam stared off into space. "Then I heard the siren and all of a sudden the room was filled with EMTs and police. They questioned me, took a statement. I asked what had happened, and one of the cops told me he'd probably had a heart attack. They found blood pressure meds in one of the cabinets. I didn't even know he was taking any."

Miranda wondered if cops usually gave out information like that when they didn't suspect foul play. She didn't have much experience with natural cause deaths.

Parker lifted a prescription bottle from a cabinet. "Diovan. A rather high dosage." He put it back and came around the counter to examine the stain on the couch.

His face grew as grim as the sinking sensation danced in Miranda's stomach. She knew they were looking at the stain from the bodily fluid the deceased had voided upon death.

Parker scanned the couch, lifted one of the cushions. "Why do you think the police are wrong?"

Sam looked up, his green eyes teary and dazed. "There was an empty wineglass on the table." He gestured at the piece of furniture. "I think it had something in it. I—what are you doing there?"

"Our jobs," Parker said coolly. "You think your friend was poisoned?"

"I do."

Miranda grabbed the cushion on the other end and dug her fingers into the creases, just as Parker was doing at the other end. When they met in the middle they'd come up with fifty-five cents in change between them but no evidence of any foul play.

She dropped the coins on the low coffee table that stood in front of the couch and blew out a breath. They needed better equipment if they were going to find anything. If there was anything to be found.

Then something caught her eye.

On the shelf under the coffee table sat another book. It wasn't like the others. Gold leaf edging and a thick cover. She pulled it out and held it up. The cover was made to look like cattle hide, embossed with a cowboy hat and a lasso in the middle.

Parker replaced the last cushion and studied it. "Photo album?"

"Guess that's what it is."

"Oh, yeah. That." Sam's tone was surly, and his lip curled in a smirk as he gestured at the book.

"What do you know about this?" Miranda asked him.

"Just open it."

She did.

Photos—in bright, bold color. First one, a clown in front of a tent holding a bunch of balloons. His head was topped with a large wig of bright blue curls. His outlandish outfit was yellow-and-green striped with big red buttons down the front. His hands were covered with big-fingered white gloves and his face was painted in the happy clown expression.

Next photo, the clown was handing out balloons to some kids. Next one, looked like he was doing a dance and making the kids burst out in giggles.

"So this is Tupper?" Miranda asked.

Sam nodded his face going tender. "That's him. Or was."

She turned the page.

First photo here was a beautiful young woman in a sparkly teal costume standing in a dramatic pose under a spotlight, a strand of silky white fabric in each hand. Next photo, she was in the air, both legs gracefully outstretched in a nasty split, each ankle wrapped in the white fabric. You could see the sheen of her teal-painted toenails.

Next shot, she was suspended from a hoop, hands and feet in the air. *Wow.*

Finally, she was on the ground, taking a bow. Her long blond hair, pulled back in a ponytail, draped nearly to the floor. Her dark eyes had a mysterious, sensual look and she wore a lot of stage makeup, but underneath the powder Miranda could tell she had a natural beauty.

In fact, she was gorgeous.

"Who's this?"

"That...is Layla." Sam said it like it was the name of a disease. "She gave Tup that book."

"Aerial performer?"

"Aerial *silk* acrobat. One of the best I've seen."

Miranda turned another page. Here were several shots of the pair out of makeup and costume, doing the typical things couples do together. A boat ride, a walk in the park, bicycling down a winding path.

She studied Magnuson's features. He seemed to be in his mid-thirties, about Sam's age, an average looking man with an average build. Short brown hair, brown eyes. Nice, apple-cheeked smile.

Layla was just as lovely as her performance photos. She wore her long blond hair in a braid down her back, and jeans and nice tops over a lean, well-formed body. She had to be in shape if she swung through the air with the greatest of ease regularly. She seemed young. Early twenties maybe.

Didn't it take years to become good at a flying act? Maybe she started young.

If Miranda was reading the smiles and looks they gave each other in the photos right, the pair was very much in love. "You don't like Layla?"

Sam chewed on his cheek awhile, as if he were putting his thoughts together. Then he strolled over to the countertop that separated the kitchen from living room.

He folded his arms and leaned against it. "Layla came to the Big Top about six months ago. Most folks in the circus know about other performers in other troupes. Nobody had heard of her or knew where she came from. She said she was from Bulgaria. She's got an accent and all. And then, just a few weeks after she's here, the boss makes her a headliner. Everyone was—well, stunned."

"Professional jealousy?"

"Sure. You work your butt off to get to the top of your game and some nobody comes along and steals it out from under you."

She studied his face a long moment. He didn't sound like he had any resentment. But Sam probably didn't think of an aerial artist as competition.

"Sounds like the other performers disliked her," she said.

Sam shrugged. "Not everybody. She had a way of charming people."

Miranda looked down at the photo book. "Like Tupper?"

Sam snorted another dry smirk. "I thought so. They hit it off right away. Tup was totally smitten. I thought she was using him. Thought maybe she'd gotten him to put in a word for her with management and that's how she got to be the headliner, but Tup swore to me he hadn't. We had a couple go-rounds about her. He'd never listen to me." He gazed blankly out the window and ran a hand over his face. "Look where that got him."

Miranda shot Parker a look of surprise. "You think Layla has something to do with Tupper Magnuson's death?"

Sam shoved his hands into his back pockets and began to pace the small floor with agitated steps. "I don't know. She was supposed to go with us to the pizza place last night."

Miranda's ears perked up. "Okay."

"It wasn't settled. She and Tupper had been at odds with each other the past few days."

"Over what?"

He shrugged. "Tupper didn't say. I didn't think it was anything big. Just a little lover's spat." He avoided her gaze as he spoke.

"I see."

"Anyway, Tup told me he'd asked her to join us, but she didn't say yes or no. He was going to wait for her here and if she didn't show, he'd meet us at Danny's. When I got here, she wasn't inside. I guessed she was still mad at him. After the police questioned me, I went over to her trailer."

"And?" Parker asked, foreboding in his tone.

"I knocked and knocked. She didn't answer. She wasn't in there."

Miranda looked at Parker. "Maybe she went out to dinner with friends."

"Like I said, she didn't have many friends in the show."

"Does she have any friends or family in Dallas?" Parker wanted to know.

Sam frowned, looking confused. "Don't rightly know that."

If she was pissed at her boyfriend she probably treated herself to a girl's night out. "Didn't she show up for the show tonight?"

"We had an off day today. Good thing, since nobody's felt like putting on a performance with Tupper...gone." He rubbed a hand over his face. "I moped around in my trailer most of the day myself. I checked her place again before I came to pick ya'll up. She's still not there."

If she had the day off she might still be in town. Maybe she went home with someone. She might not even know her fiancé was dead. Or...she could be in trouble.

They could check around for her. Stop by a few nearby watering holes or hotels.

"What's the young woman's last name?" Parker asked, thinking along the same lines.

Sam stared at him a moment, blinked hard. "She just went by Layla. Tupper never told me what her last name was."

Miranda thought they should check it out themselves.

Sam took them over to Layla's trailer, and they waited while he knocked on the door several times. There was still no answer.

Miranda tried peering through a window, but it was too dark to see anything. Deciding they'd try again in the morning, she and Parker headed back to the old red truck.

Sam thought of a few convenience stores and bars Layla might have gone to if she'd gone into town, places the performers frequented. Most spots where Tupper used to take her were closed, he said.

After making her way past several mechanical bulls, fighting through three crowds of raucous line dancers, and shouting over the loud country music and sing-a-longs to show Layla's picture to a slew of different bartenders, none of whom recognized her, Miranda was beat.

She told Sam to drop them off at the hotel and said good night to their new client.

CHAPTER SIX

When Miranda stepped inside the suite she had booked for them, she let out a long, low sigh. The rooms were quiet, smelled clean and the air was deliciously cool.

She looked around.

The living room and bedroom part was combined this time, due to the budget constraints Gen had insisted on and Miranda had agreed to. There was a large bed with a fancy embossed gold spread, a shiny mahogany desk and chair near a window. Through the glass you could see the glorious splash of colored lights—the Dallas skyline, with its sixty-story-plus bank buildings and the ball-shaped observation deck of a nearby hotel.

Two overstuffed guest chairs matching the bedspread sat against the far wall, in front of them a glass-topped coffee table matching the desk. Either there'd been a sale when they'd put the place together or the designer was really into coordinating pieces.

Over the bed were two paintings of cattle drives Miranda didn't care for, but overall the place was nice, if a bit monotonous. Maybe she should thank Gen—or not.

As soon as the bellhop left Parker scowled. "There's no kitchenette."

He was in a pissy mood, Miranda thought.

"We usually order room service," she said and with a shrug waltzed over to the fridge in the corner and opened it. Inside were soda cans and two beer bottles. "Hey, there's free drinks. Want one?"

He shook his head and moved to the suitcase on the bench at the foot of the bed. "We need to plan our next step." He began to unpack.

Miranda joined him and tugged at the zipper on her case. "Sure. I think we ought to stop by the police station first thing tomorrow and see what they've got so far."

"That was my thought." He crossed to the dresser, began laying his things in a drawer. "If Magnuson's death was indeed from natural causes, there's no need to proceed further."

Miranda followed suit and stuffed her underwear beside his tighty whities. "Don't you think it was strange for the police to decide it was natural causes so soon? And not to treat the clown's trailer as a crime scene?"

"Not necessarily. But they'll be doing an autopsy to confirm it. Let's hope they have results by tomorrow."

She ignored the implication that he'd like this case over and done as she tucked her sports bras next to her panties. "And what about this Layla character? She falls in love with Tupper Magnuson and leaves town the night he dies? Maybe Sam is right about her."

"If his facts are accurate."

Miranda closed the drawer and turned to Parker. "What do you mean by that?" She didn't mean her words to sound as defensive as they came out.

"Simply that your 'friend' may have ulterior motives."

She couldn't believe he'd just said that. "Ulterior motives?"

"We have no confirmation as yet that anything he's told us is true."

She put a hand to her head. It was starting to ache.

He gave her a dark look. "Surely you've considered the most obvious possibilities."

"Which possibilities?"

"First, that Keegan himself could be the killer."

She gritted her teeth at his words, though the same thought had flickered through her mind earlier. She raised her hands and plodded to the closet near the door where the bellhops had hung their garment bags. "If Sam is the killer why would he call us out here?"

Parker moved back to his bag at the foot of the bed. "One explanation would be to cover it up."

She pulled out her clothes and spread them on the rack. She did the same for Parker's, since he'd exerted himself enough tonight. "Cover up what? The police don't think it was murder."

"So Keegan says. What if the truth is they're about to arrest him but haven't put their case together yet?"

She spun around and stared at him. Parker was back beside the chest of drawers. Fully dressed in his business suit, he looked as deadly serious as she'd ever seen him. She couldn't believe this.

"And so he calls up a top investigative agency who would only confirm that?" But he hadn't called the agency. He'd called her. Did Sam think he could sweet talk her like he used to? She shook her head. "The police have to have their reasons for deciding it was natural causes, and apparently they don't consider Tupper's trailer a crime scene."

"According to Keegan."

"Again, why would he lie to us?"

He opened the drawer, laid some T-shirts in it. "Some years back a man hired me to find his wife's killer. It turned out it was him."

The breath went out of her. Did Parker really think Sam was capable of murder? "Did you know that guy before he hired you?"

"No, I didn't."

"Okay then. I know Sam. That's the difference." Stinging at his insinuation, she turned back to the closet and rearranged her clothes.

"We have no real proof that was the victim's trailer." Slipping off his suit coat Parker crossed to where she stood and hung it up.

The closeness of his body had always thrilled her. Just now it set her teeth on edge. She could feel his anger brewing under the surface.

"Except for the state of that couch."

"Which might have been moved there. Or the body moved to another spot after the fact." He spoke as smoothly as if he were ordering a Bacardi in the bar downstairs.

She stared at him, trying to figure out if this was just his bad mood or if he was really onto something. "Either way it would take a lot of effort. Sounds pretty extreme."

"Murder is always extreme. People go to extreme lengths to cover it up."

Still, it was a stretch. True, they had no proof except Sam's word. But that was good enough for her. For now anyway.

She watched Parker's movements, doubt and irritation vying in her brain. "What are you saying? The trailer we went to tonight could belong to somebody else? Who? Some other...clown?"

"Perhaps it was Keegan's."

She scoffed out a laugh. "So he set us up? Placed that photo album there for us to find so we'd go after the wrong suspect?"

"He wasn't expecting the two of us. He was expecting only you."

And thought she'd be an easy pushover? She remembered Sam's reaction tonight when he'd stared at the couch. It had seemed real to her. This conversation was ridiculous.

"Parker, you can't really think—"

"Which brings us to the second possibility."

"Which is?" Her temper was simmering and she almost wished she hadn't asked.

"That Sam is well aware that Magnuson passed away of natural causes. That he called you simply to see you again."

"You mean—?"

"To strike up a relationship. He's unaware that we're married, isn't he?"

She glared at Parker wondering if she were having a bad dream. How could he imply something like that? Then she saw something in his handsome face she'd never seen before. The lines around his eyes betrayed fatigue and the physical pain he'd been enduring all night but there was something else.

Something more.

She narrowed her eyes. "You're jealous."

He laughed and shook his head. "I am not jealous."

The hell he wasn't. Of Sam. But she didn't dare say that. She was too exhausted to get into a shouting match with him tonight, though that might come tomorrow.

"You're jealous I got a case on my own," she said instead. "That someone came to me."

He gave her a knowing look that cut straight through her and turned away. "I'm simply pointing out that as a good investigator, I'm sure you'll consider all possible angles."

Fury buzzed around inside her brain like an angry bee. He was giving her a headache, pissing her off royally. But she forced in a breath and managed to keep the anger under control.

"You're tired," she said. "You need rest. Why don't you take the bathroom first?"

He turned back and regarded her a long moment, as if he wanted to say something else, then thought better of it. "Very well."

She took a few steps toward him and stopped. "Do you need any help?"

"I'm fine." He picked up his toiletries.

Folding her arms, she gauged her next words. She was supposed to be in charge here, after all. She blew out a breath. "Really, Parker. I think for now you ought to stop being so cynical and give Sam the benefit of the doubt."

He turned his head toward her and gave her a long, stony look as cold and deadly as an ice storm. "Forgive my suspicious nature, Miranda. It goes with my profession."

His profession? His profession? It was her profession, too. Didn't he think she was being "objective" enough? She opened her mouth about to say so, then fought back the rage.

Instead she spun away from him, stomped over to the window and stared out at Dallas at night. "We're both exhausted. Let's get ready for bed and get some sleep."

He didn't reply.

When she heard him stride away from her and shut the bathroom door, she knew he wasn't going to. That stung worse than his words.

In the bathroom Parker leaned against the sink and stared at himself in the mirror.

The bruise under his eye throbbed and his ribs ached like the devil. The pain was both a source of irritation and a reminder of how much his wife meant to him. A few weeks ago she had risked her life for him.

She would risk her life for anyone she felt loyal to, but in his case she'd gone beyond all expectation. He loved her for that. More than he ever had before. More than he'd ever thought possible. More than his own life.

And that was the trouble.

He'd never felt this way before. Never experienced the particular sensation he'd had when Sam Keegan greeted his wife tonight with a kiss. The image lingered in his mind, simmered with its stark brashness.

He most certainly was not jealous.

And it wasn't Keegan's bold gesture that had produced these feelings. No, it was Miranda's reaction.

23

The glow on her face. The giddy smile on her lips. The joy that sparkled in her deep blue eyes at the sight of her old "friend," at the sudden physical contact with him.

The kind of involuntary response that came from deep inside. The kind he thought only he could incite in her.

Friend, he thought again with a wry grimace.

Sam Keegan had certainly been more than that to her. Precisely how much more, he couldn't say. But that glow told him they had once been lovers.

Miranda Steele had had a horrendous marriage and when he first met her, she'd made it crystal clear she wanted no part of a long-term relationship. She'd been too wounded, too angry for too many years. He'd had to move Heaven and earth to make her change her mind, but he'd done it gladly and would do it again to win her.

They were meant for each other. He'd always known that.

So how could it be anything but a shock to suddenly discover she'd had a serious relationship with another man?

Not that it would make her do anything foolish now.

Miranda would never cheat on him, he was sure of that. He had nothing to worry about on that score. She had too much integrity, too much pride. She was a good woman. Tonight she'd treated Sam as she would any other client.

And of course he couldn't hold it against her if she'd been intimate with the man long before they had met. If he did, he'd be more than a hypocrite. What really bothered him was that she hadn't been honest with him about it.

No, there was something more than that.

He ran a hand over his beard and took out his razor. He turned it on and began to shave.

Perhaps it was not knowing the precise nature of their past relationship. How long had they been together? How serious had it gotten? If it had been trivial, certainly Miranda would not be so secretive about it.

What exactly was she hiding? Had she intended to marry this man? And if she had...

The bond he had with Miranda was deeper than he'd ever known. He'd felt it in the core of his soul the moment they'd met. They were alike. Kindred spirits, fighting the same fight, driven by the same feverish passion to avenge the innocent, the victim. And now with the consultation service they were more a unit than ever.

But what if her bond with Sam Keegan had been...not deeper, that was impossible...but different? And somehow more appealing? What if circumstances in her past had worked out differently?

Ah, that was it. That was what stuck in his craw.

He lowered the shaver and let it run as the revelation struck him like a straight arm punch.

Miranda might have been just as happy with Sam Keegan as she was with him.

He scowled at his reflection. That thought sounded petty even without stating it out loud.

Still, the idea festered in his heart. She had told him many times she'd found her destiny through him. She'd found a career more fulfilling than she'd ever dreamed possible. And love beyond belief. And when they were working together and everything came together it tasted like the strains of an impossibly sweet symphony. A feeling he'd never experienced before. He knew she felt it, too. He could see the exhilaration, the excitement on her lovely face. That arousing fire in her deep blue eyes.

And yet?

What if she had gone another route? What if she had settled down with someone like Keegan and had a different life? A safer life?

A life she wouldn't have to risk so often?

He pulled himself out of his thoughts and drew a hand over his face. None of that mattered now. She was his. They'd taken the course they'd taken. They were where what they were. Who they were.

And just now they were in Dallas working for Miranda's old lover.

No matter how much that fact might irk him, he was an investigator first and so was his wife. They would do their best on this case and leave it behind. That was that. Ruminations about the past would only get in the way. There was no sense letting himself be upset over mere imaginings. That would only draw out the process.

He wasn't about to let that happen.

If Tupper Magnuson had died of natural causes, they would know by tomorrow afternoon and be on a flight out of this city by evening. But a vague suspicion that there had indeed been foul play gnawed at him along with Miranda's relationship with their client.

He was annoyed that they might have to stay on. And that realization annoyed him further. It ran contrary to all his professional ethics. He didn't drop murder cases just because he was irritated by the client. He would see this case out, no matter which way it went.

That was that.

Determining to put the irritation away for the night, he finished his shave, undressed and stepped into the shower.

CHAPTER SEVEN

The next morning Miranda wondered what Parker was up to when he treated her to a delicious huevos rancheros breakfast with extra hot peppers in the hotel restaurant. But she was relieved he was in a better mood. By the time she climbed into the silver gray sedan he'd rented and they took off, heading east down I-30, she felt like they were a team again.

The temperature was ninety-five and climbing, and she wished she could have worn shorts and a tank top. But she'd learned at the Agency how to dress like a professional, though the standard dress code would have been too formal for Dallas. So she had chosen a pair of dark jeans, a sleeveless blouse, and a lightweight jacket. Parker was in his designer jeans, a casual shirt and a blazer of deep gray that made his eyes look fierce. She was glad he could dress down a bit and hoped he'd be more comfortable.

"I did some research on Under the Big Top this morning," he told her as he braked for the big semi in front of them.

"And here I thought you were ordering me jewelry," she teased.

He'd been up and dressed and working on his laptop at the desk when she woke this morning. She was glad he was on board with this case now. After their "discussion" last night.

Crap like that would only hurt their investigation, especially since she was the one in charge.

She knew it was hard for Parker to step aside and let her make the decisions. He wasn't used to being second in command. But he'd done so graciously and patiently—for the most part—on their cases together so far. She appreciated his respect for her abilities and only wanted to live up to his expectations. And her own.

She didn't need the melodrama of current husband versus old flame.

Her remark got a smile from him. "Under the Big Top or UBT Inc. was founded seven years ago by Paxton Tenbrook, who is also its current owner."

She wrinkled her nose. "Paxton Tenbrook? Sounds like a real highbrow."

"Actually, he was raised by parents of modest means outside Houston. By all accounts he doesn't put on airs."

"Okay." She'd believe that when she saw the guy.

"Tenbrook went to Texas A&M for a few years then dropped out to become a rodeo clown."

"Has something in common with his performers."

Parker nodded. "Yes. He spent six years with the rodeo, then went to Hollywood and became a stunt man. Apparently he was in high demand but after about four years into that career, he was injured diving off a wall into flames."

"Gutsy guy."

"He seems to be. That was when he started UBT. He built the business slowly. It hasn't been until this year that he's come into some media coverage. There was a lot of publicity when the circus came to Dallas three weeks ago. In an interview he stated he wants to make UBT bigger than the Big Apple and Ringling Brothers."

"Ambitious dude."

"He said it has always been his dream to build something special where people can see performances they can't anywhere else."

Sounded like he liked the attention. Probably knew every detail of his performers' lives, at least the top ones. He might know where Layla was. "Tenbrook would be one to talk to."

Parker nodded. "He should definitely be on our list."

They fell silent. Miranda's thoughts buzzed around in her head while the A/C blasted blessedly away and Parker continued to steer them through the heavy morning traffic.

She was glad he seemed back to himself after their near fight last night. They hadn't even made love after she got out of the shower, though they'd had to do some improvising in that area lately, what with Parker recovering from injuries. But last night it had been more bruised egos than bruised ribs that had them falling asleep after nothing more than a goodnight kiss.

She hoped he'd conquered the green-eyed monster inside him.

After about forty-five minutes they got off the highway and drove a short distance through an industrial area to a spot littered with long beige brick buildings.

They turned in at a sign reading "Dallas Police Department" and found their way to the most promising looking one. They found a parking spot, stepped out and into the hot, dry air, and went inside.

They made their way down a long hall lined with cop memorials on one side and wanted posters on the other until they reached a central desk where a female clerk in white shirt and badge was answering the phone.

"Can I help you?" she asked hanging up on someone that seemed to have annoyed her. As she turned to them for a moment her gaze fixated on Parker and her lips spread into a gooey grin.

Not an uncommon reaction for most women.

Miranda cleared her throat and since she was the one in charge, spoke up. "Yes, you can. My name is Miranda Steele and this is my partner, Wade Parker. We're from the Parker Investigative Agency in Atlanta, and we've been hired to look into the death of Tupper Magnuson."

The woman blinked at her as if she'd spoken in Chinese. The phone rang again. "Excuse me." She raised a finger in the air and answered the call. "That's right," she said sweetly after a moment. "Just past the highway. You're very welcome." She hung up again.

"I'm sorry. We had a gang shooting last night and we're shorthanded."

"No problem."

The woman frowned as if trying to remember where she was. "Who did you want to see?"

"The person in charge of investigating the death of Tupper Magnuson."

The woman cocked her head in another you're-speaking-a-foreign-language look. "Who?"

"He was employed by Under the Big Top. The circus that's been here several weeks? He was a clown."

"Oh, right. I remember that incident. Night before last?"

"Yes."

"Let me see." She turned to her computer, punched in some keystrokes, waited. Before she turned back to them, she had paged through several screens and answered two more phone calls. "Here you go," she said at last. "Detective Underwood is handling that case."

"Is he in?"

"She. I'm not sure. They don't check in with me. But if she is, she'd be in the hive."

"Hive?"

She waved over her shoulder. "It's right down that corridor. Make a left and it's on the right. Unit C. You'll see the sign."

Miranda's brows shot up. No, "I'm sorry, you can't go down there?" No, "The police don't work with private investigators?" She gave Parker a glance of concern.

He nodded down the hall as if to say, "Let's go with it."

So she did.

"That was just too easy," she muttered to him as they headed down the hall the woman had indicated.

"The desk clerk was new. She must have assumed we're with the government."

"Works for me," she shrugged, though she was a little annoyed with herself for not picking up that the woman was a new hire. Parker was in fine form today.

As promised, they found the door—it was actually marked *Homicide*, Unit C—on the right in the middle of the second hall.

Miranda was debating whether to knock or barge right in when it flew open and a big bald guy with a thick waist in a cop uniform appeared.

"I'm on it. I'm on it," he cried over his shoulder as if someone had just nagged him. "Oh." He stopped short nearly banging into them. He blinked at Miranda, then at Parker. "Can I help you with something?"

"We're here to see Detective Underwood," Miranda said, hoping the officer would also assume they belonged here.

He scratched at his hairless head, then called into the room again. "Underwood, you expecting visitors?"

"Yeah. Show them in."

"Middle cube. Down that cutaway." He pointed a finger in that direction then hurried past them and down the hall.

Miranda shot Parker a surprised look.

He simply caught the door and held it open. "After you."

She stepped inside.

Hive was right.

The place was buzzing like a nest of neurotic bees caught in a vacuum cleaner. The air was noisy and warm with the hum of cop talk and printers and computers and whatever other equipment they used, and mixed with the odor of stale coffee grounds and last night's pizza.

Officers stood in groups in the spaces between cubes or with arms dangling over the canvas-covered walls, discussing the details of their cases. A couple of them were taking a civilian to an interview room. No one even took notice of the two new bodies who had just arrived.

Miranda led the way past a wall covered with maps and charts, turned in between two dividers and ended up at a cube in the middle with a sign that read *Sgt. Eloise Underwood.*

Must be the place.

A stocky woman maybe in her late thirties with short, straight, carrot-red hair sat talking on the phone, madly scribbling notes on a pad. From her profile Miranda could see she had a pert, turned-up nose, a smattering of freckles across the cheeks, big, bright eyes, and an expression that seemed authoritative and motherly at the same time.

She was dressed in a Texas working-woman outfit. A short-sleeved blue-and-white checked jacket, jeans and cowboy boots that gave her a rugged look, despite her maternal air.

The desk was crowded with all kinds of office paraphernalia. Phone, stapler, plastic organizers crammed with colored-coded folders. Papers lay all over the surface and sticky notes were everywhere. On the cube wall next to a calendar hung hand drawn pictures that must have been done by the detective's kid. Ah, that's where the motherly part came from.

A woman, a mother carving out her place in a male-dominated career. Miranda could relate to that.

"Uh huh," Underwood said into the phone. "Got it. Right. Got it. Thanks." She hung up, got to her feet and nearly bumped into Miranda. She took a step back, put a hand to her forehead. "Oh, right. You two here about the shootin' last night?" Her clipped words came out in a thick southwestern drawl.

"No, we're from the Parker Agency." Miranda took a deep breath and did the standard intro, hoping they weren't about to get the boot. "We're here about the Magnuson case."

"Parker Agency?" Underwood's eyes went wide at the sight of Parker, then she caught herself and stared at Miranda a moment as if she didn't recognize the name. "Oh, right. The circus clown. Somebody called and said you might be coming in." She snatched a stickie note off the side of her computer screen. "Sam Keegan. He was a friend of the deceased as we understand. Made the 911 call."

"That's right."

Parker gave Miranda a questioning look. She shot back a shrug. She didn't know Sam was going to call the police. She certainly hadn't asked him to.

Underwood ran a hand through her short red hair. "Sorry. We had a gang shooting last night and two recent liquor store robberies. I'm a little swamped right now."

Miranda inched inside the cube opening a bit. "We understand, Sergeant. We only need a minute of your time."

Underwood raised her hands in a shrug. "Not sure what I can tell you. The autopsy hasn't been completed yet."

Miranda gave her as solemn a look as she could muster. "Sergeant, Sam Keegan is our client. We were hoping to bring him some closure."

Underwood's lips went back and forth, but she shook her head. "I appreciate that, Ms. Steele, but we don't normally consult with civilians."

She said it kindly, but the word "civilians" stuck in Miranda's craw.

Parker had been standing quietly beside her, letting her take the lead. She caught his gaze and gave him an almost invisible nod that only he would understand. It said, "Work your charm."

With a compassionate expression, he leaned toward the woman. "Sergeant, we sincerely apologize for disturbing you at such a busy time."

"Not a problem, Mr. Parker. Thanks for stopping by." She extended a hand.

He took it like he was a suitor wooing her and continued as if she hadn't said a word. "However, since Mr. Keegan hired us, I'm hoping we can be of assistance to your unit."

Underwood wrinkled her nose suspiciously. "Assistance?"

"We intend to investigate this matter on our own, but any collaboration with the Department would only aid both of us. Wouldn't you agree?"

She pulled her hand out of his and eyed him with a cop's gaze. "You're a smooth one."

He only flashed her more charm with a wry smile. "I've been told as much."

She blew out a sigh of resignation. "Like I said, I don't know what I can tell you. As far as we know Mr. Magnuson died of natural causes."

"But your investigators went over the scene."

"Yes."

"The newish Winnebago?" Miranda asked.

"Right. They did the standard evidence gathering."

Miranda resisted the urge to shoot Parker a look of triumph.

Ignoring her question, he continued. "And your lab is conducting tests to verify COD, correct?"

"Of course, they are."

"Sergeant, is there anything, anything at all you can tell us?" His voice was so irresistibly seductive, his sexy gray eyes so hypnotic, Miranda couldn't hold back a small pang of jealousy.

Until she saw the results.

"I guess it wouldn't hurt to share our findings," Underwood said, letting out another long breath as she sank back into her chair. "But I only have a minute." She waved at a couple of wire chairs along the cube wall. "Have a seat."

"Thank you." Miranda quickly slid into one before the woman changed her mind.

"Let's see." Her fingers danced across her keyboard. After a moment she squinted at her screen, then shook her head. "Nope. Just as I said. Fingerprints are still at the lab. So are the fibers and hairs we lifted. A lot of long blond ones, as I recall."

Layla's, Miranda thought. "Sergeant, we visited the deceased's trailer last night."

Underwood spun around to face them. "You went there?"

"Mr. Keegan has a key. It wasn't marked as a crime scene."

"Guess the team finished with it." She didn't look happy about that. "I had to leave before they were done. Got the call about one of the robberies. The clerk on duty had been shot and was in the hospital. He lived, thank God."

"Thank God," Miranda repeated before pressing on. "We found a photo album in the place. We wondered why it wasn't taken into evidence."

Now Underwood looked as if somebody on her team was going to get their butt chewed, though she quickly covered it. "The CSIs must not have thought it was relevant."

Overworked cops too stressed to be thorough. That could work in their favor—or against them. "There were photos of Tupper Magnuson and his fiancée, Layla. Mr. Keegan believes she's missing."

Underwood sat back, chewed on the end of the pen she'd picked up. "That so?"

She was interested.

"We'd like to know if—"

A rough Hispanic voice echoed over the cube wall. "Underwood, you coming to interview or taking a vacation?"

"Be there in a minute, Rodriguez," she called back. She lifted her hands. "I'm sorry. I've got a witness to talk to."

About the other case, of course.

"Do you mind if we take your card?" Parker asked. "If we find out anything we'll be sure to call."

"Sure. Of course. Appreciate it." She took one from a pile next to the computer. Just as she handed it to Parker her phone rang. "Good Lord." She picked it up. "Underwood. Yeah? Yeah? Is that so? Thanks, Garber." She hung up.

Miranda leaned forward on pins and needles. This was something important.

Underwood let out a low whistle and turned to them. "Tox report's in on the Magnuson case. Residue from the wineglass found on scene's been analyzed." She put a hand to her head. "Haven't seen this before and I've been around awhile."

"What is it?" Miranda said.

"The wine was a cheaper brand. Barefoot Merlot. Contained a nice dose of NaCN. Same showed up in Magnuson's blood."

Parker's brows shot up. "Are you sure?"

"Kind of hard to mistake that. Our labs guys are good. So it wasn't natural causes. It was probably suicide."

Miranda racked her memory for what those letters meant. She thought she knew but that couldn't be right. "What are you saying, Sergeant Underwood?"

The woman sank back in her chair shaking her head in regret. "What a sad way for a clown to go. Something really must have been bothering him to make him do that to himself. It appears Tupper Magnuson drank his last glass of wine after lacing it with sodium cyanide."

CHAPTER EIGHT

"Sodium cyanide? What the heck was this dude?" Miranda growled when they were back in the rental car. "Some kind of spy?"

They were ones who took poison pills when they were captured. Not clowns.

Parker turned out of the police station parking lot, a look of deep concentration on his face. "That's a little farfetched but a remote possibility."

"Didn't the Nazis use cyanide to kill themselves before they were caught?"

"Some of them did. It's one of the most lethal substances on earth."

She stared out the window at the flat landscape of small middle-class homes along the highway. "Magnuson must have died an agonizing death."

Parker nodded grimly. "Suffocation would have been almost immediate, accompanied by acute abdominal pain and cardiac arrest. All in a matter of seconds."

Suicide definitely wasn't painless. Not in this case, poor guy. She rubbed her arms. According to Sam, all Tupper the Clown wanted to do with his life was make everyone happy. Maybe underneath all the smiles and the laughter he lived in despair.

"You think he killed himself, Parker?" There was a catch in her voice she couldn't control.

His answer was soft. "Hard to say. Most deaths by cyanide poisoning are suicides."

She knew that, but she could tell he wasn't buying it. "Magnuson had a new fiancée," she offered. "Someone to live for." Then she sank back in her seat. "Who was mad at him. Maybe mad enough to leave town."

"So we've been told."

She ignored the cynical comment. "Maybe Layla just broke off the engagement. Broke Tupper's heart. Made the otherwise happy clown feel as if suddenly life wasn't worth living anymore. Maybe Layla left because she couldn't face seeing him every day after she did that to him." But he couldn't have gotten cyanide that fast. And how could he have gotten it?

33

"Perhaps," Parker said. "If Keegan's facts are accurate."

He wasn't getting off that horse anytime soon, was he? Only one way to confirm those facts and find out what state of mind Tupper Magnuson was in before he died. "We need to go back to the circus and talk to the other performers."

"That's just where I'm heading."

CHAPTER NINE

The colossal red-and-white striped tent stretched across the wide open field like a lazy giant taking a nap. Atop its peaks flags flapped lazily in the noonday breeze near floodlights that were dark and loudspeakers that were still. A sign in big, fanciful letters curved over the broad entrance. *Under the Big Top*, it read.

But no one was here to see the show.

Parker cruised past the tent and headed for the dirt road. When he pulled up to the first row of trailers, the back lot looked different from the way it had last night. Instead of murky shadows, the sun beat bright and hard against the white siding and fanciful decals of the vehicles, giving them the look of giant sheep grazing in a field.

It was a huge spread. Seven or eight rows wide and maybe a dozen deep. Some RVs were lined up end to end with space between, others sat perpendicular, with cars and trucks for everyday transportation scattered every which way between them or parked in the big lot down the road.

Along the grassy stretches between the campers and RVs there was movement.

Life after a day of mourning the dead.

People were walking about, groups were practicing their acts, kids were playing, mothers attending to children. A whole community knit together by a common purpose—the show that must go on, despite the recent loss.

Parker drove down the narrow stretch of pavement where they'd come last night and pulled over to the side. He didn't go as far as Magnuson's place but stopped at the other end of the road.

"Good thing about it," Miranda observed, "everyone we need to talk to is in one place."

"Easier for them to get their stories in sync," Parker said wryly.

"True." Assuming they had something to hide. "Where do we start?"

He scanned the area. "Why not start at one end and work our way down?"

"Sounds good to me." She nodded and reached for her door handle.

They got out and crossed the grassy space between two campers. A light breeze made the hot air a little more tolerable, but Miranda caught herself hoping they could get some answers soon. Jeez, the heat never used to bother her. She'd really gotten spoiled by Parker's unlimited A/C.

They stepped out into the wide main path between the two rows of mobile homes and were greeted by the shouts of children kicking around a soccer ball, the barking of dogs, and the smell of hamburgers being grilled for an early lunch.

On a flat patch of dirt, a pack of young, tan, shirtless dudes with assorted tattoos and rock hard abs shot a basketball through a hoop hung on a tree.

A Hispanic-looking guy with a single dragon tattoo on his shoulder missed his shot and the ball bounced in the dirt toward Miranda. She caught it, took aim, tossed and sank it.

The whole group turned to look at her.

A couple of them whistled in admiration.

Single-Tattoo caught the ball as it came out of the net and gave her and Parker the once over with a surly eye. "You two with the show?" Thought they were new hires.

She shook her head. "We're PIs."

"PIs?" A burly, rough-looking white guy took a step toward them for a closer look. He had so many tattoos on his arms and torso he looked like he'd been dipped in an ink bottle. "You here about what happened to Tupper?"

"We are." Parker nodded to him. "What can you tell us about him?"

They looked at each other.

A dark-skinned dude with a pencil mustache and no tattoos shrugged. "Not that much. We're on the ring crew. The performers mostly hang out with each other."

"Surely you had some interaction with Mr. Magnuson."

"Magnuson? Was that his last name?"

"It was," Parker said.

"We only knew him by Tupper. Terrible what happened to him. Everybody's shaken by it. Yeah, he'd say hi to us, maybe tell us a joke or something. But we mostly keep busy taking care of the facilities."

"Yeah," Single-Tattoo grinned. "The tent doesn't go up without us."

"And the port-a-potties don't get emptied," the over-inked guy chimed in with a smirk.

Miranda was getting frustrated. "You see Tupper hanging out with anyone in particular?"

"You mean another performer?"

"Uh huh."

Single- and Uber-Tattoo looked at each other. "Laaay-la."

She decided to play dumb. "Layla? Who's that?"

"Tupper's girl," Pencil Mustache grinned. "She does a silk aerial act. Man, she's hot."

The others chimed in their agreement with the sounds males made in reaction to attractive women.

Parker smiled along with them as if sharing their lust then his face went deadpan. "When was the last time you saw her?"

"Layla?"

They all looked at each other again and shrugged.

"Night before last during the performance, I guess," Single-Tattoo said. "We were busy breaking things down after the show. Had a shower, went to bed."

The others nodded that they'd done the same.

Miranda decided to throw out a hook. "We've heard Layla's missing."

Uber-Tattoo's mouth opened. "Really?"

Single Tattoo shuffled the basketball from hand to hand. "That's weird. She's a headliner. How do you know?"

"We don't."

"Well, you can check out her trailer. It's down that way." He pointed to where the nicer RVs were parked, closer to the tent. "In fact, that's the area where all the performers live. They'd be able to tell you more than we can. They knew Tupper better."

A school bell like chime rang out over the trailer roofs.

Pencil Mustache jerked a thumb over his shoulder in the direction of the sound. "Lunch time. Sorry. We gotta go."

"Yeah," said Single-Tattoo. "If we don't get there right away, Tiny will eat all the food."

They weren't going to get much more from this bunch. "Thanks for your help," Miranda said as she watched them trot away, leaving the basketball lying under the tree.

She turned to Parker. "We're off to a terrific start."

"They told us Layla might not be missing." Proving Sam's suspicion wrong. Parker would love that.

"Unless they're hiding something."

"True."

She gazed at the lane that ran down to the trailers near the big top, the area where they'd been last night. "Let's take the crew's advice and talk to some of the performers."

"Very well."

They strolled along the grassy path, traversing the maze of various sized RVs and campers, most of them with breeze fans or window A/C units going full blast.

Each vehicle was parked to leave enough space between it and its neighbor to make a yard about fifteen or twenty feet wide. In each yard a range of belongings was sprinkled about, similar to what you might find in any typical neighborhood with kids. Shoes piled up at one door, bikes lined up against the wall. Strollers, a small wading pool like the one Miranda's father got her when she was little. Planters hanging from under awnings.

Families lived here.

Amazing how folks could make themselves at home even when they had to pick up and move every other month or so. Kind of reminded her of the way she used to live. She never cared for having a lot of things. Most of her belongings used to fit in her old car.

But Parker had come along and changed all that.

They reached a spot where several groups of performers were practicing their acts. A couple of young muscle-bound men in tight red T-shirts and blue jeans tossed colorful rings back and forth. Beyond them, a large man in white tights with a big black mustache and a Russian accent barked stern instructions to a young woman walking a narrow bar barefoot.

"Not too fast. Do not look down, Feya. It make you look like amateur."

Her scowl said she didn't appreciate the correction, but she quickly covered it before he saw it.

"That is it, Bobo. Good boy!" cooed someone in a French accent.

In front of one of the nicer RVs a bubbly woman with bright red curls piled atop her head led a cute shaggy white terrier around in a circle on its hind legs. Two other pooches sat on brightly painted overturned buckets watching the woman and the terrier, and looking like they would love to join in the antics. But it wasn't their turn yet.

Seemed odd for the place to be so animated while the death of a fellow performer still hung in the air. Guess you had to keep in practice no matter what the circumstances.

Miranda looked around wondering which one to talk to first when she spotted a small, delicate looking woman in jeans and a black T-shirt with the UBT logo in gold under a vinyl awning across the way. She was getting a couple of little boys settled at a picnic table.

"Want to try her?" she said to Parker.

"As good a choice as any."

She stepped over to her through the tall grass. "Excuse me."

The woman looked up, surprise on her face. "Can I help you?" She spoke with an Eastern European accent.

"Maybe." Miranda cocked her head at her.

Apparently people from all over the world came to work in the circus. If someone wanted to knock off a clown and head back to the Old Country to hide for a while, who'd be the wiser? But she was getting ahead of herself.

Extending a hand, she stepped up to the woman. "My name is Miranda Steele and this is my partner, Wade Parker. We're investigators looking into the incident that occurred here night before last." She purposely left out the word "private" hoping the woman would think they were cops.

The woman shook her hand, frowning suspiciously, gave Parker the once-over common to anyone missing a Y chromosome. "You mean Tupper?"

"Yes."

The woman ran a hand over her head to smooth her curly brown hair. Close up she seemed tinier, coming up just to Miranda's shoulder. Her arms and neck were thin. And though her flyaway hair hid it, Miranda noticed her forehead protruded just a tad.

"The police were here that night. We saw them over there." She gestured around the corner several trailers away.

"That was Tupper's place?"

"Yes." It was where Miranda and Parker had been last night. Another point for Sam's honesty score.

The woman eyed her closely. "Didn't they get everything they needed?"

So much for the idea of making her think they were cops. "We're private investigators," Miranda told her. "A member of your staff hired us."

The woman rubbed her arm. "Oh? Who?"

"Mama, I'm hungry." The smaller boy pounded his little fists on the table. He couldn't have been older than four and his brother beside him three. Both had their mother's curly brown hair.

"In a minute, Grigori," she told him.

He poked his lip out in a pout while the woman busied herself setting out plastic plates and utensils.

Miranda used the distraction to dodge the question. "We'd just like to talk to you a few moments about the deceased."

She laid a plastic fork next to the younger boy's blue plate. He picked up the plate and started to lick it.

"No, Vasya. Put it down." She glanced at Miranda. "I'm not sure what I can tell you."

"Did you work closely with him?"

"Me? Well, we weren't in the same act, if that's what you mean. I assist my husband. He's the human cannonball."

A real human cannonball? "That's impressive."

Keeping her gaze down she half smiled. "We were all in a few dance numbers together, but most of the cast is in those."

Miranda blew out a breath of frustration and nodded to Parker. Maybe he could loosen this woman's tongue. She was female, after all.

Parker shot her one of his to-die-for smiles. "How well did you know Tupper Magnuson, Mrs....?"

"Varga. Dashia Varga." She was unmoved by Parker's charm or maybe just too busy. Without looking up or offering a hand she laid out napkins for her sons. One blew away and the smaller boy ran after it.

She sighed aloud and folded her arms. She didn't run after him but kept a watchful eye on the boy to make sure he didn't stray too far. "I knew him pretty well, I guess. As well as I know most of the other performers. We're all family here."

"What was he like?" Miranda asked.

She turned back to face them. "Tupper? Oh, he was a joker. A funny man. He was a clown, you see."

"So we understand," Parker said in a practiced tone that made you want to say more.

Mrs. Varga pushed her hair back again and smiled wistfully. "Most clowns, you know. They're only entertaining in the ring. Tupper, he was on all the time."

"You mean he was a phony?" Miranda said.

"Oh, no. He was very genuine. He cared about everybody. That was real. I just meant he could always make you laugh, no matter how down you might be."

Miranda pursed her lips at Parker. She could tell he was thinking the same thing she was. Didn't sound like the type of guy to commit suicide.

Just then the flap on the RV door pulled back and a man appeared with a plate of hotdogs. He was tall, thick-necked and muscle-bound, and dressed in a black leotard like his wife. He might be the human cannonball, but he could have doubled as the strongman.

Not the type you'd want to meet in a dark alley.

At the sight of the dogs, the older kid jumped from his seat and started hopping up and down. "Oh, boy! Oh, boy!"

"Quiet down now. Grigori, put that in the trash," the man said to the younger one who was waving the runaway napkin he'd fetched off the ground. The man set the dogs down on the picnic table and frowned at Miranda and Parker. "You didn't tell me we had guests, Dashia." He also had an accent.

"These are private investigators, Yuri," his wife told him. "They're here about Tupper."

There was a look of shock on his face, then his expression turned dark. "I hope you can find out what really happened to him."

Miranda eyed his face trying not to stare. He was bald, with thick black brows. He couldn't have been more than mid-twenties, but a long scar ran from one side of his head, down his forehead and across his nose, which was wide and flat. Another scar ran down the side of his neck. Miranda knew scars. She had a couple of her own that would never go away and so did Parker. The cannonball's looked particularly nasty.

"Do you share the theory it wasn't natural causes?" she asked him.

He slipped a protective arm around Dashia's shoulders. "We don't have a theory. We heard a rumor the police weren't sure how he passed away. We only want things to be made right, whatever happened."

Interesting comeback. "What about Layla?"

"Layla?"

"The silk aerial artist? How well do you know her?"

Dashia glanced up at Yuri as if asking permission to speak. He gave her a slight nod.

"We don't know her very well," she said.

"Didn't she date Tupper?"

Her eyes widened as if she was surprised Miranda knew that little tidbit. "Well, yes. But she was very private."

Uh huh. "Can you tell me Layla's last name?"

"Last name?"

"Surely you know it. I understand she was from Eastern Europe."

Dashia glanced up at her husband again. Miranda knew she was about to lie.

"There you two are!"

She spun around and caught sight of Sam jogging up to join them. He had on a dark blue Harley-Davidson T-shirt, khaki cargo shorts, and a camouflage cowboy hat to replace yesterday's Stetson. His big silver belt buckle gleamed with the image of a longhorn and the embossed words "Cowboy Up," Southwestern for "man up."

"Sam," she said when he reached them. "What are you doing here?"

He frowned at her. "I live here, like everybody else."

"I mean what are you doing right here?" She pointed to the ground.

He raised his palms. "Coming to help you two out. Did you talk the police?"

She didn't answer. "Right now, we're talking to this gentleman and his wife."

Sam folded his arms. "I can see that. Have you met? This is Yuri Varga. He's our human cannonball."

"So his wife said."

"His act is absolutely amazing. He flies over sixty feet in the air at sixty-five miles per hour. Nothing scares Yuri. He missed the net once. That's how his face got messed up."

She scowled at him as if that remark was the rudest thing she'd ever heard.

"Oh, ole Yuri brags about it. Those scars are badges of honor. Right, big guy?" He gave the man a punch on the arm.

Yuri forced a smile. "I'm only grateful I lived. Sam, did you hire these detectives?"

"Yes, I did. I want to find out what happened to Tupper."

"We all do."

So it was Sam the cannonball had heard the rumor from.

Miranda wanted to give Sam a shake for spreading it. And for bumbling into their investigation and ruining the rhythm of their questioning.

But he seemed oblivious. "I thought I'd take you over to check out Layla's trailer again. That okay?"

She glared at him. Now the Vargas knew they'd been here. And to Layla's trailer. She wanted to give her new client a kick.

"If you'll excuse us," Dashia said. "We need to have our lunch. We have a rehearsal this evening to prepare for."

"Rehearsal? Isn't the circus shut down?"

"Just for today," Sam said. "Boss wants to have a memorial performance for Tupper tomorrow night. You know. The show must go on." He raised his hands and gave her that innocent sheep look she used to find endearing.

"Guess so," she said through gritted teeth.

As the Vargas were getting settled into the picnic table next to their boys Sam turned to them. "You two know Layla's missing, don't you?"

Yuri had a dark look and Dashia frowned. "What do you mean she is missing?"

"I mean she's gone. She doesn't answer her door."

Dashia looked nervously at her husband again. "Was she fired?"

Sam looked suddenly deflated. "I don't see how."

"Maybe she got a hotel room in the city. She never really liked living in the back lot." Quickly Dashia put a napkin to her face to hide her slip. So she knew the aerial artist better than she'd said.

"Let me know if you hear from her," Sam said.

"All right."

He turned to Miranda. "C'mon. Let's go to Layla's."

CHAPTER TEN

As they strolled through the grass, Sam began to chatter excitedly in his southwestern drawl. "If you want, I can introduce you to the performers who knew Tupper best. There's Yvette Nannette, the dog trainer. And Danny, the guy I mentioned last night. And Harvey. He's another clown. You'll want to speak to him. Oh, I almost forgot." He dug in his pocket and handed Miranda something.

"What's this?" she asked.

"Visitor passes for the dress rehearsal tonight. Can't get in without them."

Miranda handed them to Parker who stuffed them into his blazer pocket without a word.

She didn't appreciate Sam barging in and taking over their investigation, and she could see Parker was fuming.

"Mr. Keegan," he said in a low, ominous voice.

"Oh, please. Call me Sam." Sam chuckled as if he didn't notice there was a problem.

"We're quite capable of interviewing people without your help."

Sam stopped and turned around to face them. He looked crestfallen. "Jeez, I'm sorry. I just thought I'd help you out. Thought you'd really want to talk to Harvey.

Miranda sighed in impatience. "Who's Harvey?"

"Harvey Hackett. He's one of the lead clowns. He worked closely with Tupper, and…well, they didn't exactly get along."

Miranda folded her arms. "You think he could be a suspect?"

"Maybe. I'm not a professional like you two." He put his hands in his back pockets and gave her that shy sexy grin of his.

She narrowed her eyes and Parker narrowed his at the same time. They both knew bullshit flattery when they heard it. Still this Harvey dude sounded like he might have a motive.

She turned to Parker. "Couldn't hurt to talk to the guy."

For one infinitesimal spec of time, his gray eyes flashed dark with rage. Then he took a controlled breath to fight it back. "All right. Where is he, Sam?"

Sam brightened. "He lives right over here. Should be out practicing now. It's on the way to Layla's."

He led them past a few more RVs then made a turn between two of the larger ones. There, in what you might call the alleyway, stood a man dressed in a sleeveless white undershirt and baggy pants held up by red suspenders. He was cussing at a set of bowling pins lying on the ground.

A cigar hung out of one corner of his mouth and he badly needed a shave. He looked like a sad sack clown even without any makeup.

"Damn cheap props," he muttered.

"You'd do better if you got rid of that stogie," Sam said.

The man looked up and glared at him. "Shows what you know. It's part of the act."

"Sure it is. In the smoke-free tent." Sam strode over, snatched the stub out of the man's mouth and tossed it on the ground. Then he dug the heel of his cowboy boot into it.

The man's weathered face twisted in a grimace. "Dammit, Keegan. Who do you think you are, my mother?"

"You need a mother sometimes."

"I'm warning you, you'd better stay out of my stash. I'm missin' a pack of cigs. And a bottle."

"You're the only one who wants to touch your stash, man. And hey, you need a limit on your wine drinking, too."

Miranda looked at Parker. This guy had a drinking problem? With wine? And he was missing a bottle?

Parker took a step forward. "Sir, we're wondering if we might speak to you a moment about Tupper Magnuson."

"Sir?" He sneered at Parker, revealing a set of yellowed teeth. His tan was deeper than Sam's, and his skin had the texture of old leather. "Who the hell are you?"

Sam scoffed. "You really need to work on your manners, Harvey. This is Wade Parker and Miranda Steele from the Parker Investigative Agency in Atlanta, Georgia. I hired them to look into Tupper's death. They'd like to speak to you."

Parker extended a hand. "Harvey Hackett?"

The man eyed him up and down, then did the same to Miranda. "I got nothin' to say to either of you."

With that, he stumbled over to the steps in front of his trailer door and sank down onto them. Miranda noticed a small garden filled with red rosebushes. The grumpy clown had a green thumb? She eyed his small trailer. He couldn't have grown them in there. He must have gotten the plants from a local nursery. She wondered if he left them there for the next trailer park guest when the circus left town. Despite his crude demeanor, perhaps he had a soft spot for growing things.

Harvey put his cheeks in his fists and scowled at the bowling pins. "I can't do Tupper's act tomorrow night."

Sam sat down next to him and patted his knee. "Sure you can, Harvey."

He shook his head. "Damn thing is, I taught him the routine. He stole it from me, really. But he made it his own. His signature. I can't do it the way he did."

Miranda gave Parker a let-me-try-this look and squatted down next the man. As she did, she got a nice whiff of old clown BO. She ignored it.

"How did the act go?" she asked in a gentle, warming-up-to-you tone.

His eyes brightened. "Oh, it's a good one. First you do some bragging business with the bowling pins and some patter, you know. Talk to the crowd, get them going, so they expect you to be the greatest juggler they've ever seen. Then you toss all three pins in the air and let them drop. Big laugh."

He got up and strolled over to the bowling pins on the ground, put his hands on his hips. "Then you do some shtick, blaming the pins." He shook his fists at them. "You try it again, same thing. A few more times, then you plop down on the floor and cry." He did so, pantomiming kicking his legs and wiping his eyes with twisting fists. "Then you beg the crowd for help and while you do, Jubjub sneaks up behind you. She's the clown dressed like a fairy princess. Real cute costume. The crowd tries to tell you she's there, but you don't get it. Just then Jubjub sprinkles you with fairy dust—that's just glitter confetti—and you get up and go after her, grabbing the pins like you're going to hit her over the head with them, but instead, you magically start juggling them. Two. Three. You pick up a fourth one..."

He started tossing the pins in the air and catching them while he was talking. It was as if telling the story brought back the muscle memory. He was really good.

"Fifth one." He reached down and grabbed it, tossed it up with the others—and dropped them all. "Shit!" He shuffled over to the steps and sank down again. "At least I've got the dropping part down."

"You just need practice," Sam told him.

"Mr. Hackett," Parker said as if there'd been no interruption. "It seems you were close to Tupper Magnuson."

He shrugged. "Sure. We were both in the troupe. Most of our acts were together."

"Can you tell us what sort of mood he was in lately?"

"Mood? Tupper didn't have moods. He was always in good spirits. So freakin' happy it was sickening."

"He was in love," Sam said flatly.

Miranda glared at him. She didn't need him supplying answers to this guy. But he only frowned at her. She thought about what Detective Underwood had called her and Parker. Sam was the real civilian here.

She took a breath and picked up the questioning. "We understand Mr. Magnuson was recently engaged."

"Yeah. To that fine piece of—" He looked up at Miranda and cleared his throat. "To that aerial artist who climbed the silk ropes. She's a looker, all right." He squinted at Miranda. "You're not so bad yourself, come to think of it."

"Thanks," she grimaced. Just what she always wanted. A come on from a dirty old clown.

"Was there any trouble between the couple?" Parker asked.

"Trouble?"

"Did they argue? Fight about anything?"

He waved both hands. "Maybe once or twice. Minor shit. They'd make up right away. You couldn't keep those two apart. They were always lovey-dovey, kissy face. Couldn't get enough of each other. Like I said. Sickening."

Parker put a foot on one of the steps and pressed a little harder. "Are you sure you didn't notice anything unusual around the time Mr. Magnuson was found in his trailer?"

Harvey scratched his beard. "Come to think of it…"

"Yes?"

"They did have a row recently. Bigger than usual."

"When?"

"Let's see. When was that? Sometime last week maybe? I saw them." He chuckled and gestured toward the end of his RV. "I've got a view of Tupper's front door just around that corner. It was right before the show. I'd come outside to stretch and warm up for my act. Layla was standing at Tupper's door, yelling at him. He was talking to her, trying to calm her down. Both of them sounded really mad."

"Did you hear anything specific?"

He shook his head. "Naw. I mind my own business."

Sure he did. "What happened?"

"They shouted at each other a bit, then she stomped off." He shrugged. "Like I said. Not my business."

"When was this exactly?"

His lips went back and forth in an exaggerated gesture he no doubt used in his act. "I don't know. Late last week sometime."

"The night Tupper expired?" Parker said.

"I don't think so. Maybe the night before. It's hazy. They all run together when you've been around as long as I have."

And when you're into the bottle a lot, Miranda thought.

"Anyway," Harvey said. "I didn't think anything of it. I knew they'd make up again and go right back to all that gooey stuff."

Sam got a wistful look in his eyes. "Tupper told me you encouraged him to pop the question."

Harvey curled a lip. "I hoped he'd leave the show. Some do when they marry."

"But he didn't," Miranda said.

He shook his head. "Shouldn't have gotten my hopes up. I knew he was a lifer."

"But he ended up dead instead."

Slowly Harvey raised his gaze. "You sayin' I had something to do with it?"

"You wanted him out of the way. Maybe so you could have a chance with Layla."

He shot to his feet. "You're out of your mind. Okay, I didn't really like the guy, but I'm no killer."

Miranda looked down at her fingernails. "That's what all the guilty say."

"Hey, girlie. You take that back."

He lunged at her, but Sam caught him before he could take a swing. "Take it easy, Harvey. She didn't mean it."

Miranda glared at Sam, irritation burning in her. Suddenly she didn't know who she wanted to punch more. This old clown or her cowboy client. He hadn't understood what she was doing and he'd ruined her interrogation tactic.

There was no reason to keep going now. They'd get nothing more out of this guy.

"Sam," she said, stuffing down her anger. "Why don't you take us to Layla's place now? Harvey needs to practice."

CHAPTER ELEVEN

Now pissed as well as hot, Miranda trudged angrily beside Parker under the trees with Sam on the other side. "You really don't need to put your two cents in when we're questioning someone, Sam," she grunted.

He looked at her as if she'd just slapped him. "What did I do? Harvey's hard to talk to. I was greasin' the skids for you."

"We can grease our own skids just fine."

He kicked at a patch of dirt as he took a step. "Jeez, I was only trying to help."

"Just try to keep quiet next time, okay?"

"Sure. Whatever you say." He started to sulk.

Good grief.

Parker wore that hard iron look, keeping his focus straight ahead. He was upset over Sam again. This time she couldn't blame him.

They turned in at an RV with a rear ladder and a red-and-blue pin stripe design and found the second trailer they'd visited last night.

In the sunlight it looked bright and shiny, with a wavy teal striping design along its side and friendly girlish curtains hanging in the windows.

Miranda ascended the two metal steps at the door and knocked hard.

No answer.

"Layla? Are you in there? We're with the police. We need to talk to you about Tupper Magnuson."

Still no answer.

Miranda turned back and raised her hands. "Looks like she's still not home."

A funny feeling started to nest in her stomach. What if something awful had happened to this woman?

Parker's eyes took on a hard look and he began to scan the area. He ran his hands over the side and found a latch to one of the compartments that covered hooks ups and batteries for the vehicle. He opened the latch and lifted the flap.

He put his hand inside and felt around for a long moment. Then he straightened again and pulled out a key.

"Voila!" Miranda said, beaming with pride.

She wanted to add she knew she'd brought him along for something, but that might give Sam the wrong idea.

Instead she climbed down the stairs as Parker stepped up to the door and inserted the key.

The door opened.

"Are you sure we should be doing this?" Sam said.

"You want us to find her, don't you?" Miranda snapped at him.

"Sure, sure. I just thought...never mind."

Once more Parker slipped gloves out of his pocket. Miranda put hers on and handed a pair to Sam. "Here. And be careful not to move anything."

"Okay," Sam grumbled, pulling them on.

She was tempted to give Sam a quick lecture on crime scene contamination, but it would probably be wasted.

Instead she turned and followed Parker inside.

Layla's trailer had a faint musty smell mixed with the scent of girlish perfume. Like Tupper's place last night, all the windows were shut. The A/C was on but not set very low. The place was sweltering.

Miranda switched on an overhead light. "Electricity's still on." Not that that meant much.

"It's supplied by UBT," Sam told her.

Okay, it meant the circus didn't consider her missing. Yet.

She strolled through the place hunting for any sign of what had happened to its occupant.

This RV was smaller and had light-colored fake wood cabinetry. On the opposite side a foldout couch had been left open under a shaded window, the sheets and blankets rumpled on the mattress.

Miranda searched a tiny closet in a cramped corner while Parker went through the storage space under the bed. Sam stood in a corner using his camouflage cowboy hat for a fan. She was glad he was keeping out of the way.

She found several skimpy, glittery costumes, leotards in an assortment of colors. White, blazing reds, flaming pastels in a tie-dyed pattern. Ballet slippers, stilettos, a boa. A couple of dresses, but no jeans or Ts or every-day clothes of any sort. Nothing like she'd seen in the casual photos in Tupper's place.

No suitcase.

"Blankets and towels in here." Parker closed the under-the-bed drawer and straightened.

"Did you see a duffle bag in there?" she asked him.

"None whatsoever."

A narrow chest stood on the other end of the bed. Miranda picked her way over to it and opened the drawers one by one. Stage makeup, a big handheld mirror, more fancy, glittery hosiery that seemed to go with the costumes in the closet.

No underwear.

She shut the last drawer and looked around.

Sam ogled her as if he were outraged she was violating Layla's privacy. She ignored him.

On the other end of the space stood a small laminate computer desk. She and Parker took that next. No sign of any equipment. No cell phone left behind. Stray papers and receipts stuffed in the drawers along with a paperback romance novel. No pictures of Layla and Tupper like they'd found in the clown's place. Maybe they'd kept them all in the album. Maybe she took them with her.

Miranda left Parker to sort out the sales slips while she examined the kitchen.

Small stove and sink next to the desk. No dishes in it. Nothing on the counter but a dry dishtowel neatly folded. She opened a cupboard overhead. Whole wheat cereal, organic oatmeal, a bag of tortilla chips. Pretty normal fare.

Miranda picked it up and checked the date. Not that old. She went to the fridge. Water bottles, a jar of sweet pickles, sandwich fixing. A Styrofoam container of leftovers from a Mexican restaurant. She opened it and gave it a sniff.

Also not that old. Other than her job, it looked like the woman led an ordinary life.

"You satisfied?" Sam said as if he'd won some kind of victory. "She's gone like I said."

Parker gave the computer desk another gaze. "Did Layla have a laptop?"

"No," Sam told him. "She barely had more than the clothes on her back when she came to UBT six months ago. Bought most of her stuff at the local Walmart."

"As these receipts confirm," Parker said. "There's nothing out of the ordinary here."

"Looks like she packed a bag with essentials and took off."

Parker put the papers back in the desk drawer. "It seems we can rule out abduction."

"Yeah."

Sam's face took on a look of alarm. "Abduction? You think Layla might have been kidnapped?"

"No," Parker said with strained patience. "I just said we could rule that out. Kidnappers generally don't allow their victims to pack a bag first."

"But she still could be in danger, right?"

Ignoring him, Miranda wiped sweat from her forehead with the back of her hand.

Maybe Layla had been on the run when she joined up with UBT. A traveling circus was a good place to hide, but then she got to be the headliner. She was known to the public. Time to vamoose.

She thought of what Harvey Hackett had told them about Layla fighting with Tupper. Maybe she wanted to break up. Maybe Tupper wouldn't let her alone. She might have offed him to stop his advances, but not with cyanide. Where would a young woman with little money and no Internet access get cyanide from anyway?

No, the most reasonable explanation was Sergeant Underwood's. Poor ole Tupper killed himself. Who knew why people did such things?

Layla's disappearance had to be either the cause of him ending his life or just a coincidence. Maybe the aerial artist had gotten tired of dangling in the air on strands of silk and wanted to try something new.

There could be a hundred reasons for a young woman to up and take off. Nobody knew that better than she did. It had been her own modus operandi before she met Parker.

"Layla might have gotten cold feet about her engagement." Her eyes locked with Sam's and they shared a moment, a memory of their history.

Not a good one.

She looked away. Shouldn't have brought that up. Really shouldn't have brought that up, she thought, when she caught Parker frowning at her.

She stepped to the doorway. "Okay, Sam. You've proved she's been gone for a few days. Your next rehearsal's tonight?"

"Yeah, at seven."

"She'll probably be back by then." If she just went to visit someone.

Sam set his hat back on his head with a scowl. "You don't know that for sure. You need to find her."

"We need to find out the truth."

"Yeah. The truth about who killed Tupper. What if Layla did it?"

Tired of his badgering, Miranda folded her arms. "Sam, Tupper was poisoned."

Sam stepped back, sank into a chair. "What? Poisoned?"

"The police think it was suicide."

He stared up at her, his green eyes growing moist. "It couldn't have been suicide. Tupper would never have done that."

Funny reaction for the guy who found the body. Didn't he see there was no blood? No bullet wounds? Maybe he was too rattled to notice. Or maybe he'd assumed natural causes and called her just to see her again like Parker had surmised.

"How do you know what Tupper would have done?" she said.

"Because I know my friend."

"What about what Harvey said? Tupper and Layla were fighting. Maybe she left because of him and that was the trigger."

From the other side of the room, Parker cleared his throat.

Miranda glared at him. He thought she'd told Sam too much. That set her off more than Sam had. She was hot and tired and frustrated with both of them.

"I'm tired of this bullshit." She turned on her heel and headed out the door.

Her temper fuming, she hurried down the steps and into a nice warm breeze. Even in the hundred-and-one degree heat, it felt good after that trailer.

As she might have expected, Sam came trotting after her. He grabbed at her arm. "Miranda, do you think it was suicide, too?"

She turned to him, spotted Parker at the top of the steps. He looked like he was simmering like a volcano himself, ready to burst forth any second.

Professionalism, she thought. "We don't have an opinion yet, Sam," she told him flatly, making sure he caught the "we" part. "That's why we're still investigating."

"But Layla will…she'll get away if somebody doesn't go after her."

"We've looked for her, Sam. It isn't as if we have any terrific leads on where she might have gone." And it wasn't as if there was no one else with motive. The Vargas were definitely hiding something, and Harvey Hackett as much as admitted he was jealous of Tupper. "If we spend time going after her and she didn't do it, the real killer will get away."

They were short-handed here. Until they could give the police something to convince them this wasn't suicide, they were on their own. She wasn't about to explain all that to Sam. Parker was right. She'd already told their client too much.

She put her hands on her hips and watched Parker return Layla's key to the compartment where he'd gotten it.

She braced herself for him to dress her down. Instead he glanced past her.

She turned and realized he was looking at a young woman in an electric blue leotard doing a cartwheel in front of the RV across the lane.

The woman came upright and gazed back at Parker with a haughty look. "I thought breaking and entering was illegal."

CHAPTER TWELVE

Miranda shot across the street to the acrobat just as she turned and started another cartwheel, this time front to back.

"Excuse me, could we speak to you a moment?" she asked as the young woman's feet landed.

She flipped up with her nose wrinkled, her dark brows drawn together on a delicate Asian face. "Who are you? And why were you snooping around in Layla's trailer?"

Her frame was small. She wasn't much more than a girl. Maybe in her very earlier twenties or as young as nineteen. About five or six years older than Mackenzie. And with an attitude similar to Miranda's daughter's when she'd first met her.

Her long hair, dark with brassy blue and auburn streaks, was pulled back in a braid, and her pretty features glistened with sweat from her workout.

"That's who we want to talk to you about," Miranda told her. "Your neighbor."

Before the girl could answer, Sam appeared at Miranda's side.

"And what were you doing over there, Sam?" Layla's neighbor wanted to know.

Parker reached her other side just as Sam gestured toward her with a ring master's flourish. "This is Miranda Steele and Wade Parker. They're the detectives I hired to find out about Tupper."

A look of shock came over the young woman's face. "What about Tupper?"

"You know, about what happened to him." At least Sam was trying to be delicate this time. It was an improvement.

The girl squinted at him. "I thought the police said it was natural causes."

"They were wrong," Sam said.

So much for her client's improvement. Miranda gritted her teeth and gave him a warning look.

He scowled back but didn't say anything.

Miranda focused her attention on the neighbor. "And what's your name?"

"Biata. Biata Ito." She gestured to the RV she stood beside. "I live in this trailer with my older sister, Chavi." She pointed over her shoulder to the vehicle parked behind it in the next row. "Our parents live in that one, and my brother and his wife live in the one next door. We're the Flying Itos." Her tone oozed with pride.

"Trapeze artists?" Parker asked.

Biata looked at him and went typically gooey-eyed for an instant before jutting out her chin. "Yes. Some of the best in the world. I've been flying since I was ten."

No shortage of ego around here.

Miranda resisted the urge to clear her throat. "Ms. Ito, we're trying to find out more about Tupper and what might have happened to him. We don't know anything for certain right now about how he passed away."

"Okay." She folded her arms. "You're detectives?"

Miranda nodded. "From the Parker Investigative Agency in Atlanta."

"That's a long way to come."

She wasn't about to get distracted with an explanation of why they were here. Instead she got straight to the chase. "Ms. Ito, did you notice anything unusual the night Tupper Magnuson was found dead in his trailer?"

Her frown grew deeper.

"That was the night before last," Miranda prompted.

She blinked at her, looked at Sam, then at Parker. "Yes, I know when it was. We had finished the late show. We were done around nine. Surely you don't think I had anything to do with it."

"We're simply doing preliminary questioning right now," Parker said in a reassuring tone, since the young woman's gaze lingered on him.

"Did you see or hear anything unusual that night?" Miranda repeated.

Again Biata looked at Miranda, then as if she didn't know what else to do with herself, she bent over at the waist to stretch. "No. Nothing out of the ordinary. I had dinner with a friend, came home, took a shower, watched some TV, went to bed. Same as most nights after a show. I didn't hear about what happened until the next morning."

So far this interview was a big fat zero. Miranda pressed on. "How well did you know Tupper Magnuson?"

"Not very well. I don't hang around with the clowns much. But he was always over at Layla's." She gestured across the path at the trailer they had just searched. Then she bent at the waist, this time the other way, arms stretched over her head.

Miranda waited for her to come up again. "How well did you know Layla?"

Her thin shoulders went up and down under her blue leotard. "Enough to say hi. We didn't hang out or anything if that's what you mean."

"Had she been acting strange lately?"

Her shoulders bobbed again. "No stranger than usual. She was kind of an odd bird."

"In what way?"

"I don't know. Just different."

Everyone around here was different. "When was the last time you saw her?"

"Let me think." She drew her foot up and raised one leg in the air with her hand. "The last show. She did her act. I passed her in the tent backstage. We were in the final dance number together. That was it." The first leg came down, the second one went up.

"You didn't see her at her trailer later that night?"

She frowned, shrugged. "Not that I recall."

Miranda studied the young woman, wondering if she was telling the truth.

Sam took the opportunity of the pause to jump in. "You know Layla's gone, don't you, Biata?" His tone was demanding.

Miranda shot him another glare, wanting to give him a push and make him go away.

He folded his arms and shut his mouth. She hoped he'd keep it shut.

Unfazed Biata nodded across the way. "It's been pretty quiet over there. I wasn't sure what happened." She lowered her leg and shifted as if she was about to leave.

"Did you see Layla with a bag or a suitcase that night?" Parker asked.

She cocked her head and gave him a half grin. "Not that I recall."

Miranda stepped around her to block her path. "But you said you were a trapeze artist. Didn't you and Layla work together? Didn't you have any personal conversations backstage?"

"No," she said with condescension. "Layla did an aerial silk act. It's completely different. She worked alone." Biata paused to sneer. "If she had worked in a troupe, she wouldn't have gotten away with the things she did."

Miranda glanced at Parker. Now they were getting somewhere. "What do you think she got away with?"

Biata peered down the path to the big top as if she didn't have time to explain. Then she sighed in resignation. "When Layla came here to Under the Big Top, she was an unknown. She had no background. No name, no circus family. Nobody knew where she came from."

"Doesn't everyone start out that way?"

The trapeze artist rolled her eyes, shaking her head at Miranda's ignorance. "No. My family, for example, has been with the circus for five generations. My great-great-grandfather started with PT Barnum in the nineteen twenties."

"Impressive."

Her dark eyes flashed. "It's more than impressive. All those years of passing down the traditions and skills of the trade? All those years of hard work and risk? It's the guarantee of an outstanding act."

Miranda resisted the urge to tap her foot in frustration. This didn't tell her anything about why the silk aerialist had left so suddenly. "But from what I hear, Layla's act was pretty good."

Biata put a hand to her forehead. "I...I don't know how to explain it to an outsider."

Oh, brother. Miranda folded her arms. "Try me."

"There was just something...weird about her...'phony' maybe that's the word. That act she does with the hoop? The way she suspends herself, draped over it backward?"

Miranda remembered seeing that in the picture in Tupper's photo album last night. "Yeah, what about it?"

"It's not the way it's done. I mean, if you do that, you have to have some sort of anchor holding you. Usually that's the wrap of the fabric. It's part of the skill, the art. The way the aerialist wraps the fabric around various parts of her body to secure herself. Sure, it's a daring act, but there's always something keeping you up there. The hoop is a little different, but it's more obvious."

"Obvious?"

She let out a frustrated breath as if she didn't know how to talk to this uninitiate. "There was this one bit she did with the silk where Layla didn't have anything holding her. Not that you could see. She was cheating somehow."

Miranda didn't know what to make of that. So the girl had good balance. If you pulled something off and made it look like you were suspended in air more or less, didn't that just make you a better performer?

This young lady was jealous of the competition.

As if she'd had enough of this annoying conversation, Biata swept around Miranda with the grace of a ballet dancer. "Like I said, I don't really know anything about what happened to Layla or Tupper. And if you'll excuse me, my family is waiting for me in the tent."

She turned to go.

Miranda didn't think they'd get anything more out of her and was ready to let her be when Sam suddenly reached out and grabbed the young woman by the arm.

"C'mon, Biata. You're Layla's neighbor. You had to have seen something the night she left. We think Layla knows who killed Tupper."

Biata's dark eyes blazed as she glared at him, both with shock and outrage. She pulled out of his grip. "I repeat. I don't know anything. I have to go now, Sam. I'm late."

And she turned and trotted off toward the tent.

Miranda was so furious, she couldn't think straight. What in the hell did Sam think he was doing telling her they thought Layla knew who killed Tupper?

She spun around to him, about to read him the riot act. "Look, Sam. I know you're trying to help, but—"

Parker's low, ominous tone drifted over her shoulder. "A word with you, Miranda."

She turned to him.

He looked cool and calm, but she could see under that unruffled surface he was ten times madder than an angry volcano. Without saying anything else, he gestured to a vacant area between the trailers across the path.

Leaving Sam to wonder what was going on, she followed her partner to the spot.

Parker shifted to face her as soon as they were out of earshot. His expression was harder, hotter under the quiet exterior, than she'd ever seen it. "I've had just about enough of this, Miranda."

He meant Sam, of course. She raised her hands. "I know, but—"

"Do you really think you're conducting this investigation properly?"

What? He was turning this on her? "What do you mean, Parker?"

"Dragging the client along on interviews?"

She didn't drag him. He butted in. Suddenly she turned defensive. She shoved her fists on her hips. "He's an in. He knows these people."

"He's feeding them answers. Leading them. Telling them details and conclusions he has no business voicing."

"Of course, he is. He doesn't know what he's doing. I was just about to tell him to find something else to do."

"You should have done that when he first arrived. It's a little late now."

Why was he suddenly being such a hard ass? "Are you saying I'm not capable of heading up this case? If you think that, why did you offer to take turns when we started?"

"Of course, you're capable." Somehow that came out as more of an insult than a compliment. "But on this one, your judgment is slipping."

She wanted to sock him. She was hot and tired and hungry. Her temper was ready to blow.

"Look, Parker," she said through gritted teeth. "My judgment is just fine. What's slipping is your ego."

He caught her drift and took a threatening step toward her. "Don't go there Miranda."

She raised her chin. "Or what?"

He opened his mouth, but she never got to hear what he had to say next.

Shrill screams tore through the air. A woman's screams.

"*Non! Non! Non!*" French accent. More shrieks. Heartbreaking cries for help.

Miranda spun away from Parker and hurried into the path between the trailers.

People were scurrying every which way. A crowd was gathering in front of Harvey's place.

She ran toward it.

CHAPTER THIRTEEN

When she reached the edge of the group, all Miranda could see were flailing arms and bright red curls flipping this way and that.

It was the woman with the dogs. *"Mon Dieu! Mon Dieu!"*

Someone was holding her from behind. Miranda recognized the scarred head of Yuri Varga, the human cannonball. "Calm down, Yvette."

"Calm? How can I calm down? My poor leetle Bobo! *Mon petit chouchou.*"

What the heck was going on? Miranda shoved her way through the circus folk to the corner of Harvey's trailer—and cringed at the sight. Right beside the spot where the clown had been practicing lay the shaggy white terrier.

He wasn't moving.

"Everyone back!" Parker's voice rang out strong and clear behind her.

She turned and watched him step past her and into the space between the trailers. She followed him as he quickly slipped on a plastic glove he'd used at Layla's trailer and bent down beside the pooch. He put a gentle finger to its throat, looked up at Miranda and shook his head.

"Oh, non. Non, non, non!" cried Yvette. "I must hold him. I can bring him back. He needs me now."

"Stay back, ma'am," Parker said to her. "It might not be safe here."

"What do you mean?"

But Miranda had already spotted what he meant. She put on her own gloves and gently pulled back the flowers of the one of the rosebushes. Parker stood and moved to her side.

Together they peered down at the liquid still dripping from the leaves and thorns. The poor, curious dog must have lapped some of it up.

Its source was wedged into the branches at an angle allowing some of its contents to spill over onto the plants. From where she stood Miranda could read the label clearly.

It was a bottle of Barefoot Merlot.

CHAPTER FOURTEEN

"What in the frick-fracking hell is going on here?" A big, gray-headed man with a booming voice stepped through the crowd like a giant striding across a mountain pass, and the people parted before him like fearful slaves.

He made his way over to the edge of Harvey's trailer.

"It's my poor leetle Bobo," the French woman told him. "Someone has keeled him."

Without entering the yard the man stared down at the poor pooch and his neck and face turned red with rage. Miranda noticed his wide nose was crooked, like it had been broken in several places. His face wore the rugged look of an old cowboy who'd been around a long time.

"Another act gone?" He let out a string of curses that would make the guys on the ring crew blush. Then he glared at Miranda and Parker. "Who the hell are you two?"

He was massively tall, almost as big as Yuri, the cannonball. He had thick curly gray brows, curly gray hair combed back at the sides and long at the neck. Over wrestler's arms and a muscled chest, he had on a fire-engine red T-shirt with the UTB logo and a leather vest. Very worn jeans and a pair of snakeskin cowboy boots completed the look. Plus a belt buckle featuring a cowboy on a steer and the word "Rodeo."

Sam stepped out of the crowd. "Mr. Tenbrook, these are the detectives I hired."

Tenbrook. As she had guessed, this was the big cheese around here. The owner.

A head taller than Sam, who was no shrimp, Tenbrook turned to glower at his employee. "I didn't tell you to hire any detectives, Keegan."

Sam tipped his Stetson back and glared at his boss as if he was about to get into it with him. "It's a free country."

Miranda opened her mouth, about to spare Sam by giving the owner the latest update when another shout came from the back of the crowd.

"Stand back! Official police business."

59

Again the audience moved aside and Sergeant Underwood appeared, followed by the big bald guy they'd seen at the station earlier. Somebody called the police already?

"What seems to be the problem here?" Underwood stepped into the grassy yard between the trailers and looked down at the body. Her cheeks glowed hot. "We don't do animal deaths."

"You'll want to see this, Detective," Parker told her and gestured to the rose bush.

With a this-better-be-good glare, she marched over to where he indicated. When she saw what lay wedged between the thorny branches, her shoulders sank.

"Peluso," she said to the officer with her. "Get the CSIs over here. I think we just located our murder weapon."

Before Peluso could move to carry out the order, the trailer door banged open and Harvey appeared still in his undershirt and baggy pants. "What's all this ruckus?" he growled as if he didn't notice there were police in his yard.

Underwood shaded her eyes with her hand and scrutinized him. "Are you the owner of this trailer, sir?"

Harvey shrugged. "It's the one I've been assigned to. The circus owns it."

"We'll need to speak with you. Step out of the trailer, please."

Harvey's mouth twisted in a bizarre grimace. "You've got to be joking. I'm taking a nap. We've got rehearsal tonight."

Underwood's shoulders went military stiff. "Please step out of the trailer, sir. It's regarding the matter of Tupper Magnuson's death."

"What?"

Tired of arguing with the man, Underwood simply gestured for him to come down.

After lifting his arms to the sky with an exaggerated eye roll, as if he were in the ring, Harvey shuffled down his front steps.

Peluso took him by the arm and led him through the crowd to a police car for questioning.

CHAPTER FIFTEEN

So Sam was right. Tupper had been murdered.

Miranda stood in the crowd rubbing her arms, kicking at the dirt and watching the few police officers Underwood had available interview the circus employees one by one.

"Looks like we've been shoved out of this one," she muttered to Parker under her breath.

"We'll get back in," he said, his gunmetal gray eyes fixed on the CSIs processing the rose bushes.

But now that they'd pointed the police in the right direction, he just might take the first opportunity to call the case closed and head home. She could tell his ribs were aching, though no one else would have noticed.

"Do you think Harvey did it?" she asked him.

Parker's grim expression turned thoughtful. "He had opportunity."

"And motive and means, too." A jealous clown with a drinking problem and easy access to Tupper's trailer. "I wonder how long he was napping. I didn't see the bottle when we were here before."

"We might have missed it," Parker said.

She didn't think so. "One thing we know for sure. The killer doesn't care who he hurts. One of the kids around here could have come by and gotten into those bushes."

"Indeed. It was bad enough the dog did."

Miranda could see the death of an innocent animal bothered him. Parker had a soft spot for all living things. It upset her as well. She could still hear the cries of the poor owner in her head and knew they'd stay with her a while.

"And another thing. If the killer put the bottle there after we saw Harvey, it couldn't have been Sam. He was with us the whole time."

"Unless he put it there right before he found us with the Vargas."

She scowled at him. He just wasn't going to give Sam a break.

Her heart heavy, she turned away and gazed across the yard.

Sam was trotting over to them, his hat in his hand, his face lined with worry.

He shook his head as soon as he reached them. "Looks like Harvey's in bad trouble."

Yeah. A tippler with a cyanide-laced wine bottle hidden in his rose garden. The police were going to latch onto that like a shark on a bloody leg.

"I'm sorry, Sam." It was all she could think to tell him.

He looked up at her in shock. "You don't think he did it, do you?"

"He's a likely suspect," she said.

"No. Harvey didn't do it. He couldn't. I know him."

"He'll need more than a character witness to prove his innocence, Mr. Keegan." Parker had that annoyed tone in his voice again.

"Look, I hired you. I want you to find Layla. She's got to know something about all this."

Miranda watched Parker's face turn to stone. *Uh oh. Here it comes.* This case was over.

"You there!"

All three of them turned toward the booming voice of the circus owner. He strode across the grass like Paul Bunyan through Texas, batting the air with his hand. "Keegan. I want to see you and your two PIs in my office pronto."

Sam didn't like that idea. "Mr. Tenbrook, the police still have to talk to me and I—"

"I've already arranged it. Detective Underwood will call me when they're ready for you. This way." He gestured with his big hands.

"Yessir." Sam hung his head and started away from the crime scene.

"Let's see what we can learn from the owner," Parker murmured in her ear as they followed behind.

"Right," she nodded.

CHAPTER SIXTEEN

The twenty-four-foot trailer that served as Tenbrook's office was nicer than Miranda expected. Its walls were oak panels, its floor pale beige tiles, its L-shaped desk and chairs executive-style. Plus it was wonderfully cool and it really felt good to get off her feet and sink into soft cream-colored leather.

Tenbrook reached inside a small fridge unit and pulled out chilled bottles of water. He passed them out without asking if they were wanted. Not that anyone would refuse a cold drink after spending the afternoon tromping around in the hundred-degree heat, but the circus boss was obviously a man who didn't take no for an answer.

Miranda eyed a tall whiteboard along one wall that was covered in chicken scratch she took to be the list of acts. Tupper's name had several question marks beside it and a big arrow pointing to Harvey's name.

Tenbrook sank into his executive chair with a groan. He pressed his bottle against his forehead and waved his free hand at the board. "So now I'm down two clowns, and I'm a total of three acts short."

Sam swallowed a swig of water and wiped his mouth against his arm. "Yvette told me she could go on with Winky instead of Bobo."

"The Chihuahua?"

Sam nodded. "Right."

"Are they ready? Is she...steady enough to perform?"

"She seemed pretty insistent on it when I spoke to her just now."

"We'll see how she is a little later. That woman's as fickle as..." he trailed off.

Tenbrook pointed his bottle at Parker. "How's this investigation I wasn't just informed about going? Do you concur with the police? Am I going to get my clown back soon?" Meaning Harvey.

Parker paused to take a dignified sip of water before answering. "We've only begun, Mr. Tenbrook. It's far too early to tell you anything."

Tenbrook scowled at that reply and stared at the board.

Miranda studied the photos that hung on the opposite wall over a pair of small beige filing cabinets. In addition to a gaudy *Under the Big Top* flyer were pictures of the younger Tenbrook. Tenbrook performing as a rodeo clown. Tenbrook riding a motorcycle through a blaze of fire as a stuntman. Tenbrook leaping off an exploding building. Tenbrook on fire running from a demolished car.

At the far end were several photos of the man today. He stood smiling under a spotlight in the middle of the ring, dressed in top hat and a sparkling gold suit coat.

"You're the ring master?"

He studied her a moment before answering. "That's common for the owner. I'm also the lead creative director. I have assistants, of course. But UBT is my brain child. My baby."

"I see." Talented guy. Miranda looked at the photos again. They were all of the owner. "You have family, Mr. Tenbrook?"

He grinned. "Three ex-wives and five children of assorted ages. You can see why I have to wear so many hats. Alimony." But he didn't have any pictures of his kids in his office. In fact, he didn't seem too concerned about anything but himself, his show, and his wallet.

"Then you'll realize how lucky you were that wine bottle was found before any of the children here got hurt," Parker pointed out.

Tenbrook narrowed his eyes at Parker then raised his water bottle in agreement. "You're right, Mr. Parker. Astute observation. And UBT would have been liable. I guess I owe you two a debt of gratitude."

"Guess you do," Sam said, as if hoping his boss ought to give him some credit.

Tenbrook ignored him and studied his whiteboard. "This is all starting to sink in now. Sorry, you'll have to give me a minute." He set his bottle down on his desk, got to his feet and turned his back. Running his fingers through his wavy gray hair he began to mutter half to himself. "I've had trouble with Harvey for some time now. His drinking really gives him an attitude. And he was viciously jealous of Tupper. A week didn't go by that he didn't come to me and complain about this or that."

"Such as?" Miranda asked.

The large man turned around and his body seemed to take up half the space in the trailer. "Oh, how Tupper stole his bowling pin bit. How Tupper didn't have the credentials he did. How Tupper was 'cheating' when he went to hospitals to entertain kids. I don't know where he got that idea. For a long time, I've thought he was losing it. I encouraged him to get help, but he didn't listen. Now I wish I'd been firmer about that."

Hard to imagine this guy not being firm about anything having to do with his show, his "baby" as he put it.

He sat on the edge of his desk and ran a hand over his face. "I guess the police have the right man after all. Too bad." He let out a long sigh that almost made Miranda feel sorry for him. "We'll have to postpone the memorial show for Tupper a day. We can't have the dress rehearsal tonight without a lead clown."

Sam shot Miranda a look of annoyance. "Mr. Tenbrook?"

"What is it, Sam?"

"I think...I mean...what about Layla?"

"What about Layla?"

"She's missin', you know." Part of Sam's charm was stating the obvious in that boyish way of his. But this was news to Tenbrook.

Miranda watched the circus owner's rugged face go from sorrowful to shocked.

"What do you mean she's missing?"

"She hasn't been home. Not since the night Tupper passed. We just went to her trailer. It looks like she—"

"Mr. Tenbrook," Miranda interrupted sharply, more irritated with Sam than ever. "We think Layla may have left for a few days. Did she say anything to you about being away?"

Tenbrook stared at Layla's name on the whiteboard. Once again he pressed a massive hand to his massive forehead. He looked like he was getting a massive headache.

"No," he said in nearly a whisper. "She...she didn't say anything to me." He turned to them, eyes glazed. "Are you saying something happened to my star performer?"

"We don't know that," Miranda said. "That's why we're asking questions. Did she have family in the area?"

"Not that I know of."

Sam looked like he was about to explode. "Doesn't anybody think it's funny Layla disappeared at the same time Tupper was killed?"

Tenbrook folded his arms. "How do you know that?"

"I went to her trailer right after the police were done with me that night. I knocked and knocked but she wasn't there. We were just over there when...all the commotion broke out just now. She's gone."

Tenbrook frowned. "Tupper and Layla were engaged two weeks ago," he explained to Miranda and Parker.

"Yes," Miranda said. "Sam told us that."

He lifted his big shoulders. "Maybe she found the body and got spooked, ran away?"

"Without even telling anybody what had happened? Without calling 911?"

Tenbrook's gaze shifted from Sam to Miranda to Parker and back again. Wheels were turning in his head. But there seemed to be more he was considering than Layla's possible motives for bolting. "Do you think she was...involved?"

Sam took a long while to answer. "I don't know. Maybe," he said at last as he gestured at Miranda. "I want them to find her."

Tenbrook rubbed his chin. "That might not be a bad idea."

Miranda turned to Parker with a frown. His expression telegraphed his thoughts to her.

"Mr. Tenbrook," she told him. "We're not even sure Layla's aware her fiancé is dead. She may be back shortly. And we need to see what further information the police have gathered about the current suspect first."

Tenbrook was still back at the murder scene. "Layla might have seen something that night. Perhaps Harvey threatened her."

It was a thought that had been running through her head and Parker's as well, she knew.

"Yeah," Sam agreed. "Harvey and Layla didn't exactly get along. She pretty much avoided him."

"According to her neighbor Biata, she pretty much avoided most people," Miranda said.

Tenbrook gave her a hard look. "That was another thing Harvey complained to me about. He had a powerful crush on Layla. He hated it when she took up with Tupper." He got to his feet and reached for a drawer in his desk. "If it's a matter of money, I'd be happy to cover your fees and expenses."

"That won't be necessary just yet," Parker told him. "But if you have any background information on Layla, it would be helpful."

"Background information?"

"Her last known residence? State of birth?"

"I believe she was born in Bulgaria somewhere. Where was it now?" He scratched his head. "Khaskovo?"

"Then I assume she has a green card or a work visa. You would have a record of it in her employee file, wouldn't you?"

"Employee file? Uh…" He grinned sheepishly and pulled out a few drawers, closed them again. "You know, that's the one thing I have trouble keeping up with. Paperwork, what a bitch," he chuckled. "Pardon my French," he said to Miranda.

"Mr. Tenbrook," Parker said and Miranda caught the annoyance in his voice. "We don't even know this woman's last name. Or her real name, if Layla is a stage name."

"Last name? It's…uh…" He pressed a hand to his forehead as if he could squeeze it out. "You know, I don't think she ever told me her last name. Do you know what it is, Sam?"

Sam shook his head. "No, sir."

Disgusted, Miranda got to her feet. "We'll see what we can do, Mr. Tenbrook. Right now, we need to give our statements to the police."

"I understand. Certainly. I appreciate your help in this matter." He extended a hand to her, then to Parker. "The sooner we can get this all settled and behind us, the better."

"We'll do our best," Parker said.

But the tall order of finding the clown- and dog-killer had just gotten taller.

CHAPTER SEVENTEEN

It took another hour and a half for the police to finish with the circus personnel they were interviewing. While she and Parker waited, Miranda decided they needed to do more of their own questioning while everyone was out.

They spoke to the jugglers, an acrobat team, a dude who rode a unicycle, the distraught Yvette Nannette. They also found Danny, Sam's friend, whose last name turned out to be Ackerman.

Danny Ackerman was a tall, dark-haired guy, who looked as innocent as his baby face. Not that that proved anything, but his account of the night Tupper was killed matched Sam's. With him, as with the others, they learned nothing new.

Except that the police had taken Harvey Hackett into custody.

A cop called Miranda away to take her statement, and by the time he'd finished with her, she'd lost track of Parker.

As she tromped around the grounds hunting for him, she passed the Vargas's trailer and spotted the petite Dashia taking clothes down from a line.

She stepped through the grass toward the woman. "Mrs. Varga, I was wondering if I could ask you a few more questions."

The woman laid the sheet she'd just finished folding into her basket and glared at Miranda. "I have already spoken to the police, Ms. Steele."

"Mrs. Varga, one of your coworkers is dead. And another appears to be missing."

With a hiss, she pulled a clothespin off one of the boy's T-shirts and put it in her pocket. "I'm very well aware of what has gone on here the past few days. I do not need a reminder."

"I'm not trying to upset you." Miranda reached for a second shirt to help.

As she touched it, Dashia yanked it out of her hand. "I barely knew Tupper or Harvey."

"What about Layla?"

She paused, another clothespin in midair. Then shook her head firmly. "I didn't know her well."

Of course, she didn't. "If you can remember anything, any little detail, it would really help."

She shook her head again, making her flyaway hair even more flyaway. "No. No details."

Drop it, Miranda told herself. The woman wasn't talking. But she couldn't help pressing one more time. "If you heard anything unusual. Saw anything."

Dashia picked up her laundry and spun around, the basket almost swallowing her small frame. Anger lit up her features like a spotlight. "I told you before, Ms. Steele. I don't know anything. I didn't see anything. I didn't hear anything. Now please. Leave me alone."

And she turned on her heel and took the basket into the trailer slamming the door behind her.

So much for the close-knit circus family, Miranda thought as she stood staring at the door. But there was one thing she knew for certain now.

That woman was lying through her diminutive teeth.

When she finally found Parker, he said he was ready to call it a day and she agreed.

They plodded through the yard to the rental car in silence, both of them deep in thought.

"I think we ought to focus on Layla," she said at last, feeling spent.

Parker's gaze was fixed ahead as he mulled over the bizarre events. "Has Keegan convinced you she knows who the killer is?"

Miranda shot him a scowl. "She might know. Besides she's a missing piece of the puzzle. Where is she? What the heck happened to her? Did Harvey do anything to her?"

He frowned. "Difficult to reconcile that with the state of her trailer."

Meaning it looked like she had packed a bag and taken off.

Miranda thought a moment. "Okay, how about this? She breaks up with Tupper and decides to leave after the show night before last. She's heading out with her bags when Harvey spots her."

"And he grabs her? And incriminates himself?"

"He's not thinking about that. Tenbrook said he had a 'powerful crush' on Layla. He's just offed his rival, he knows he'll get his spot in the show. Now he wants it all. Maybe he takes her somewhere. He could have her bound and gagged in some sleazy hotel in the area."

Parker's face went grim. "Or, if she was a certain type of person, she might have been the one to kill Tupper and hide the bottle in Harvey Hackett's rose bushes to put the blame on him."

"And the little dog tipped it over and took his last lap." Feeling miserable about that, Miranda pulled at her hair. "At any rate, there are just too many questions around Layla. We need to find her. But how are we going to do that with no data on her at all?"

"We can look at hotels, as you said. We can also do some research on the Internet." Among many other things, Parker was a master at e-research.

"Yeah. Okay."

They had just reached the car when Miranda's stomach grumbled. She hadn't had anything since breakfast and it was past dinnertime.

"Perhaps we should eat first." Parker gave her a tender half smile.

He was right. She couldn't think with her head clouded by hunger.

She was about to tell him she was starving when the rumble of an approaching engine caught her ear. She turned and saw Sam pulling up on a midnight blue Harley.

He swung over to the side of the narrow road. "Sorry, I lost track of you two."

Miranda wasn't sorry, but the sight of that ride had her suddenly drooling. It made her think of the bikes Parker bought for them when he was trying to win her over.

"We were about to get a bite to eat, Sam," Parker told him, with an implied "alone" in the statement.

Sam ignored the insinuation. "Say, I know of a great Texas Barbeque place you'd really love." It sounded like an open invitation, but Sam was staring straight at Miranda. And his cagey, boyish smile seemed to be saying, "Let's dump him."

Plus Sam knew her well enough to know she wouldn't be satisfied riding in a rental car when she could be on the back of a Harley. He was making a play for her.

Did he really think she'd go with him without Parker? Was he out of his mind?

She needed to straighten him out. About her relationship with Parker and about sticking his two cents into their investigation. Tell him thank you very much, but they didn't need his help.

"Look, Sam. Parker and I—"

"Go ahead, Miranda."

She spun around and stared at Parker. "Huh?"

He gave her a smile so cool, the temperature seemed to drop twenty degrees. "You and Sam have dinner together. I'll start that research and get something back at the hotel."

"What?"

Parker watched the look of shock and outrage in his wife's deep blue eyes. Those vivacious eyes with their black, razor-sharp lashes that had stolen his heart the first time he'd gazed into them. They told him she would never betray him. Not that he needed reassurance.

He was convinced by now Keegan was just what he said he was. Someone close to the victim who wanted to know who'd killed his friend. Not the one who'd done it.

He was also convinced Keegan had ulterior motives regarding Miranda. And that she carried around unresolved feelings about this man. They had some sort of primal connection. In this personal matter between his wife and their new client, she didn't know her own heart. At the moment, Parker wasn't sure of it either.

All he knew was, if he didn't let those feelings play out here and now, they might follow them home. They might fester there. Simmer and bubble under the surface until they exploded—and drove her away from him.

And Keegan would be sure to take advantage of that. Even from eight hundred miles away.

He studied the way the man was looking at her. It took all he had not to march over to him, tear him off that motorcycle, and knock the grin off his face.

But that wouldn't put out the lingering fire between Miranda and this man from her past. That would only rekindle the flame. Only make it burn hotter. And bring resentment as well.

Though it took all the resolve he had, he knew he had to risk letting that fire blaze to its fullest…or it would never burn out.

Miranda couldn't catch her breath. Parker was really telling her to go have dinner with Sam? She didn't know which one of them was crazier. Or maybe she was the one losing her mind.

Last night, he'd acted like a jealous lover, and now…he wasn't even going to protest? Wasn't going to guard her from this marauder in he-man style? Wasn't going to fight for her?

Suddenly that thought made her madder than a charging bull at a rodeo. She gave her hair a snippy flip and strode toward the bike.

"Sure. I'll go." She swung her leg over the backseat. She'd set Sam straight, then set Parker straight as well. "I'll see you back at the hotel then."

Parker just nodded. "Until then."

While she was still reeling from his cold response, Sam waved goodbye and wasted no time in heading down the narrow back lot road to the highway.

CHAPTER EIGHTEEN

The place Sam had in mind for dinner was Buckin' Bronco Barbeque just off I-30 on the outskirts of the city. They parked the Harley in the lot behind the place and went inside.

Loud country line dancing music hit her when she stepped through the door. The walls were lined with spurs and saddles and pictures of cowboys roping steers, and the air was filled with the scrumptious odor of slow cooked meat.

Soon a friendly waitress led them to a wooden table with a plastic red-and-white checkered tablecloth. They got settled, ordered, and the waitress disappeared leaving them with an awkward silence between them.

Sam hung his hat on the rung of a nearby chair. "What a day, huh?" He looked weary and very sad.

"Yeah."

"I hate what happened to Yvette's dog. Bobo was a real star in her act. Poor little thing."

She studied his good-looking face for any trace of insincerity but couldn't find it. "You like working in the circus, Sam?"

"Oh, yeah. It's great. Guess I've got sawdust in my blood." He chuckled quietly. "I'm lucky UBT has kept me on three years. They let some folks go after the first year's up."

"I see."

His smile faded as he shook his head. "I meant what I said before. I don't think Harvey could have hurt Tupper." He raised a hand as if to ward off her protest. "I know he was jealous of him. I got an earful of that myself. But in the circus, we're all family. We might scrap with each other some, but deep down we all respect one another. We love each other."

Really? Miranda resisted the urge to drum her fingers on the table. Even family members sometimes killed each other.

But that wasn't why she was here. She leaned forward, trying to look as businesslike as she could. "Look, Sam. When we're talking to someone I need you to—"

"Here we are." The grinning waitress arrived at their tables and set two overflowing plates down before them. Then she refilled their glasses from an icy pitcher. "Can I git you anything thing else, sugar?" she said to Sam.

"I'm fine."

"You, honey?" she asked Miranda.

She could only shake her head and stare down at a half slab of juicy ribs, potato salad and jalapeño-laced *charro* beans. Plus loaf bread and sweet tea on the side. It was a feast. More than she could eat right now with the way she was feeling.

"Let me know if you need anything. I'm Judy."

"Sure."

The woman disappeared.

Despite her distress over the case and her concern for Layla, Miranda couldn't keep her mouth from watering. Still it felt weird to be dined, and ice-tea'ed—if not wined—by Sam instead of Parker.

The man in question picked up a rib from his own plate. "Well? What are you waitin' for, darlin'? Chow down."

Darlin'? But she was too hungry to debate what Sam wanted to call her. She lifted the first rib and bit into it.

Oh, yum! Succulent and flavorful and just what she needed. Sam always did know good food.

"It's East Texas style. Thought you'd like it because of this." He slid a small green bottle toward her labeled "Bull Snort Texas Sweat."

"Sure." She snatched it up and shook it over the ribs like it was ketchup.

"Be careful with that," Sam started to say then raised a hand. "Never mind. Forgot who I was talkin' to."

She took another bite. This time along with the juicy meat, the spicy hot sauce sizzled and snapped on her tongue. Just the way she liked it.

"Mmm. Good," she said with her mouth full.

Sam chuckled and shook his head. "Same ole Kick-Ass Steele. Remember the time back in Phoenix when you ate that big guy under the table in jalapeños?"

Miranda shrugged. She'd done that in a lot of places.

"Oh, c'mon. You had him turning red and cryin' like a baby before you even broke a sweat."

She thought a moment and a vague recollection came back of Sam at her side cheering her on. "Oh, yeah. What was the name of that place we used to go to?"

"Rosie's." His boyish half smile made her feel suddenly warm and nostalgic as he pointed a saucy rib at her. "Remember those two thugs you flattened one night? They were harassing one of the overworked barmaids."

She gnawed on her rib as the memory came to her of a burly guy and his buddy lying on the peanut-shell strewn floor, crying for mercy. She hadn't done that alone. "You helped."

"But I'll bet those guys haven't forgotten you, Steele. You made a real impression on them."

She drank some tea and grinned. "Mostly with the new dents in their foreheads."

"Yep," he drawled, his forest green eyes twinkling with admiration. "I've thought about you a lot over the years."

Feeling uncomfortable, she reached for a wipe and began to clean her hands.

Before she could finish, Sam caught one in his. "I've missed you, Miranda."

Her breath stuck in her throat as a flutter went through her. She sat up and gently eased her hand out of his. "Sam, I need to tell you something."

His smile disappeared. "What?"

She took a minute to get her thoughts together. She didn't like telling clients her marital status for fear she'd be treated like the little wifey, just along for the ride instead of the full-fledged investigator she was. But Sam wouldn't think of her that way.

She decided simple and straightforward was best. She looked her dinner partner right in his sexy eyes. "I'm married, Sam."

"Married?" Shock spread over his face like a herd of longhorn crossing a plain.

"To Parker."

For a moment she wasn't sure he wouldn't get up and stalk out of the place leaving her to find a ride home. As last he puffed out a breath and shook his head. "That explains a lot. I never figured you for a hyphenated woman."

"I'm not hyphenated. I kept my own name for business reasons."

He studied her a long moment with an expression she couldn't read. "So you married the boss, huh?"

I married the man I love, she wanted to say. Instead, different words came out. "Guess so."

He considered that a moment. "Is that what your relationship with him is? All business?"

"No." What the heck was he implying?

He leaned forward and took her hand again. "Are you happy, Miranda?"

What was he planning to do if she told him "no?" Thank God she didn't have to. "Deliriously happy," she said flatly and pulled her hand out of his again.

He raised a brow. "Really? Didn't look like it to me this afternoon."

Good grief. He'd heard them arguing. Over him. She shifted in her chair and wiped her hands some more. "All couples fight sometimes."

"If you say so. We never did."

Now he was making her mad. She wasn't sure she'd have called them a couple. "We never got that far," she snapped.

His eyes blazed back at her. "Can't blame me for that."

"Look, Sam—" Just then her cell went off. Damn. She was about to mute it when she saw the call was from Fanuzzi. Saved by the best friend back home. "I've got to take this," she told him and turned away as she answered. "Steele."

Fanuzzi's sarcastic Brooklyn accent rang in her ear. "Oh? I'm sorry. I must have dialed the wrong number. I was trying to reach my friend who was supposed to call me two days ago."

Miranda sighed, remembering her conversation with Becker in the office before she left. "I know. I know. I'm sorry I didn't get back to you. I'm on a case."

Fanuzzi's tone immediately turned worshipful. "A case? With Parker? A juicy one?"

"Uh...can't really talk right now." She glanced over at Sam and saw he was eyeing her with wounded curiosity. "I'm with a client."

"Oh. Sorry, Murray. I didn't know. I'll call back later."

"No, it's okay." A chewing out from Fanuzzi was better than facing Sam right now. "We're just...uh, finishing up. What did you want to ask me?"

She could almost hear Fanuzzi shaking her head. "I wanted to talk to you about the anniversary party I want to throw you and Parker. Dave said he mentioned it?"

"Oh, yeah." Now guilt flooded her like a dry gulch after a downpour. Her first wedding anniversary was coming up soon, and she'd hardly given it a moment's thought. "What about it?"

"I need a date. I have to work it around some personal plans."

Of course, she did. Fanuzzi and Becker tied the knot just a few weeks before she and Parker had.

"I'm thinking the Saturday before the actual date, since your anniversary falls on Sunday. Will that work for you two?"

"Uh..." How the heck should she know? "I'll have to check with Parker and get back to you."

"Yeah, right. I'll call you. But it'll be soon. Like I said, I've got some things going on, too."

Relief hit her hard. She'd just let Parker handle the arrangements. "Okay. Thanks."

"No problem. Oh, and Murray?"

"Yeah?"

"Don't forget Wendy's skating in the Atlanta Open next Saturday. We're all going to be there."

Oh, crap. She didn't even know if they'd be done with this case by then. Or if they'd have another. But she had to be there. She couldn't miss the big event of the girl she'd grown so close to the past year.

"You didn't forget, did you?"

Miranda cleared her throat. "No, of course not. Why would you think that?"

"Anyone ever tell you you're a really bad liar?"

She almost growled under her breath. "Thanks for reminding me anyway. I'll be there." Somehow.

"Good to hear it. Talk to you later."

"Later."

She hung up and saw Sam had already paid the check and was studying her pensively. "You've changed."

"What do you mean?"

"Sounds like you've got a personal life now. You used to be pretty much of a loner. No matter how hard I tried to change that."

He'd wanted to get close. He'd wanted to be a couple back then. Right now, she didn't want to talk about it.

She wiped her mouth on her napkin and got to her feet. She was tired of this walk down Memory Lane. "I need to get back to the hotel, Sam."

He stood, stretching his long, attractive body, took his hat off the rung of the chair where he'd stashed it and tipped it to her. "Sure thing, ma'am."

CHAPTER NINETEEN

When she unlocked the door to the downtown hotel suite and stepped inside, Miranda found Parker sitting at the fancy desk in the window working away at his laptop, an expression of intense concentration on his handsome face.

A plate of crumbs and a coffee cup sat on the desk beside him. Remnants of a lonely meal.

The sight filled her with anguish.

Why did she have to go off with Sam? What had she been trying to prove?

She closed the door and moved up behind him quietly. "Hi there."

"Hello," he said without looking up from the screen.

Her heart sank at his chilly tone. "Missed you at the restaurant," she ventured.

"I had something here."

"So I see." She picked up the plate, moved it to the coffee table, and settled a haunch on the table next to him. Get to the chase, she decided. "I told Sam we're married tonight."

That got his attention. He stopped staring at the screen and turned to look at her. But she couldn't read him. She waited several long minutes for the news to sink in.

Parker studied his wife's face for any sign of delusion, of misdirection, of deception. Not that he thought she would lie to him. But that she might lie to herself. He saw nothing but honesty.

Had the flame of the past reawakened and died out as quickly as he'd hoped it would? Or had her dinner with Keegan left a coal smoldering under the embers? He couldn't be sure and he hated being unsure of anything. Especially when it came to the woman he loved.

The whole time she'd been away he'd been struggling with the urge to fight for her, to claim what was his, to find Keegan and tear him limb from limb. But he wasn't a caveman. And Miranda wasn't a piece of meat, a prize to be won. She was an intelligent human being with feelings and opinions of her own.

76

Feelings she had a right to.

Had she discovered those feelings were stronger for Keegan than for himself? He chafed at the very thought. He sounded like a jealous schoolboy. But he knew this wasn't jealousy. No, this was facing reality. A reality more painful than the beating he'd taken a few weeks ago.

His wife did in fact have feelings for this man from her past.

So she'd told Keegan they were married. And what else?

Death had taken two women he'd loved dearly. He'd feared he'd lose Miranda that way sooner or later. He never thought, even for an instant, he'd lose her to...another man.

His mind began to race as if out of control. He'd always believed in the sanctity of marriage, but he refused to keep Miranda with him against her will. Dear Lord, how could he live without her? He couldn't imagine. His life would be empty, meaningless. But if she would be happy—and above all, safe—with the man who had come before him, that would be all that mattered.

He drew in a breath to steady himself. "How did Keegan take the news?" he dared to ask.

She rolled her eyes with a disgusted expression. "Not real well. You know how men are." She reached over and punched him on the arm.

Miranda grinned at him, then stopped when he didn't respond. His reaction was like an icy spike through her heart. It made her angry. "What do you want from me, Parker?"

His muscular chest rose and fell. "What do you think I want?"

Stop answering a question with a question, she wanted to scream at him. He was interrogating her like she was a suspect.

Instead she jumped off the desk and began to stomp around the space between the desk and the bed. She didn't want to be caught between two men. For years and years, she'd never wanted any man in her life. How did she ever wind up with two of them?

She pulled at her hair in sheer frustration. She had no idea why Parker was acting this way. All right, maybe she shouldn't have had dinner alone with Sam, but Parker had suggested it, dammit. And she'd only done it because he'd made her so mad.

Suddenly she knew what he wanted from her. The truth.

She stopped pacing, spun on her heel, fisted both hands on her hips with a snarl. "Okay, smartass. I slept with him. Are you happy now?"

His expression didn't change.

"Not tonight."

"No," he said calmly. "When you knew him before."

He'd known, hadn't he? He'd known all along. He'd probably guessed it at the airport. No, when she first came to him with Sam's case in his office. She should have realized that. He could always see straight through her.

He drew in another slow breath as he fixed her with that cold, gun-metal gaze of his. "Why didn't you tell me?" This time his voice had just a touch of tenderness in it.

It broke her.

She sank down on the end of the bed and put her head in her hands. "Hell, I don't know, Parker."

He was quiet a long moment before he spoke again, even more softly than before. "Miranda, didn't we make a promise not to hide things from each other anymore?"

She stared at him.

After their last case they had vowed not to keep things from each other, not to hide things, as he said. Things about the case and how they intended to solve it. Not this kind of stuff.

"Professionally," she said. "That promise didn't apply to our personal lives."

He uttered a wry laugh laced with pain. The first human emotion he'd openly shown tonight. "Are you saying we'd have to make another vow not to hide our personal lives from each other?"

It sounded so awful when he said it like that. "No. I don't know."

She rubbed her hands over the thighs of her jeans. She had to tell him the truth. The whole truth. There was probably a Bible in the drawer she could swear on if he didn't believe her.

She didn't want to. She'd had enough of reliving this part of her past tonight. But it was only fair. He deserved to know.

She took a deep breath and began. "I met Sam Keegan when I was making my way around the southwest, passing through Phoenix."

He sat back, leaned an elbow on the desk, ready to listen.

"I got a job with a drywall company. We did hotels, high rises, apartment buildings, that sort of thing. Sam was a framer and I came on as a finisher trainee. He showed me the ropes, trained me, really. We hit it off."

Slowly he nodded. "And?"

"We...started hanging out together after work. We'd go out to a bar, get in a few fights with the local scumbags. You know."

"Um-hmm." Parker knew her background only too well.

"We had fun. He was the one who taught me to ride a motorcycle."

He shifted his weight and she knew that had to sting. "I see."

She could see his mind go back to the time she mentioned a pal in Phoenix who taught her how to ride.

"Sam was...the first nice guy I'd ever met. We hung around together maybe five or six months. Longest I'd stayed in one place. And Sam, well. He started getting serious. Really serious. Talking about a future together."

Parker folded his arms. He was still listening.

"And I got...well...nervous. You know how I was."

"I do."

"Then one night, we had a little too much to drink and I ended up going home with him." God, this was awkward. "He started kissing me, things got out of hand, and I ended up in his bed." She could still see the small apartment, the beer bottles and empty pizza boxes in the kitchen. The manly smell of the sheets on his bed. "Guess I was lonely. He told me he loved me that night."

Parker rose and came to sit down next to her on the bed. He took her hands in his and stared at them as if wrestling with himself. "What happened after you slept with Keegan?"

"What do you mean, what happened?"

"How did it end?"

She let out a long sigh. "I left."

He frowned. "Left?"

"Got up the next morning with a bad case of cold feet, packed up and took off. Didn't even leave him a note. Pretty rude, huh?" She tried for a laugh without success.

"I see." His voice was even more quiet and thoughtful.

He must not have guessed that part. Even though she'd tried to do the same thing with him—and failed.

Back then she didn't *do* love. She'd been done with that kind of crap after Leon. Until she met Parker. She hadn't wanted to have feelings for her boss, had fought them, fought him, with all she had.

But he was too good to her, too sexy, too mind-blowing. And he loved her with such a stubborn steadfastness, she had no defenses against him. In the end, she'd lost the battle. She just couldn't help falling in love with him right back.

Parker studied her long fingers and wrists that seemed too delicate for such a strong woman. She had her weaknesses. He'd thought he'd known them all. So Keegan hadn't been the one to break it off. That was a relief. That meant it was less likely there were residual issues to be resolved on Miranda's part. For Keegan, it was different. Perhaps that was why he'd gone after Miranda without even questioning if she was in a relationship. Perhaps he was looking for an explanation after all these years.

Miranda laid her hand on her husband's lap and forced out the words she knew she had to say. "Parker, do you want to drop this case and go home?"

He turned his head to face her, the shadow of a smile on his lips. She'd surprised him. "What do you want to do?"

"I want to find out who really killed Tupper. And about Layla. I want to find out why she's missing. I'd like to see it through. For professional reasons. Not because of Sam."

He studied her face for a long while as if he were looking for any small vestiges of her long ago mini affair. He must not have found any because at last he nodded and got to his feet.

"Very well. Let me show you the research I've been doing."

He took her hand and led her over to the desk, seated her in the chair.

"I found exactly two cut-rate motels in the area near UBT. Both of them small. No one matching Harvey or Layla's description had checked in during the past two days. And the maids had cleaned all the rooms in both establishments by this afternoon. They hadn't seen anything unusual."

Miranda let out a breath of relief. "That's something, then." Didn't mean she wasn't somewhere else, or Harvey hadn't killed her and tossed her in a field somewhere.

Parker pressed a key on his laptop and switched to an open browser window on the screen. "I've found some information on Harvey Hackett that might be pertinent."

She took the mouse and scrolled and read. Divorced. Ex-wife living in Houston. No kids. Arrested for DUIs several times over the past year. Treated for depression. She sat back. "This certainly impugns his character, but where would a guy like Harvey get cyanide from? He doesn't seem capable."

"He could be more resourceful than he appears. Or he could have an accomplice."

"Sam?" Was that what Parker was thinking?

"No, not Keegan. But perhaps someone else he knows." He pressed a key and flipped to a new page.

This one was a website for Yvette Nannette, the petite, vivacious dog trainer. Lots of pictures of her and her little dogs. Videos. Information about how she got started in the circus. She was born in a small town outside Paris, acquired a few miniature poodles and trained them to do funny stunts, started going to the festivals. She'd worked in Denmark, Finland, Croatia. No mention of a rap sheet.

Miranda clicked to another page of Parker's work. This was about Biata Ito and The Flying Itos. Again, nice photos and videos of performances. The trapeze artist's claim about her family history was correct. They started out in LA with Ringling Brothers and had worked every circus on the planet. Or so it seemed from the list.

Next page. Yuri and Dashia Varga. Just a photo of Yuri being shot out of a gaudily painted cannon, smoke everywhere. No videos. No bios. Just a short description of their act. That seemed odd.

Miranda looked around for another page. She'd reached the end. "What about Layla?"

"Nothing on her," Parker told her.

"Nothing at all?"

"Except for her photos on the UBT page, there's nothing. She doesn't even have her own website."

"Odd for a performer."

Parker let out a low breath of frustration. "Of course, it would help if we had a last name."

"Yeah," she smirked. "If you type in *Layla*, you'd mostly get links to the Eric Clapton song."

"And some pornographic sites."

"Well, you must have had fun while I was gone, then." Her joke died on her lips. She turned back to the Vargas's sparse web page with the exploding cannon and thought about how evasive the pair had been, how uneasy Dashia had been when she last talked to her. Especially about Layla. "I got a vibe from these two. They're hiding something."

"I got the same impression."

"In fact, I caught Dashia alone after the police took my statement this afternoon. She clammed up tight."

"Mmm," Parker murmured and let his gaze rove over his wife's lovely, lean body.

He loved watching her work, watching the fiery passion in her come to life with the skills he had taught her. At the moment, the sight distracted him, aroused him. At the moment, he didn't mind one bit.

"Okay. What do we do now?" Miranda pivoted around in the chair to face him.

"Now?" He lifted a strand of her hair, moved it between his fingers as his gray eyes locked on hers. "We do this." He slid his hand around her neck and drew her lips to his.

Their mouths met and her heart flooded with a sharp pang of joy.

He kissed her gently, caressed the back of her neck softly, as if she were a china doll, so fragile she might break.

The heck with that.

She jumped to her feet, yanked her sleeveless blouse over her head and reached for his knit shirt.

As she struggled with the fabric he sank his face between her breasts. "Miranda," he murmured.

"Parker," she whispered back to him, relishing the very sound of his name on her lips.

She gave up on the shirt and simply let her hands slide under it, let her fingers run over his muscled back. It felt so good. He felt good. It was as if they'd just met again after being separated for years.

He ran his fingers around her waist sending shivers through her core, and then he undid the button of her jeans and slowly pulled down the zipper. She did the same for him. Together they stepped out of the clothes and kicked them aside as if they were doing a choreographed dance move.

He pulled off his shirt, then went for her bra.

And then they both stood there panting and naked, eyeing the other's body as if they'd never seen each before. She wanted to touch him. Feel his flesh. Feel his skillful hands all over her.

She leapt into his arms, wrapped her legs around his waist, then regretted it when she saw him wince.

"Are you—?"

"I'm fine." And he took her mouth with his in a voracious kiss that was hot and furious and filled with the pent-up passion of weeks.

He moved them both to the bed, with her still clinging onto him and laid her down on her back. He began to work her over like a top MMA fighter in the ring works an opponent. His fingers seemed to take on a life of their own as they moved over her skin, her arms, her sides, her stomach. He was driving her insane. She felt crazed and giddy and more aroused than ever from the impossibly delicious sensations bombarding her. Surge after surge, wave after wave, until she cried out from sheer pleasure.

This was what she wanted, what she longed for. She loved him. Only him.

"Parker," she murmured, her voice little more than a soft muddled gasp. She wanted him. Now. She couldn't wait another instant. Though she was too overcome to form the words.

As if he read her thoughts, as if the desire he aroused in her had sparked from her body and into his like a lightning bolt, he locked his gaze on hers, hovered over her, and finally, at last took what was his.

CHAPTER TWENTY

In the white lab coat she thought of as her uniform, she paced the sterile floor of the observation room. As she did every night, she scrutinized the readings on each of the bank of monitoring machines and recorded her findings.

"D242, vitals satisfactory," she said into the speaker in her hand. "E311, progressing nicely." She moved to the next screen and frowned. "F412, development still appears somewhat stunted." She moved on.

Overall this new batch was doing better than the last. She hoped they wouldn't have to destroy any of them this time. Though the process was painless, it disturbed her.

But no need to be discouraged. Not at this point. They'd come a long way after more than twenty-five years of research and experimentation. Those first years had given them false hope. Success they hadn't been able to duplicate since. Out of an even dozen implantations nine had survived. A promising ratio.

But one by one, the successes had turned to failures and had had to be terminated. All but three.

The following year all the implantations had failed and she'd almost suspended the project. The Director wouldn't hear of that and so she'd continued on with her faithful staff. The third year there had been five successes out of nineteen. Only one had made it to full maturation.

They had kept on. After all the research was vital. It would change the world. They tried to keep the implantations alive. They performed surgeries as needed, provided the best care. But most lingered in an unsatisfactory state.

And so she had put all her hopes on the one success begun twenty-one years ago.

And now? What would happen to that success?

There was a knock on the door. It opened and the Director entered the room. He was a handsome man, in his late fifties now, with distinguished gray at his temples. She'd always thought him attractive.

"Have you made any progress yet?" he said.

She shook her head. "I have no idea where she is."

His face told her he wasn't happy with that answer. "None at all?"

"I told you. If only you had allowed tracking devices to be implanted before we released them—"

"And I told you that was too risky. What if they went through an airport and the device showed up on some scanner? It would lead straight to us."

She sank into a chair feeling bone weary. "Yes, you're right."

They couldn't let this facility be discovered. Not yet. Not before they were ready to make their findings public. Once they were truly successful, humanity would be advanced beyond anything that could currently be imagined. Many would not understand that. Many would try to stop them.

She refused to let that happen, to let all her years of work and struggle come to nothing.

She turned to a system, pressed a few keys on the keyboard. "I've been trying to plot her thought patterns. Extrapolate where she might have gone with the data we've collected on her since she was born."

The Director bent down and together they studied the complex maze of lines and graphs on the screen. She felt his breath against her neck and it made her skin tingle. Her mind filled with memories of the love they'd shared once upon a time. A love that had evaporated away years ago, like the dew.

"I think she might go west."

"That's all you have?" He was angry.

"All for now. I'll keep working at it. We know her. We created her. Surely we can find her." Though deep inside she feared it would take too long.

"I'll leave you to it then." The Director rose and went to the door. His hand on the knob he turned back, his face betraying a deep seated dread. "You'd better hope we get to her before the authorities do."

"Yes, yes. I know."

"I hope you do. If they find her first there will be hell to pay, Dr. Tenbrook."

CHAPTER TWENTY-ONE

The air was warm and scented with wildflowers. She smiled at the rush of it blowing against her face, through her hair as she rode along. The cycles' motor purred gently in her ears.

She felt free.

The highway was wide and smooth and they easily rounded the gravel embankment dotted with yucca trees. The air was hot and dusty, but she felt happy, lighthearted.

She hugged her arms tightly around his lean, muscular body and leaned her head against the strong back that lifted fifty pounds of drywall material all day. She could smell his earthy cowboy scent. Yes, she was happy. She hadn't felt this way since...not for years.

But it wouldn't last. She knew that. Knew she had to live for the moment. For special moments like this one.

The craggy mountains loomed in the distance, covered with cactus and sage. They were heading there for a picnic. A picnic that would probably end up in some sort of romantic wrestling match.

A tingle flittered through her belly at the thought.

And just as it did, the sky went dark. Overhead thunder clapped and black clouds twice as big as the mountains began to form.

Suddenly they were in the mountains. Racing down dark, narrow paths that twisted around the cavernous rocks, a stomach-churning drop on the other side.

And he was gone. She was alone.

Her fingers gripped the cycle's handles. The motor beneath her growled and sputtered. And then she heard another sound. Another motor.

Someone was behind her.

She was heading around a hairpin curve. As the cycle took the bend, she dared to glance behind her. She saw him. The black slits of his eyes, the dark stringy hair, the face full of hate.

No.

She rolled the throttle and sped up, the cycle's tires squealing around the turn. The engine sputtered again. A loud crack of lightening erupted over her head. A brilliant flash sizzled through the handlebars.

The engine gave out.

The cycle broke into pieces against the mountainside. She tumbled down, down, down until she was swallowed up in darkness.

And then she heard that too familiar voice in her ear.

I always said you were a whore.

Miranda woke with a start.

Her chest tight, her heart pounded wildly she gasped in air and tried to figure out where she was. She could barely breathe. Still half in her dream she groped the mattress for Parker.

Empty.

She opened her eyes. He wasn't there.

She raised her head in alarm—and heard the sound of the hotel room shower.

Exhaling an open-mouthed breath of relief she let her head fall back on the pillow. She ran her hands over her face.

Why in the world had she dreamt of Leon?

She hadn't had a nightmare like that since Lake Placid. Did his ghost haunt the Arizona desert?

Last night came back to her. Parker's hands and body. All the delicious sensations of his powerful lovemaking. At last they'd had a chance to express what they felt for each other with raw animal lust again. She thought everything was fine between them again. How could she have dreamed of Sam after a night like that?

What kind of a person was she?

She didn't have those kinds of feelings for Sam. How could she? She'd left him high and dry back in Phoenix. It had been over before it started.

Then an odd thought came to her. What if she hadn't left? What if she had tried to make a go of it with Sam all those years ago? Would it have worked out? Could she have loved him? Had she loved him? Did she now?

That was crazy. She loved Parker. Sam was just a guy.

No, he wasn't just a guy. She'd had feelings for him in the past. Stronger than she'd realized apparently. But not anymore. What was it that made her dream about him then?

What did it matter anyway? She was married to Parker and that was that.

Parker was the one she'd chosen, the one she'd said *I do* to. She loved him more than she'd ever thought she could love anyone. She was nuts about him. She'd never do anything to hurt him.

Not intentionally anyway. Unintentionally, she'd hurt him a bunch of times.

Feeling shaky again, she got up, reached for a robe and went to the window. She looked out at the city she thought she knew. Did Leon's ghost haunt this place, too? He'd lived near here once.

Was Layla out there somewhere, hoping someone would come and rescue her? Or maybe it was her ghost haunting the place.

Miranda didn't know. All she knew was she felt something deep down that was making her very uneasy.

Somewhere out there was something very bad.

There was a knock on the door and she almost jumped out of her skin. That had better not be Sam, she thought, stomping across the floor to answer it.

"Room service."

She opened the door and a bellhop rolled in a small table laden with silver-covered dishes. The smell of bacon and fresh-brewed coffee hit her nose, and her mouth started to water.

The bellhop uncovered the dishes for her perusal and Miranda leaned over to have a look. Shiny polished silverware, fancy china cups and saucers, steaming plates of delicious-smelling breakfast food.

It was so Parker.

He had thought of everything, hadn't he? Sam might know she liked hot sauce, but Parker knew more than that. He knew she liked her coffee black, her eggs hard-scrambled, and her bacon extra crispy.

She got some cash from a drawer, tipped the bellhop, and he headed out the door with a smile.

The next instant the bathroom opened and Parker stepped out, a towel around his waist. His dark, salt-and-pepper hair was wet and falling over his forehead. His muscular chest and shoulders seemed even hotter and sexier than they had last night.

She hurried over to him and gave him a big sloppy kiss. "Good morning," she said, her lips still against his.

"It seems to be," he murmured, kissing her back.

She ran a hand down his side, heard him wince. She pulled back and saw the pale marks along his ribcage. She touched them gently with her fingertips. "Did we make it worse last night?"

He smiled lustily. "It was worth it." Then he caught her hand. "And if you don't stop that, we may never get any work done today."

She let her arms go around his neck and lingered there, wondering if that wouldn't be such a bad idea.

He looked past her and eyed the table with a frown. "I meant to finish in the bathroom before breakfast came. I didn't want to wake you. You had a restless night."

Had he known she'd been having a nightmare? She pulled away from him, feeling awkward. "I was already awake." She pulled a chair over to where the food sat. "Hey, let's eat before this stuff gets cold."

"All right." He grabbed another chair, disregarding his ribs and held it out for her.

She indulged him and sat, watched him while he took his place opposite her, bare-chested and still in just a towel. This was where they belonged. On a case, together. Body and soul.

She waited for him to pour coffee, then gulped it greedily. She needed fortification. She doused her eggs with hot sauce and dug in.

After a few bites, her mind began to focus. "So we've got Harvey Hackett with a grudge against the vic, a crush on the vic's fiancée, and a bottle of the same wine used to kill the vic wedged in his rosebushes." She sighed aloud. "Pretty good circumstantial case."

"It appears so." He took a thoughtful sip of coffee.

"Yeah." She took a bite of toast, chewed on it slowly. "If they've charged Hackett some judge is probably hunting up a grand jury right now."

"If the DA has agreed the evidence is strong enough."

She broke off a bit of bacon and popped it in her mouth. "The police are ready to close this case. They think they've got the killer."

Parker reached for the pepper. "They may be right."

"Or wrong." She sat back cuddling her coffee cup. "It just seems too easy. Too...staged."

"Hackett is a circus performer."

She didn't buy it. "And we still haven't found Layla. If Sam's right, she could tell us if Harvey did it or not."

Thoughtfully, Parker nodded.

He hadn't even flinched at Sam's name. That was progress.

She imagined the layout of the back lot. "Everyone in that whole freaking circus had opportunity. They're all neighbors. It's like a little commune. A family, Sam keeps telling me."

Now Parker frowned at the mention of Sam's name and set down his own cup with a click that was a little too noisy. The progress was short-lived. "According to what we've learned so far, only Hackett had motive."

"Yeah, his hatred and jealousy of Tupper."

"Everyone else seems to have loved the lead clown." Parker rose to put on a shirt and pants while she finished.

"So they say." She leaned forward again, put her coffee cup in its saucer. "Okay, let's talk about means. What does Hackett do that night? Sashay over to Tupper's trailer with a bottle of Barefoot Merlot spiked with cyanide? They'd just finished a show. That time of night, there'd be people all over the place. Wasn't he worried about being seen?"

Parker pulled up the zipper on his jeans. "Perhaps there's a path between the trailers that's hidden from view."

She pointed a finger at him. "We should check that out."

He nodded, sat down again for another cup of coffee.

"And what the heck does he say to Tupper when he gets there? 'Hi, ole buddy, ole pal. Look what I brought you?'"

"You're right. It doesn't seem likely if they were at odds."

"Or maybe it went, 'Look, I know I've been an asshole, but I've had a change of heart. Let's have a drink and be BFFs.'"

"Hackett burying the hatchet?"

Miranda winced at the bad joke. "Good point. It just doesn't sound right."

"If he did something on that order, there would have to be a second glass at the crime scene."

"Yeah. Underwood didn't mention anything like that." Not that the sergeant had been a fountain of information yesterday. "Maybe Hackett—or whoever the killer was—took it with him."

"Or her."

"You think Layla did it?" She was surprised to hear that.

He took a final sip and set his cup down. "Layla's always been a possibility. We know nothing about her to confirm or deny what she did that night."

He was right. But she was one of too many possible players. Suddenly Miranda put down her fork with a clink.

Parker sat forward, concern on his face. "What is it?"

"I just had a thought. That trapeze artist said she didn't know Layla's circus background. Her resume. What if Layla joined the circus because she was running away from a boyfriend? What if he caught up with her and saw he had a rival? A rival he had to get rid of. He might be the killer."

Parker considered that a moment, his face growing grim. "It would be easy for an outsider to get on the lot if he knew where to go."

They had certainly gotten there without any trouble. Somebody could have stalked Layla, maybe followed her back to the lot when she went to town for groceries or something. A chill went down her spine. "She might be dead, too."

"Or still on the run."

She hoped the girl was alive and unharmed somewhere. She didn't want another murder. But just hoping wouldn't make it so. "We need to find her," she murmured.

"Yes. The sooner the better."

She swallowed the last bit of coffee and got to her feet. "Let's go see Underwood and tell her we want to talk to Hackett. If he knows anything about what happened to Layla he may tell us now."

Parker rose and moved to the closet to finish dressing while Miranda headed to the shower. "If the sergeant will give us permission to see him," he said.

She turned back and beamed at him. "If you work your manly charms on her like you did yesterday, babe, she'll give us anything we want."

"I'll do my best," he said.

And he made her heart leap when the lines around his sexy eyes crinkled into a cocky grin.

CHAPTER TWENTY-TWO

Underwood was three times as busy and in five times as bad a mood when they reached her desk at the police station an hour later.

Miranda sat with her leg bobbing up and down as she waited for the petite woman to answer about fifty calls and do several interviews. When she returned from the last one, she eyed her and Parker with a you-two-still-here? leer in her eye.

"Ms. Steele, Mr. Parker, what can I do for you this fine Texas mornin'?" Her tone said what she'd like to do was boot them out of her cube.

"Sergeant Underwood," Miranda began. "We stopped by to see what progress you've made on the Magnuson murder." She chose the word to emphasize it had been murder, not natural causes or suicide as Underwood first thought.

Underwood's thin strawberry brow rose. "The Dallas police would like to thank you for helpin' us find the primary suspect."

It was an invitation to say goodbye, but Miranda just sat there in the hard metal chair, wagging her crossed leg. Might as well shoot straight from the hip. "What information do you have on Layla?"

Underwood frowned. "Layla?"

"The victim's fiancée."

"Oh, yes." She thumbed through a few folders on her desk that looked like the reports her team had written after interviews yesterday. "Okay. Several of the residents of the circus trailer lot mentioned her. What about her?"

"Did they mention she's missing?"

She sat back with a wary look. "No."

"According to our client, she was supposed to be at Magnuson's trailer just before he arrived." Better to go with that version, though Sam had made it sound iffy.

"That would be Mr. Keegan? The one who called in the incident?"

"Yes. He told us after he called and spoke to one of your officers that night, he went to Layla's trailer to tell her what had happened. She was gone."

"Gone?"

"We went to her trailer the night we arrived and again yesterday afternoon. She didn't answer the door. The place looked deserted." No need to mention they'd gone inside.

Underwood blinked at her. "Has anyone filed a missing persons report?"

"Not yet." Miranda sat back again and let the information sink in. Then she slid a glance at Parker as a cue.

He smiled kindly at Underwood with that irresistible face. "Sergeant, we're wondering if we might have a word with your suspect. He may know something about what happened to Layla that night."

She tapped her unpolished fingernails on her desk and narrowed an eye at Parker. Miranda could read her thoughts. Didn't want to file a missing persons report. Thought they could handle it better on their own.

The truth was Layla could get erroneously listed as a violent criminal if they weren't careful. If she were a victim that would only complicate things.

The sergeant shook her head. "I'm afraid I can't. Mr. Hackett lawyered up after we charged him."

"I see." Parker pretended to study his nails. "Then you can't question him any further."

"Not without his attorney present. He hasn't arrived yet."

Parker's grin turned deadly sexy. "But we can. And we may be able coax a little more out of him." A little more than the big goose egg the cops had apparently gotten.

Underwood rocked back in her chair, considering the idea that the two PIs actually might get some information out of their suspect that could bolster the DA's circumstantial case. She looked at Parker, then at Miranda, then back at Parker.

The charm was working.

She took long enough to mull over every pro and con in an entire legal library, but finally she gave them a curt nod. "I'll have someone get him and we'll see if he'll talk to you."

Miranda had been sitting beside Parker in the narrow interview room down the hall from Underwood's cube for what seemed like an hour. Her butt was so numb from the metal chair, she was thinking about chipping in to a donation to the policeman's fund for cushions. And for some A/C. It was stifling in here.

Probably easier to get confessions that way.

The torn padding on the walls was making her feel claustrophobic. That and the stale air reminded her of the days when she'd been the arrestee.

Like the night she and Sam had been hauled in after getting into a bar fight with the sheriff's son. Hadn't known he was the sheriff's son when she'd kicked his balls in. He'd been just some arrogant asshole who thought he was God's gift to women instead of the pain in the tuchus he actually was.

Parker sat next to her, concentrating on his phone. There was a wry half smile on his handsome face.

"What are you doing?" she asked him.

"Having a text conversation with Joan Becker."

She wrinkled her nose. "Who?"

He looked up at her and raised a refined brow. "Fanuzzi."

"Oh." Her shoulders slumped. Damn. She'd forgotten all about that. "She wants to throw us an anniversary party."

"So I understand," he murmured, pecking at the display and smiling smugly. No doubt they were discussing her antisocial foibles.

"What are you telling her?"

"That if you're agreeable, I can make sure our calendars are clear for the date she's suggested."

"Uh…when was that again?"

"The Saturday before. Sunday is our actual anniversary. Are you?"

"Am I what?"

"Agreeable. I told her to keep it small."

Miranda shifted in her seat. She'd never been into parties, never had friends to celebrate anything with. Never had had much to celebrate. This life with Parker was so different from the way she used to exist. But he went for that type of thing. All the to-do, all the fancy social niceties. He was raised with it. A party, like their wedding, would be mostly for him. As well as for Fanuzzi and the others in their little circle.

She leaned in close to him and poked him on the arm. "Can we spend Sunday alone together?" she whispered.

Parker's handsome face broke into a smile of naughty delight. "Just what I was hoping you'd say. I have several things planned I think you'll like."

She raised her hands, unable to think of a way out of the party the day before. "Then it's okay by me. As long as we have Sunday."

"Oh, we will have Sunday. Glad you agree." He turned back to his phone. "And Joan will be saving us seats at the Atlanta Open next Saturday."

Wendy's big day. They had to get home by then.

She nodded and glanced at the two-way mirror wondering if the officers had had to wrestle Harvey into a straight jacket to get him here.

She studied Parker a long moment. Her boss, her mentor, her lover. He was everything to her. The best detective on the planet. And that wasn't just her opinion.

She leaned forward again, catching the mix of his cologne and his natural, clean scent. "You take this one."

He seemed surprised. "Are you sure?"

She grinned at him, glad they weren't at each other's throat any more. "The sooner we get to the bottom of this case, the faster we can get out of here and go home. Might as well use our best resources to do it."

He took her hand in his. "Your own interrogations skills are nothing to underestimate."

Her heart fluttered at the compliment.

"Let's take him together."

"Okay."

The word was just out of her mouth when they heard shuffling in the hallway and the door opened up.

A weary-looking officer led Harvey Hackett into the room.

In his orange jumpsuit and booties, his wrists linked behind his back, Harvey actually looked a little better than he had outside his trailer yesterday.

He'd had a shave and probably a shower as well.

But his long bushy black brows drew together in a scowl as soon as he saw who was waiting for him. "Good God," he groaned. "Not you two again."

"In the flesh," Miranda said.

The lines of his shriveled leather face looked deeper under the harsh lights. "Like I said yesterday. I got nothin' to say to you." He nodded to the cop. "Take me back to my cell."

Parker rose with the dignity of a king. "Mr. Hackett, I believe we can both be of mutual assistance to each other."

A corner of Hackett's mouth lifted into his cheek revealing his smoke-stained choppers. Oops, guess they'd run out of toothpaste in the prison.

"Assistance?" he sneered. "You think I was born yesterday?"

"We only desire a few moments of your time to go over a few details. Then we'll be on our way."

Man, he was smooth.

Hackett pulled his lips to one side of his mouth and eyed the large cop who stood, big arms folded, barring the door.

"Have a seat, Mr. Hackett," he commanded.

Hackett rolled his eyes. "Guess I don't have a choice." And he let the uniform usher him over to the end of the table.

The cop pulled out the chair with a noisy creak and set the old clown down in it.

He eyed the two investigators with disgust. "Okay, I'm here. What do you want?"

Friendly sort.

Parker sat down and settled back with a casual ease only he could pull off and smiled at the man. He waited three uncomfortable beats before he spoke in his rich Southern accent. "How are you doing, Harvey? Is everything going well for you in here?"

Hackett showed his dingy teeth again. "What the hell kind of question is that? It's a jail."

"I understand. You've had a rough time lately, haven't you? In fact, you'd had it rough for most of your life."

Hackett sat back, a threat in his eye. "How do you know about that?"

"We private investigators have our sources." Implying that the cops might know what Parker knew as well, but that he and Miranda weren't bound by the same laws.

"So? I've had a couple of rough patches in my life. Everybody does."

"True." Now Parker's tone turned compassionate. "I don't mean to put you on the defensive, Mr. Hackett. I only want to convey, again, that we might be of help to you."

Parker had used a version of that line on her once upon a time. From this vantage point she could appreciate it.

"Help convict me, you mean."

Not unlike her own reaction. Or anyone who'd been accused of murder, whether guilty or innocent.

Parker glanced down at his phone as if consulting his facts. "You were treated for depression a number of times. You seem to have a problem with alcohol."

"I can control it."

Parker's sad smile made him seem like a concerned friend. "The primary characteristic of an addict is self-delusion. Exactly how deluded are you, Mr. Hackett?"

Harvey brought a palm down on the table with a sharp slap. "Not too self-deluded not to get a good lawyer," he growled. "My brother's one of the best defense attorneys in Dallas. He'll get me off. He'll be here any minute and as soon as he works his juice, it'll be bye-bye hoosegow." He wiggled his fingers.

Miranda sat as still as she could, fighting the urge to shake the guy.

Brother's a top attorney and he ends up an alcoholic clown working for the circus? Had to be some family history behind that.

She sensed her cue. "Must have been hard growing up with an over-achiever," she said in an offhand way.

That got his interest. "Tell me about it. Why can't you get good grades like Jeremy? Why can't you make the football team? Why can't you go to college?"

"Brutal." She shook her head in sympathy.

"I was a klutzy kid. All I could do was trip over my own feet. But it never failed to get a laugh from the other kids. So when I grew up, I decided to make a living at it." He folded his arms and sat back as if to say that was that.

"And you were doing just fine at it, too. You were the lead clown act," Miranda said.

"Until Tupper Magnuson came along," Parker added grimly.

Hackett gritted his yellow teeth, his dark eyes flaring. "That rat bastard. He took away everything I'd worked for."

"It's no wonder you didn't like him," Parker said.

"You must have hated him," Miranda agreed, watching as Harvey rubbed one hand over the other. They were getting into his emotional quicksand and he didn't like it.

Harvey's gaze darted back and forth between them. "Yeah, okay. I hated him. So what? Not big news to hate your competition in this business. But I didn't kill him."

She jumped up and leaned over the table, close to his face. "But you wanted to, didn't you? Bet you thought about it all the time. Bet you went over every detail in your head step-by-step. You knew his patterns, his habits. You knew when he'd be alone in his trailer. It wouldn't be hard to catch him off guard. He was an unassuming kind of guy."

Now the hand that came down on the table was a fist. Bang. "I didn't kill him."

Miranda swooped in closer. "But you wanted to," she repeated. "Especially after he took up with Layla."

He pulled away as his eyes went hazy. "Layla." He said it like he was chewing on a sweet piece of candy. "Okay, I lusted after her like every red-blooded male on the lot. Never did anything about it, though. She was Tupper's girl. I'm not that kind of man."

Sure you aren't, Miranda thought. "So you loved her from afar?"

"Pfft," Hackett replied, shaking his head. "I'm not that romantic. I wanted to get in her pants. That was it. Me and her could never have hit it off."

"Why not?"

"In the first place, she's young enough to be my daughter. In the second." He waved a hand. "I've said enough."

Miranda got up and strolled around a bit, then began a different tack. "Tell me about your rose garden."

"What about it?"

"Why do you have one?"

"I like to garden. Is that a crime now?"

"Unusual for a circus performer."

"When it comes to circus folk, we're all unusual. Haven't you ever heard of a freak show?"

She fisted her hand to hold her tongue, waiting for him to say more.

"Okay, my father owned a nursery. I used to help him out. It reminds me of him. We got along. Not like me and my mother. Nothing wrong with having a rose garden," he added quickly.

"Nothing at all. But there is something wrong with hiding a wine bottle laced with cyanide in it."

"Pfft," he said again, rolling his big eyes. "If I were trying to get rid of something I'd kill somebody with, I'd have hidden it better."

Good point.

"Anybody could have stashed that bottle in my flower bed. I know it. You know it. The cops know it."

"And why would they do that?"

"How the hell should I know? Isn't it your job to find that out?"

Miranda just stared at him.

"Maybe Layla did it."

"Layla?" He let out a nasty laugh. "Yeah, that's right. Didn't you say she's missing? Maybe she killed Tupper and has been sneaking around the lot, watching you detectives chase your tails."

Or maybe she was locked someplace where Harvey had taken her. The idea made Miranda's skin crawl. "You think she killed Tupper?"

He shrugged. "Like I told you, they fought all the time."

"Lover's spats, you said."

He folded his arms and shrugged. "Guess they were worse than I thought. I mind my own business."

"Where's Layla, Mr. Hackett?

"Hell if I know."

Miranda brought her fist down on the table hard. She'd had enough of this bullshit. "Are you sure you didn't grab her and take her somewhere? Do you have her locked up in some room somewhere? Did you kill her?"

Hackett jumped and glared up at her like she was crazy. He hugged himself defensively. "I'm not saying anything else. Jeremy told me not to talk to anybody."

"What happened to Layla, Mr. Hackett?" Miranda demanded. She wasn't about to let him off the hook now.

"How the hell should I know? And you two don't know what you're dealing with."

"What do you mean?"

"I mean, that Layla," he shook his head. "There was something off about her."

Same thing most everyone said about the aerial silk artist.

"What do you mean by 'off'?" Parker asked.

Hackett rubbed his chin. "I don't know. I've been around circus folk for thirty years. This one wasn't circus."

"Can you clarify that?"

"I don't know how to explain it to outsiders. She didn't have the background. The experience. I could tell the first time I saw her perform. She must have been one of those high school prima donnas, you know? Then she probably did a few carnies before she came to us. But Tenbrook didn't care about her resume. He was mesmerized by her when he saw her act."

Maybe this clown was jealous of Layla, too. "How close were you to her?"

He rubbed his nose with the back of his hand and sniffed. "Not very. Like I said, she wouldn't have gone for the 'mature' type."

Huh. "Did you ever ask her out?"

"Hell, no." The anger was back in his eyes. "She started dating Tupper right away. Amend that. She started dating Tupper after she dated Sam."

Miranda sat down again her body rigid. With all that was in her, she fought not to yelp out in sheer surprise. Had this clown just said what she thought he'd said?

Avoiding Parker's sudden glare, she cleared her throat. "Layla dated Sam?" Parker's ways must be rubbing off on her. That came out smooth as silk.

"Sure. Took her out...oh, two or three times. Nutty guy, he fell for her hard. But after she went out with Tupper, that was all she wrote."

There was more to ask. So much more. She wanted to grab Hackett, turn him upside down and shake the details out of him like a kid shaking coins out of a piggy back. But she couldn't think of another question.

The knock at the door made her jump.

It opened and a gray-headed officer popped his head in. "Colburn," he barked at the other officer. "Mr. Hackett's attorney is here. He's demanding to see him."

Harvey turned to his interrogators with the air of a triumphant conqueror. "Detectives, this interview is over."

CHAPTER TWENTY-THREE

Miranda sat in the rental car, her arms tight around her. Her teeth were chattering. She was shivering with cold like the freaking Ice Age had suddenly descended with a whoosh upon all of Texas.

She tried to stay calm, tried to make sense of what she'd just learned.

But her thoughts galloped around in her head like a stampeding herd of angry Angus. No, she was the one who wanted to stampede. She wanted to dig her hooves straight into Sam Keegan's skull.

Her old beau hadn't exactly lied to her. But he'd sure left out some pertinent details. "I can't believe this, Parker," she muttered at last, gazing out the window at the heavy Dallas traffic. She didn't dare look him in the eye.

"We need to stay rational," Parker said. His smooth voice resonant with the tranquility of a deep blue lake.

She spun around and glared at him openmouthed. "Are you sticking up for Sam now?"

"I'm simply pointing out we both need to stay objective."

Objective. His byword.

But how could she stay objective? "You were right, Parker. Sam could be Tupper's killer."

"Circumstantial, Miranda," he warned.

"He dated Layla. He 'fell hard' for her, according to Harvey Hackett. He had motive and opportunity and means."

"As many others did."

She didn't understand why Parker was suddenly defending him. "So he hires us—no, hires me—his old girlfriend he thinks he can wrap around his little finger, and brings me out here to make his case before he's caught. He says Tupper was his best friend. He wants us to find Layla—" She stopped talking and let out a gasp.

Parker remained silent while she caught her breath.

"Oh my God, Parker. Sam could have killed Layla. He asks us to look for her, we find the body, and then he looks innocent. Nobody would believe the guy who hired us to find her is her killer."

"Which is why we need a lot more proof before we pass judgment on anyone."

She sat back and forced herself to inhale. Of course. Parker was right. She was jumping the gun. Going off halfcocked on the word of an old drunken clown who might have killed Layla himself. That wasn't like her. Sam could push her buttons even when he wasn't around. The thought made her want to punch something. Like his nose.

They needed more facts. More evidence. More details. She was going to get them. She and Parker would find out exactly what happened to Tupper Magnuson and his fiancée.

She looked up and saw Parker was turning the rental car onto the paved street in front of the UBT tent. She sat up. "What are we doing here?"

The stern look in Parker's eye was as strong-willed as a bucking bronco. "We're going to locate Keegan and find out what else he's been keeping from us. And why."

He'd read her thoughts.

She smiled. "Corral the steer and get it straight from the horse's mouth."

He nodded. "And mixed metaphors be damned."

CHAPTER TWENTY-FOUR

As soon as she got out of the car and started marching through the grassy lanes between the RVs and motor homes, Miranda knew something was wrong.

Well, not wrong exactly. Different.

No one was outside practicing jumps or tossing rings or bowling pins. A couple of kids rode miniature bikes a few rows down, somewhere a dog barked once or twice, but otherwise the lot was still.

Then she heard the faint music. Happy circus music. It seemed to be coming from inside the tent in the distance.

"They must be rehearsing in there," Parker said, shielding his eyes as he peered at the back of the big top.

"Yeah," she sighed, frustration puffing out of her mouth.

She'd like to get a look at Sam's place without him in it, but she didn't want to risk another B&E charge. Besides they didn't even know which one was his. And wasn't that funny? He'd shown them Tupper's trailer, Hackett's trailer, Layla's trailer. But not his own.

No, she needed to see him face to face. She waved a hand at the tent. "Let's head over there and find him."

"Yes," Parker agreed.

With him at her side, she went down the lane with long strides, passing the places they'd been yesterday. The Vargas's RV was vacant, and more laundry hung on a line. The spot where the jugglers had tossed colorful rings back and forth was also bare, as was the area where Yvette Nannette had been practicing with poor little Bobo.

She took two more steps and the happy music from the tent stopped. Maybe someone had missed their cue.

But there was another sound. Also music, but this time slow and sensual. Still circus style, though. And it wasn't from the tent.

Slowly she turned her head. It was coming from Harvey Hackett's trailer.

She shot Parker a frown. "What's up with that?" Hackett couldn't have made bail and gotten back here this soon.

His face was grim. "Let's check it out."

She tromped over to the place, ascended the meager steps and found the door open.

She stepped inside and the music filled her ears. The place smelled faintly of old beer and dirty laundry, but that wasn't what caught her attention.

Sitting rigid on the edge of a ragged recliner, his eyes fixed on a fifty-two-inch flat screen against the wall—was Sam. And what was playing on the TV?

Layla. Performing her act.

Miranda watched the mesmerizing images on the screen.

Under a dramatically lit background, dressed in the glittering blue-and-pink tie-dyed outfit with the matching tights Miranda had found in her trailer, the lovely young woman hung in midair, her long blond hair flowing down her back.

Her body was positioned in a swanlike pose. Two pink stretches of fabric hung from overhead. She had one strand wrapped around her waist, the other around one leg, as she spun gracefully while the music played.

Eyes closed, her face was a study of artist ardor and exotic beauty. Hypnotic.

She uprighted herself, kicked off the silk strand around her leg and climbed up farther with both hands, swiveling her body. When she had ascended several yards, she threw her legs over her head, got the fabric around her waist, and dropped to hang upside down.

The audience applauded.

As if ignoring them, she spun from the waist, unwrapping the fabric that held her and ended in a drop, arms and legs outstretched as if she were suspended by nothing. Only one strand with a single wrap around her waist held her. She wasn't even holding onto it.

The crowd gasped, then broke out in cheers.

That was it, Miranda thought.

That was the trick Biata Ito had told her about. The part Biata thought was cheating. Miranda had to admit, it looked downright supernatural from her perspective.

But right now, she had bigger fish to fry.

She turned back to Sam. The glazed enthrallment in his forest green eyes told her more than she needed to know.

She spotted a remote on a stained coffee table near the recliner. She marched across the tiny room, snatched it up and shut off the recording.

"Huh?" Sam grunted, coming out of his trance. "Miranda. What are you doing here?"

"No, Sam. What are you doing here? I didn't realize you were Harvey's roommate."

He glowered at her.

Parker strolled over from where he'd been standing in the doorway, taking in the scene. "Isn't there a rehearsal going on in the tent that you're missing?" He sounded like a stern father correcting his son.

Sam shot him a surly grimace. "We're having a technical run-through before the dress rehearsal tonight. I'm not up again for a while."

Miranda laid the remote back on the table and folded her arms. "That doesn't explain why you're here."

He sat up, ran his hands over his face as if he were trying to wake himself up. "Harvey asked me to bring him some cigarettes. I was rooting around in here and found this DVD. I just wanted to see what was on it."

"Uh huh." And why had his tongue been hanging out to the floor? Why had he been so glued to the image?

"I didn't know Harvey had the hots for her. Not this bad."

Harvey had the hots for her? Miranda wasn't buying any of this crap. She'd had enough sweet talk from this cowboy. "Are you sure it's not *your* DVD, Sam?"

He glared up at her. "No. What are you sayin'? What the hell are you sayin', Miranda?"

She thought back to their first night in Dallas. Sam said he'd had a few go-rounds with Tupper over Layla. She just bet he had.

"Do you know where Layla is, Sam?" Parker asked in a low voice that sounded a lot like a growl.

He gaped at him, then at her. Then he shot to his feet and stomped over to the screen. "How in hell should I know? Why would I have been begging you two to look for her if I did?"

Miranda fought back the urge to kick him. "Oh, I don't know. Maybe to set us up? Maybe to make yourself look innocent?"

"Innocent of what? You sayin' you think *I* killed Tupper?" His voice went up two notches.

Miranda started to pace back and forth like a lioness in a cage. "Guess what we did today, Sam? We went to talk to Harvey at the police station where they're holding him. Funny thing, he claims he's innocent, too. And that he doesn't know where Layla is. Just like you."

Sam ran a hand through his wavy hair. "I didn't think he did."

"And do you know what else he told us?"

"What?"

"That you dated Layla before Tupper. You 'fell hard' for her according to ole Harvey. She dumped you for your best friend, didn't she?"

"She...I..."

"And that made you mad. Real mad. So mad you started plotting how to get rid of him, right?"

His eyes went wide. "How can you say that?"

"Did you kill him, Sam? Did you kill Tupper? Did you kill Layla?"

"What?" He turned a little pale.

"You're the one who seems so comfortable going inside other people's trailers. Did you go back to her place and pack up her things so it looked like she left town?"

Sam could only stare at her now.

She lowered her voice and hissed out the next words. "Where did you hide her body, Sam?"

His eyes began to fill with tears. "I can't believe you're sayin' this to me. Don't you know me anymore, Miranda?"

Suddenly there was a sharp rap on the door and it swung open. "Sam, there you are. What are you doing in Harvey's trailer?"

A pretty young Asian woman wearing the same electric blue leotard Biata Ito had worn yesterday stepped into the trailer. Her long dark ponytail had the same brassy blue and auburn streaks as Biata's, as well. She seemed just a bit older. Had to be the sister.

"Tenbrook is pitching a fit," she said. "You missed your cue."

"I gotta go." Sam started for the door.

Miranda shot out an arm to block him. "Not so fast, Sam."

"What are you gonna do? Arrest me or something?"

The young woman blinked at Sam in surprise, as if she'd just realized she'd walked in on a private conversation. But she took another step toward Miranda. "Are you two the detectives my sister talked to yesterday?"

"Your sister is Biata Ito?" Parker asked, his voice sounding remarkably calm.

"Yes. She told me you spoke to her. I'm Chavi."

"Wade Parker." To diffuse the tension clouding the room, he extended a hand. "This is my partner Miranda Steele."

As Miranda shook hands with the young woman, she caught the glare of resentment in Sam's eye. No doubt he wanted to give her an earful, but he kept quiet with the trapeze artist present.

"I wanted to speak to you," The older Ito sister said.

"About what, Ms. Ito?" Parker said smoothly.

Her Asian features, as delicate as her sister's, grew solemn. "Are the police right? Did Harvey kill Tupper?"

"We're sorry, Ms. Ito," Miranda said. "We can't answer that at this point."

"Oh." She brushed away a strand of dark hair with the back of her hand. "They say he might get out on bail. If he does, my father's talking about leaving the show and going back to Europe. My sister and I don't want to go. Are we safe if we stay here?"

Miranda didn't know what to tell her. Now that the news Tupper was murdered was out, the other performers must be getting antsy.

"Again, I'm sorry," Parker said. "All we can tell you is that we're doing our best to put the right person behind bars."

The trapeze artist nodded and drew in a nervous breath. "Biata told me you were asking about Layla."

Miranda glanced at Parker. "Yes, we were."

Again she nodded and lowered her gaze to the floor. "Layla and I were friends, sort of. At least I tried to be friendly with her. We talked some, but she never opened up much. And then she started spending all her free time with Tupper."

Miranda tensed. "Did you happen to see her leaving the other night?"

She looked up, her eyes big and anxious. She bit her lip. "Layla came over to my trailer. The one I share with Biata. It's right across from hers."

Miranda nodded, feeling a tingle up the back of her neck. "We saw the trailer when we spoke to Biata."

Chavi Ito's fingers began to play with her long dark ponytail. "Layla had a bag with her. She asked me to take her to the bus station."

"And did you?"

"Yes."

"What time?"

Brows knitted, she thought a moment. "It must have been about ten or so. She was in a hurry. She seemed scared."

Miranda took a step toward the woman. "Of what? Did she tell you about a boyfriend or a husband she might have been running from?"

Looking surprised by that question, Chavi rubbed the arms of her leotard. "No. She didn't say much that night."

"What about other times. Did she say anything then? Anything at all?"

"No. Like I said, we weren't that close. We just used to chit-chat back stage sometimes. You know, work off the nerves before going on. She always told me how great I was. She said watching me was a thing of beauty. I never told her anything like that. Now I wish I had. She's so much better than I am."

"Which bus station did you take her to?" Parker asked.

"The one on Lamar Street."

Miranda's eyes met Parker's. Did they have a hope of finding her now? "Did Layla say where she was going?" she said to Chavi.

Chavi frowned, looking even more nervous. "No. It might have been California. She talked about going out there once or twice. Am I in trouble? I hope I did the right thing. Do you think Layla's in danger?"

Without replying, Miranda glowered at Sam who was huddling in the corner. He was off the hook for Layla for now. She still wasn't sure about Tupper.

"Aren't you going to go look for her?" he snarled.

Parker fixed him with a stern glare. "We're just about to do that."

CHAPTER TWENTY-FIVE

The bus station was on a busy street in the middle of downtown Dallas. After stashing the rental in a public parking lot, they made their way across Lamar Street and into the tan-colored building.

The place was crowded with travelers.

Men and women of all races and ages stood in lines or sat in uncomfortable looking benches, some half asleep, others reading, others on their phones.

With the heels of Parker's dress shoes clicking along the faux parquet floor, Miranda fought her way through the crowd and followed blue signs past the rows of waiting passengers, the vending machines dispensing cold drinks and popcorn, and mothers with crying babies playing on the floor.

At last they reached a ticket counter.

By some miracle at the moment, the clerk wasn't busy.

"Help you?" snarled the rotund, middle-aged man with dark skin and hair and a horseshoe mustache. He had on a short-sleeved blue shirt and tie but looked hot and uncomfortable. Must really enjoy his job.

Parker took the lead. "Good afternoon, sir. We're private investigators, looking for a missing person."

He wrinkled his thick nose. "Missing person?"

"Have you seen this woman?" Miranda slid Layla's picture under the glass to him.

He took it and eyed it appreciatively. "Lovely lady." She seemed to have that universal effect on men.

"Yes, have you seen her?" Impatience slipped out in her words and made the man's mustache twitch.

He slid the photo back. "Don't think so." He turned away.

"We think she caught a bus three nights ago," she said. She tried to sound friendly, but it came out more like a bark.

He turned back with an I-don't-give-a-crap expression in his dark eyes. "Look at this place, lady. I don't remember the last person I sold a ticket to much less who was here three nights ago."

"Certainly you'd remember a woman like this," Parker said, sliding the photo back under the glass. "She was in the circus that's in town. Under the Big Top. Have you seen one of their shows?"

The pudgy man inhaled and took the photo again in his stubby fingers to study. "Yeah, the wife wants to take the kids, but I don't have the time."

Great dad.

"You've heard about the incident there, haven't you?"

His thick curly black brows twisted in time with his mustache. "What incident?"

"One of the clowns in the circus was murdered."

"Santa Maria! I'm glad I didn't take the kids, then." He seemed to suddenly come out of a worker bee stupor and gave Parker and Miranda the once-over. "You two with the police?"

"We're private," she told him.

"Is this woman involved?"

"We don't know. She may know what happened. We need to talk to her."

"I see." His mustache moved back and forth as he thought about it. "What time was she here?"

"Shortly after ten, as far as we know," Parker told him.

"Last Sunday night?"

"Yes."

He scratched his chin. "I wasn't working then." He turned to another guy at the next counter. He was skinny and younger. "Mendez, were you on duty Sunday night?"

"Hell, yeah. Had to fill in for that slacker Peterson."

"They haven't canned him yet?"

"Nope."

"You sell a ticket to her?" He handed Mendez the photo.

The younger guy took it, turned it one way, then the other. "I don't know. Maybe. Awfully pretty." He handed the photo back.

"These two gumshoes want to talk to her. About a murder at the circus."

"Murder at the circus? Oh, that clown? I saw something about that on the news this morning."

Great. Now they were making headlines. "You would have remembered someone like her, wouldn't you?" Miranda said to the younger clerk.

"Not really. We serve so many customers."

"We think she came here shortly after ten."

"It gets pretty crowded then." His eyes went hazy. "Wait. Does she have an accent? Like…from Russia?"

Miranda's heart jumped. "Eastern Europe, yes."

"I do seem to remember a young woman with an accent like that asking questions. Like she was trying to figure out where to go. How much it would cost and such."

"And?"

"And that's it. I don't think she bought a ticket."

106

"Did she leave?"

"I don't know. Oh, that's right. I told her if she didn't know where she was going, she'd have to step out of line until she decided. I told her if she had cash, she could use the automated ticket vendors." He gestured in the direction of a row of red machines along a wall.

"Okay. Where was she asking about?"

"Everywhere. I told her she should look at our schedule. It's posted right over there."

"Did she buy a ticket from a machine?"

He lifted his shoulders in a shrug. "I didn't pay attention to her after that. Sorry."

Miranda's heart fluttered down to the tile floor like a piece of litter someone might pick up on the bottom of their shoe.

"Thank you for your time," she heard Parker tell the clerks as she turned and sulked away.

"Shit," she said to him under her breath.

"Let's take a look at the schedule." Did he really think that would give them a clue?

They walked to the electronic board against the wall that was flashing the arrivals and departures.

Depending on which direction she took, Layla could have headed to Amarillo or Abilene or Houston or Lubbock. Albuquerque or Phoenix or Tucson. Atlantic City, Las Vegas, Connecticut.

Miranda groaned out loud, not caring if anyone heard her. "How are we going to track her down? She could have gone to Missouri or Kansas or Colorado."

"Or be on her way to LA, as Chavi Ito thought."

Miranda studied the information on the board about the route to LA. "That line takes less than two days to get there. She's had more than enough time to get there and disappear." She felt a headache coming on. "Hell, she might have gone to Mexico. We'll never find her there. What are we going to do, Parker?"

He stared at the board another long moment then turned to her looking as disgusted as she was. "Let's have some early dinner and think it over."

CHAPTER TWENTY-SIX

The restaurant Parker chose was Mexican. High-end Mexican.

Sexy, slow salsa music. Old World-style chandeliers. White tablecloths. Gleaming silverware and china. Art Deco Aztec designs along the walls.

Miranda stared down at a plate of veggies, guacamole, and red snapper bathed in what they called Diablo sauce. Parker was trying hard to make her feel better, but it wasn't working.

She picked up her fork, noticing it glistened as if it had been personally polished by the maître d', and sighed. "I don't really feel like eating."

"You need something," Parker said, a tad of insistence in his voice.

In addition to comforting her, she couldn't ignore the feeling he was competing with Sam. Sam takes her for Texas barbeque, Parker counters with haute cuisine à la southwest. But she didn't comment. She couldn't deal with battling male egos now. More than that, she was worried about Layla and frustrated with their lack of progress finding her.

Dutifully, she picked at a bit of the spicy sauce and snapper and put it in her mouth. Despite her mood it tasted wonderful. Okay, her man had an edge. Sam might know good food, but Parker knew great food. Her appetite surfaced a little and she took another bite.

She reached for her water glass and decided to state the obvious. "I'm still wondering if Sam is connected to Tupper's murder."

Parker watched her tenderly, the image of that afternoon lingering in his mind. The one of his wife shoveling out only a fraction of her fury on their client in Harvey's trailer.

There was still far too much emotion, far too much passion in her when it came to that man. Especially when she caught him watching a video of another woman.

He knew what she was thinking. He'd taken her to this restaurant as some sort of competition with their aggravating client. That wasn't entirely true. Primarily he wanted to make sure that she was fed. But it hadn't hurt to remind her of what she had with him, though money meant little to her. He was well aware of that.

He waited for her to take another bite before he replied, weighing the options of appealing to her rational side. She was a good investigator. Logic would take over sooner or later. But it would be petty and unprincipled not to point out the facts.

Once again his professionalism won out. "Keegan didn't do it."

Miranda put her fork down in shock. "I thought you wanted me to consider that possibility."

"I did. And you have."

"And now you're changing your tune?" Of course he had. Otherwise, he would have been pointing out the reasons why Sam was guilty every step of the way. "How come?"

Parker picked up his wineglass and swirled the amber liquid in it. "For one thing, he contacted you, as you said."

"Me. His old lover. Someone he thought he could wrap around his little finger." She was still burned about that.

"But he learned he couldn't do that. He also learned I'm in the picture."

"And?"

"And he would have tried to get rid of us if he were the killer."

She narrowed her gaze on him. "Maybe, maybe not." There'd be reasons why he'd keep them on, mostly that it would make him look guilty if he'd fired them and sent them packing at this point. "That's not the reason you don't think Sam's the killer."

She watched the corners of his eyes crease in a sexy, confident smile as he sipped his wine. "You know me too well."

"So what is?"

"Think about how Tupper was killed."

She considered it. "With cyanide. It was methodical. Planned. Had to be well-timed."

"Does that sound like Keegan?"

Now that he put it that way…she let out a groan. "No, not at all."

Sam had always been a spur-of-the-moment guy. If he killed someone it would be out of passion, because he'd gotten pissed beyond his endurance. And the evidence would be all over him. He'd have to cover it up. He wouldn't have thought it all out ahead of time.

She stared down at the half eaten fish on her plate. "Okay. So Sam's not the killer. Where does that leave us?"

Parker set his glass down with an air of satisfaction. "What are your impressions of Harvey Hackett?"

She made a face like she'd bitten into a sour apple as she considered the man. "He's disgusting, but…I don't know." An old drunk planning Tupper's murder? That was as unlikely as Sam. "He just doesn't feel right."

"Not to me, either."

So who else did they have as suspects? They'd talked to a lot of the performers but hadn't had time for everyone. UBT must have had over a hundred employees. And Underwood hadn't indicated there were other leads, though she might not have shared that information.

Then she remembered the family. "The Vargas," she murmured.

"What about them?"

"They looked like they were hiding something."

"True. Or they simply wanted to stay out of it."

They were guilty of something, but she had no proof they'd done anything. Just a gut feeling. Suddenly she felt a slight chill on her skin, as if winter had suddenly blown into the dining room.

"Layla?" she asked in a whisper.

Parker studied his wine again. "We know the young woman attempted to leave town shortly after Tupper was murdered. It appears she was either running to something or running from it."

Miranda thought of the beautiful performer with the graceful moves hanging from her silken strands high in the air. Nobody knew where she came from, who her family was. She was mysterious. And yet, she had an air of innocence.

"My money's on running from it. And I don't mean she killed her fiancé."

"You think she saw something that night?"

"Maybe. But it's not so much of a threat to keep her from going back to her trailer and packing a bag."

"And getting a ride from Chavi Ito," Parker added.

"Had to mean the killer didn't see her."

"Or she was the killer."

"Yes. I know that's a possibility." She felt more frustrated than ever. "We need to find her, but we have nothing to go on. She probably doesn't even have a credit card to trace. You could do a search on her with the fancy databases the Agency has access to if we just had a last name."

Parker finished his meal, wiped his mouth, set down his napkin. His face was pensive. She knew he was coming up with something.

"What?" she had to know.

"Keegan's expecting us at the dress rehearsal tonight, isn't he?"

"I guess so." She tapped her fingers on the tablecloth and envisaged the performance. "It would be a good way to watch everybody—all the folks we haven't talked to yet—see if anything jumps out. And I'm not talking about the acts."

He nodded, not smiling at her joke. "Yes, that's important. But more important, everyone will be there, including Paxton Tenbrook."

"He's the ringmaster and the creative director. I'm sure he'll be there the whole time."

"And not in his office."

She blinked at him. Was he thinking what she thought he was thinking? "You think he's got some information on Layla in his office?"

The waiter laid the check on the table and Parker reached for his wallet. "Don't you think Tenbrook was evasive the other day?"

She thought back to his nicely furnished office, his big frame, his distraught demeanor. "He seemed disorganized. And obsessed with his show, his 'baby'."

"He made excuses not to show us any paperwork on Layla."

"He offered to pay us to find Layla."

"To get us out of his hair."

She agreed with that assessment. She thought about the big man rifling through his desk drawers. "Yeah, his behavior about the paperwork did seem kind of odd. But I chalked it up to his being a typical boss."

He raised a brow.

"Present company excepted. Wait a minute. Are you saying…?"

He nodded slowly. "While the rehearsal is going on, you keep an eye on Tenbrook, and I'll pay his office a visit."

She had to gulp down a mouthful of water on that one. Parker was going to break into the circus owner's office while he was performing?

And he thought she took too many risks.

But Parker was right. If Tenbrook was hiding something, they had to dig it out. She gave him a nod. "Sure. I can do that. Do you really think you're going to find something about Layla?"

With a wry grin he rose and reached for the back of her chair. "You never know, my dear, until you look."

CHAPTER TWENTY-SEVEN

Sam sat in front of the mirror in his trailer applying the final row of dots to the brown and peach makeup outlining his features.

He tossed down the pencil and stared at his own image.

What a damn screw-up he was. He could still hear Miranda's voice accusing him. *"Did you kill him, Sam? Did you kill Tupper? Did you kill Layla?"*

How could she think that about him?

He yanked the towel off his head and ran his hands through his thick hair. He grabbed a comb and began to style it, every so often reaching for a dab of stage mousse mixed with glitter.

No one had ever made him feel the way Miranda did. He still remembered the ache in his heart the first day she'd sauntered onto his job site, acting so tough and defiant. Talk about falling for someone.

He'd been trying so hard to win her back, but she'd never love him again. If she ever had. Still, how could she have married that stuffed shirt Wade Parker? He wasn't her type. Not the match for the Kick-Ass Miranda Steele he knew.

Except…she was different now. She was a razor-sharp PI.

She'd caught him dead to rights. Yeah, he'd fallen hard for Layla. Real hard. Thanks a lot, Harvey, for letting her know about that.

But Layla had dumped him for his best friend. He might have wanted to kill him for that for maybe a minute, but how could anyone stay mad at Tupper? He was the kindest, most generous human being Sam had ever known.

Finished with his hair, he wiped his hands clean and stepped into his jeans. He stared down at the gold embossed belt buckle. A wild cowboy on a bronco wielding a lasso. A gift from Tupper.

He pulled up his pants, let out a long, painful sigh.

And now Layla was gone, too. Was she dead? Maybe. Or so far away, he'd never see her again. He knew she hadn't killed Tupper. She loved him with all she had. She could never hurt him. But she had to know something about it.

Just like he did.

He'd just wanted Miranda to find her.

Everything was so messed up now. If only he could talk to Miranda. Be straight with her. Tell her everything.

As he pulled on his midnight blue sequined vest with the fringe, and set the matching cowboy hat on his head, he made his decision.

If she came to the rehearsal tonight, if he got a chance, he'd do just that.

CHAPTER TWENTY-EIGHT

The sun hung low in the Texas sky behind the big tent, casting a golden glow over the skyscrapers of the tech-and-cow town stretching lazily along the horizon.

Miranda sat in the rental car in the parking lot across from the main entrance, watching people in casual clothes strolling from their cars and across the street to the UBT entrance beyond.

After they'd left the restaurant, she and Parker had gone back to the hotel for a nap and a change of clothes. She had on dark skinny jeans, a metal gray tank top and a light jacket. Parker was in his designer jeans with a black T and sexy dark blue blazer.

"Didn't think a rehearsal would be open to the public," she said, wondering if the small crowd would spoil their plan.

Behind the wheel, Parker studied the pedestrians with a cautious eye. "Special guests. Contributors, most likely."

"Whatever." She reached for the door handle and stepped out before Parker could come around to do his Southern gentleman thing and open it for her.

She wasn't thinking about manners and niceties. All she could think about was the hope Parker could dig up some information on Layla tonight.

If the mysterious young woman hadn't already slipped through their fingers completely.

They made their way across the street, and Parker ushered her inside the huge tent. He handed their passes to a ticket taker, and they settled into seats about midway up.

There was just one ring. European style, she'd learned somewhere.

Several rows of padded theatre seats done in a cinnamon color encircled the entire circumference, except for the aisles. Under a tall French blue canopy, scaffolding rose high overhead. The tubular system held lighting, various cording, and the trapezes for the flying act. Miranda recognized a couple of the ring crew guys clad in black like stagehands, giving the cables a final adjustment.

The seats were comfortable, the air cool and scented with an indeterminable circus tent smell. A/C must cost a bundle. Somewhere corn was popping. Around them conversations buzzed.

Miranda eyed the other "guests" chatting with each other and sharing a laugh or a private story. Finally she spotted Tenbrook making the rounds, schmoozing some folks in a nearby row. He was in a sparkly yellow vest, fuchsia pants with yellow swirls and a matching top hat. An outfit that definitely shouted, "I'm the top banana around here."

It didn't take long for the man to get to them.

"Good evening, Detectives." He grinned, shaking hands with Parker then with her.

Both of his big paws swallowed up Miranda's hands while he worked her arms like she was a water pump.

"Nice to see you, Mr. Tenbrook," she forced herself to say.

"We're looking forward to this evening's performance," Parker said smoothly.

Tenbrook shook his head. "It was a miracle we pulled it together, but we've really got a dedicated bunch here."

"You must have."

The ring master glanced over his shoulder then leaned in, his voice low. "Harvey's out on bail."

"Is he?" Miranda said. His lawyer brother must be good.

"Seems there's not as much evidence against him as we thought. He insisted on doing his act tonight, though some of the other performers are a little nervous about having him around."

So nervous some of them were thinking about leaving the show, Miranda thought, recalling what Chavi Ito had said.

Parker nodded in sympathy. "Understandable."

"I hope you two can straighten all that out?"

What did he mean? Prove Harvey did it? Miranda was about to remind the owner they didn't work for him, but Parker spoke first.

Not a bit rattled, he simply smiled. "We'll do our best."

His bushy gray brows drew together in a sour expression he tried to conceal from the rest of the audience. "Layla isn't back. Have you learned anything about her whereabouts?"

"No, we haven't." Parker's demeanor didn't change a bit.

"Shame. She'll be missed tonight. The Ito girls are doing an extra set to replace her. They're good, of course. But they're not Layla."

"Not many people are," Miranda told him.

Tenbrook shot her an odd look, but nodded. "Well, if you'll excuse me. I need to greet the others."

"Of course."

After Tenbrook had moved on, Miranda turned to Parker. "I'm beginning to see what you mean about that guy. He does seem to be hiding something."

He gave her an almost imperceptible smile and nodded to a tall woman across the aisle. "Popcorn?" he said to Miranda as if he'd really come to see the show.

"No, thanks."

When the woman looked away, he whispered, "Make sure you keep an eye on Tenbrook tonight."

"Roger that," Miranda replied.

And just as the words were out of her mouth, the lights went down and Tenbrook took center stage.

CHAPTER TWENTY-NINE

"Patrons and friends, thank you for coming to our show!" Tenbrook removed his hat and addressed the audience with a solemn face.

"As you all know, we at Under the Big Top carry a heavy burden in our hearts tonight. For one of our own is gone, snatched from us all too soon, at the very zenith of his career. A bright, shining star we all dearly loved."

His voice seemed sincere, but there was a whole lot of theater in it.

"But, as they say, the show must go on. And no one would have wanted that more than Tupper Magnuson. And so in his honor tonight we give you our very best." He suddenly went into ring master mode as he climbed onto a platform. "Ladies and Gentlemen!" he cried. "Welcome to our show."

Drums began to roll. Tenbrook's costume sparkled under the spotlight like gold. He spread his arms, intense excitement on his face. *Man, what a showboat.*

"Get set for the most stunning, the most exciting, the most titillating entertainment experience of your life. We're about to amaze and dazzle you. Take you to another place. Transport you to a strange, mysterious world of sheer fantasy."

Airy flute music started to play as he spoke, as if evoked by his words.

"A world of wonder and enchantment and yes, even fear. A world that exists only...Under the Big Top."

The music turned spunky, with a sort of half-rock, half-carnival beat and a whole hoard of performers marched out singing a loud, rousing welcome-to-the-circus song that really did seem to take you to another world.

A place where anything was possible.

They began to dance around in a choreographed number that already had Miranda feeling carried away with the enchantment. Was it something in the air?

The number ended. Before she could catch her breath, the guys she'd seen in the yard tossing rings scampered out. Only now they were in skintight, silver blue costumes, and their rings were lit in a rainbow of colors.

Armed with six rings each, they tossed them back and forth, muscles flexing, the rings climbing higher, higher, until they seemed to reach the scaffolding overhead. The guys caught them again and began to roll the rings over their arms and bounced them off their heads, all while dancing and spinning to more funky music.

Everyone applauded.

Tenbrook, Miranda thought, with a flash of panic. *Where'd he go?*

But just as the jugglers trotted out of the ring to a round of applause, Tenbrook stepped into the spotlight again and began to address the crowd. Before he could get the words out, the music turned zany and a pack of clowns came galloping down the aisles and into the ring, creating total chaos. Tenbrook acted angry and agitated, chasing one clown then another as they ran around with buckets throwing colorful confetti at the audience.

The crowd broke out in peals of laughter, even more so when one of the clowns got doused with a bucket that wasn't holding confetti, but real water.

One of the troupe, with wiry orange and blue hair and a big green nose ran toward Miranda and growled at her. She reached for Parker's hand, flashing back to a time her father took her to the circus as a little girl and she'd ended up in tears over a clown.

"Coulrophobia," Parker whispered in her ear.

"Fear of clowns?"

He nodded. "I believe I contracted it when my father took me to a Ringling Brothers performance in New York when I was five."

She had to smile. The bold, fearless ace detective Wade Parker was afraid of clowns? But who was she to talk? On the other hand, she thought squeezing his fingers entwined around her own, it was kind of nice to share the same affliction.

The Russians came next. They danced around, did some flips and handstands, then the two men held the bar while the Russian woman swung her body around and over it, then began walking it while they tossed her in the air.

Next up was Yvette Nannette with her little dogs. The obedient pooches sat on their platforms, jumped over each other, leapt through hoops and danced around on their hind legs in time to waltz music.

Miranda watched her closely, but the woman was stoic behind her stage grin. And yet underneath that makeup, Miranda thought she saw darkness under the woman's eyes. She was still grieving for her beloved little Bobo.

After the dog act there were more clowns, and Harvey did his bit with the bowling pins. It went off without a hitch and got a big laugh. Miranda peered hard at the old man, but all she saw was someone who was relieved to be back at his job.

At the clowns' exit there was a ba-da-ching from the drums, and suddenly the music turned exotic. Eastern Europe exotic.

The lights went down and a single spotlight illuminated Tenbrook at the far end of the ring.

He raised his arms mysteriously as from the opposite side of the ring, a huge silver cannon emerged.

"Ladies and gentlemen," Tenbrook cried. "Are you ready to witness one of the greatest events of the evening?"

"Yes!" everyone shouted back.

"Then it is my pleasure to give you the most outstanding. The most stupendous. The most unbelievable...Yuri from Slovakia!"

Yuri Varga stepped out from behind the cannon, dressed in shimmering red spandex and a gold cape. He turned one way, then the other, waving to the audience while Dashia, in a matching costume gestured to him as if he were a god.

Everyone applauded and cheered.

"Yuri is about to attempt one of the most dangerous and thrilling stunts in any show on earth."

Tenbrook waved his arm and a drum roll began.

Yuri removed his cape and handed it to Dashia. Then he strode proudly to the end of the cannon and began to climb its length.

Miranda leaned forward, squinting hard to see his face. Even though it was covered with makeup, there was something there. Something in his expression, the way he climbed up the cannon's barrel. And Dashia, too. She saw the same nerves and worry she'd seen the other day.

"There's something about those two," she whispered to Parker.

"Yes, I see it, too."

Yuri reached the mouth of the cannon and slid down inside it.

Tenbrook raised both arms again and the drum roll stopped. For a long moment the place was dead still. Then he began to count. "Five...four..." The audience joined in. "Three...Two...One!"

Boom!

Smoke shot out of the big gun's muzzle. Yuri blasted from the cannon's mouth and flew high into the air. He landed in a net on the other end of the ring that nobody had noticed.

The band played a traditional *ta-dah!* while the audience whistled and shouted. Yuri climbed out of the net, and he and Dashia took victorious bows before scurrying up an aisle and disappearing behind a curtain.

The guy had nerve, Miranda had to admit. Nerve enough to kill a fellow performer?

After that, there were more clowns and jugglers, this time with colorful lighted balls. The Flying Itos appeared. Clad in gorgeous gold and blue outfits, they performed some daring stunts on the trapeze. Biata and Chavi were like graceful birds twirling in the air before being caught and soaring away to the platforms.

There was an acrobat and a tightrope walker. And just when Miranda thought the show was almost over, country music began to ring out and a huge teal blue cage was wheeled into the ring.

A thrill danced up her spine though she didn't know why.

"That's Sam's act." She reached out to grab Parker's arm. Not there. She turned to look at him.

But he was already gone.

CHAPTER THIRTY

Parker slipped inside the dark room and shut the door behind him.

He stood in the dimness stock still, listening. All he could hear was the faint sound of music and another sporadic burst of applause coming from the tent. He'd taken a back way, winding a circuitous path between three rows of the various RVs and vehicles parked on the grounds.

No one had seen him. He was certain of that.

And even though no one was outside the office just now, he slid along one wall to the large window and slowly pulled down its shade. He did the same on the opposite wall.

Then he pulled out yet another pair of gloves—his supply was running low—and after putting them on, took a pen out of his pocket that doubled as a small flashlight.

He switched it on and swept it over the room.

Guest chairs, coffee table, desk, the self-indulgent photos and posters along the wall. And finally the two short beige filing cabinets.

Parker reached them in three strides.

He curled his hand around one of the handles and pulled. It came right open. Unlocked. Which probably meant there was nothing in it. Nothing that pertained to the case.

Tenbrook would have what he was looking for tucked away in some hiding place.

Parker felt around inside the cabinet drawer but didn't find any hidden compartments. He did the same for the other three drawers. Nothing.

Then, being thorough, he went through the hanging folders one by one. He found the expected financial reports and business papers going back several years. Nothing unusual there. File upon file of UBT employees, past and present. Miscellaneous receipts for equipment and circus supplies, budgeting for the food, the salaries, the cost of doing business.

But there was something he didn't find.

He glanced over at the L-shaped desk and remembered Tenbrook rifling through its drawers when he'd asked about Layla's papers.

He came around to the desk's other side and ran his light over its surface. Papers lay scattered every which way. He leafed through them but found nothing of importance.

He began going through the desk drawers.

He found drawings and schematics for various acts, notes of scattered ideas from brainstorming sessions. Paperclips and rubber bands and chewing gum.

What he was looking for wasn't here. Perhaps his hunch had been wrong.

He was about to leave when he noticed the side of the desk along the wall. It had no handle. It appeared to have a panel for show instead of an actual drawer.

Except there was a break along the top of it that wasn't quite flush with its neighboring piece. And the corner of a very small bit of paper stuck out through it.

Parker leaned over and peered at the space between the desk's end and the wall. It was about a foot wide. Narrow, but just long enough for a drawer to open at the side instead of the front. As he bent to examine it more closely the small beam of his light fell on something silver and shiny.

A lock.

This was it. Tenbrook's hiding place.

He slid his hand under the bottom of the drawer and gave it a tug. It didn't budge.

Quickly Parker pulled the tools he always brought with him out of his pocket and got to work. It didn't take long before he had the lock open. He felt inside the drawer and his heart sank to the tiled floor.

There was nothing more than old accounting records in here. Why keep those locked up? The circus owner certainly didn't seem to have a penchant for organization.

Parker was about to close the door when his light fell on something else. One of the hanging folders had slipped down behind the others. No doubt from sloppy handling. It probably contained nothing and he needed to get back before he was missed.

But dutifully, he pushed the other files aside, dug around and pulled out the one on the bottom. He laid it out on the desk and opened the manila folder inside.

And curved his lips up in a slow smile.

He paged through the documents, stood blinking at the papers for what must have been several minutes, unable to make sense of what he was seeing. But of course it made perfect sense. Up to a point.

He put the pen in his mouth to steady the light, began snapping photos of the documents one by one. He was about to snap the last one when the music from the tent stopped.

There was applause. Rather loud applause. Was the final act over? His heartbeat picked up. He had to get out of here and get back to Miranda.

He steadied his hands, took one more shot. Then he replaced the file under the others just as he'd found it, did the same for the lock and stepped over to the window to raise the shade.

As he moved to the door, he felt a burst of hope. Finally they were getting somewhere.

CHAPTER THIRTY-ONE

Parker must have snuck out while the Ito's were dangling in the air, Miranda thought, as she forced herself to appear relaxed and settled back in her seat. Made sense. It was the least likely time for Tenbrook to notice.

But it set her nerves on edge that he hadn't told her when he left.

The country music blaring in her ears, she turned her attention to the show, keeping her eyes peeled for the ring master.

Ladies in scanty, glittery cowgirl outfits were dancing around the big mesh globe while two of the clowns pretended to haul the heavy contraption to the center of the ring. It was the guys on the ring crew doing the actual work, but the clowns panted and wiped their brows as if they had borne all the weight.

Tenbrook do-si-doed his way through the cowgirls, laughing and smiling until he reached a platform on the other side of the cage.

The music went low as he addressed the crowd. "Are you ready to witness one of the greatest events of the evening?"

"Yes!" the audience cried, along with shouts and catcalls.

"We've saved the best for last." He gestured to the side of the cage and two ring crew members unlatched and raised a door in its side then lowered a ramp.

"First up, we have Pistol Pete Pierson and Wild Bill Boyle."

There was a loud, echo of rumbling motors, and two guys came rolling down opposite aisles on dirt bikes.

They were dressed like cowboys, in jeans and spangled fringed vests and matching Stetsons. Their cycles were black with orange flames.

They revved their engines, rode around the ring under the spotlights a bit then headed inside the cage. The crew guys locked the door, the music got loud and they started to ride.

Miranda's insides started to shiver with anticipation. This was the motorcycle act Sam had told her about. Way cooler than what she'd imagined.

First the two riders circled the lower part of the cage, each one opposite the other. Then one of them circled up, climbing the wall of the enclosure. The second rider followed. The music keeping time, the pair repeated the motion, looping up and down, up and down, higher, higher, faster, faster. Until they were riding horizontal—sideways around the center of the mesh globe—like two birds circling a nest.

The crowd cheered and Miranda's heart beat in time to the riders' revolutions.

Tenbrook chuckled into his mic. "Oh, you ain't seen nothin' yet."

While the first two were still going round and round, more engines roared from offstage and two more cycles rumbled down the aisles.

"Say hello to Texas Tate and Quick Draw O'Leary."

The crowd cheered and shouted as the cowboys rode around the globe and waved. This pair sported lavender bikes and had on cinnamon colored vests and hats.

The crew raised the door and they puttered up the ramp and into the cage.

They hovered a moment at the bottom while the first two still circled the center, as if picking their time. The lower bikes began the same looping motion, back and forth, back and forth, like rocking chairs. Back and forth, back and forth, then up and into two slots between the first two riders.

How they found the right spots without banging into each other, Miranda couldn't imagine.

Round and round they rolled while the music grew more frenzied. Another few circles and two of them—Miranda couldn't tell which two—broke from the others and rode in higher circles closer to the top of the cage. One went one way. The other the other way, forming a big circular X. Round and round they went while the first two still looped the center.

How in the heck did they do that? Miranda wondered as the crowd whistled and clapped.

"Would you like to see more?" Tenbrook laughed as the crowd cheered. "Give a big hand to Mad Dog Danny and Johnny 'the Cisco Kid' Ferguson."

Two more riders barreled down the aisle, this pair riding electric blue bikes and wearing purple vests and hats. Miranda recognized one of them as Sam's friend, Danny Ackerman. The pair entered the cage and joined the others, first rocking along the bottom, then zooming up to take their place in the mad swirl of riders. Six of them. Amazing.

But wait. Where was Sam?

Just as the thought formed in her head, Tenbrook's laugh echoed in Miranda's ears, sounding almost evil. "And last but not least, our very own star…Yosemite Sam!"

The crowd went wild. Sam sped into the ring and circled the cage, waving his hat to the crowd like a bronco rider in a rodeo.

The spotlight caught the joy on his painted face and set off the flaming Ferrari red of his bike. She didn't want to admit it, but in his sparkling outfit of deep midnight blue, he looked sexy as hell.

As he drank in the cheers his eyes twinkled with delight. He was in his element.

"Sam! Sam! Sam! Sam!" the crowd began to chant. He was a star.

Miranda couldn't help getting carried away with the excitement and joined in.

"Sam! Sam! Sam!" they kept on chanting as the door opened yet again, and the object of everyone's attention rolled into the cage.

He rocked back and forth just as the others had, but somehow he made it seem more dramatic.

Up he went, then back down. Up again. Back down. He huddled on the underside a moment, peering overhead as if he wasn't sure he wanted to take the risk. But the crowd kept chanting his name and finally he pushed off and joined the six other riders.

Round and round they blazed along the center, like an eclipse of frenzied moths around a flame.

Seven at once. Incredible.

The colors of the costumes blurred so you couldn't tell one rider from another. The music got really wild and the riders broke apart and made impossible-looking formations. Crisscrossing orbits like neutrons in an atom that was about to explode.

They seemed to ride that way over ten minutes.

And then one by one, they settled back down until they all were at the bottom. The door was opened and each one rode out of the cage, greeted by thunderous applause. As they circled the ring on their bikes, the other performers jogged down the aisles and joined them.

Everyone was laughing and singing and dancing. It was the last number. A good-bye, farewell, hope-you-enjoyed-the-show song, designed to leave the audience with the last bit of glittery magic from the world of the circus.

The performers took their bows, applause died down, and it was over.

The lights went up and people started to head for the exits.

Shaking herself out of her reverie with some reluctance, Miranda glanced around. Parker wasn't back yet. Damn.

She eyed the ring.

Tenbrook was at the far end talking up some audience members, probably working them for a bigger donation. Sam was a few yards away, signing autographs.

She couldn't be obvious, but she had to keep the ring master here in the tent just a little while longer.

She headed down toward Sam.

CHAPTER THIRTY-TWO

"What a show. What a performance," Miranda called out.

Sam spun around to her, his green eyes gleaming with excitement, his face glistening with sweat and gaudy makeup that made him seem a little surreal. "Did you really like it?"

She waved her arms with enthusiasm that was only a tad exaggerated. "Are you kidding? You were amazing. How did you do that?"

"Practice." He gave her a cocky grin. "And extraordinary talent."

"Oh, bull." She gave him a sock on the arm. "I bet anybody could do it."

That earned her a playful scowl.

She glanced over Sam's shoulder at Tenbrook. He was finishing up with his schmoozing, getting ready to leave.

She turned back to Sam, put a hand on her hip. "Bet I could do it."

His brows shot up. "You think you could?"

"Why not? Want to give it a shot?"

It was the same sort of thing she used to say to him when they rode cycles around Phoenix. She always pushed him to do something risky. It was almost as if she had a death wish back then. Maybe she had.

He considered it a moment, eyeing her with teasing pleasure. Then he turned around. "Mr. Tenbrook, can you spot us a minute?"

Tenbrook's bushy gray brows drew together. "What are you talking about, Keegan?"

"You'll see." He took Miranda's arm, led her over to his bike.

They headed for the cage. Sam reached out to open the door. Close up Miranda could see it was made of heavy steel and held in place by a mass of thick cables.

Tenbrook galloped over. "What the hell do you think you're doing, Keegan?"

"It's okay. She's an experienced rider. And I'm just going to have her on the back."

Miranda put on a pout. "Aw, I don't get to ride a bike of my own."

"Not the first time, sweetie," Sam grinned, as if he knew he held all the cards.

Not quite all of them, Miranda thought. She shrugged. "Guess I'll have to settle for that."

"Keegan. UBT is liable for any injury—"

Sam shot out a hand. "I'll take full responsibility, Mr. Tenbrook. Hop on, Miranda."

She did and he revved up the bike and rolled inside before Tenbrook could say anything else.

A couple of dudes from the ring crew hurried over to latch the door.

"You got guts, Keegan," one of them chuckled.

"That's what they tell me, Jerry. Hold on tight, little lady."

Miranda threw her arms around Sam's waist and pulled them together in a hard squeeze around his solar plexus. "Don't you 'little lady' me," she whispered in his ear.

"Okay, ease up, now, Kick-Ass."

"That's better," she laughed.

Sam began to roll the cycle back and forth, back and forth just like in the performance. Miranda's stomach quivered with the motion.

Up and higher. A loop, and back down. "Wow," she breathed.

She could feel Sam grin. "We're just gettin' started."

Up again, a higher loop this time. And another. Another. Another.

And then they were sideways, riding around the middle. Miranda's hair hung down and blew back as a dizzying thrill shot through her. The seats and faces below her blurred.

"Yaaa-hoo!" she shouted.

She heard Sam laugh. "But I've got more. Ready for this?"

He looped again, climbing higher. Higher. Up to the top. She was upside down for half a loop, then sideways, then straight again, then sideways again, then upside down. Round and round they went.

The motor roaring in her ears, she lost her equilibrium.

Figures had gathered around the outside of the cage. People were whistling and cheering. She started to giggle uncontrollably.

Sam's circles began to narrow and he started to descend. By the time he settled back to the bottom and stopped, she was insanely giddy.

The door opened and they rolled out of the cage.

"That was wild, Sam. Thanks." She fought to pull her hair out of her eyes as she climbed off the bike.

Glancing around as she got her bearings, she realized their audience starting to head out. Where was Tenbrook?

Sam dismounted and pulled down the kickstand with his cowboy boot. "You've always brought out the wild side in me, Miranda."

"Yeah. Guess that's mutual." Nothing wrong with that, was there?

He took a step toward her. "I want to tell you something, Miranda."

"What?"

She looked up, saw him reach out to her, felt his arms slip around her.

"This." He pressed his lips to hers.

Her leg jerked in the automatic reflex of a groin kick, but she caught herself in time and held back. She didn't want to hurt him.

Instead she let his lips roam over her mouth, sucked in the earthy smell of his greasepaint and sweat—and felt temptation. Suddenly she was back in Phoenix, ten years younger. Wild and free without a care in the world.

But that wasn't who she was anymore.

She saw that now. Clearer than ever. Whatever she had once felt for Sam suddenly disappeared into thin air like a clown's magic act. She was a different person now. For the first time, truly her own person. Why couldn't she make Sam see that? She had a new life. She was married. She was a private investigator. She was on a case. His case.

Case.

Oh, my God. Tenbrook.

Her heart hammering with panic, she tore herself out of Sam's embrace and glared over his shoulder.

Tenbrook was heading out the far exit.

Damn, she thought. But before she could go after him, a sharp, familiar shout pierced her ears.

"Miranda!"

She spun around and saw Parker marching toward her, the coattails of his dark blazer flaring behind him as he moved.

There was fire in his eyes.

CHAPTER THIRTY-THREE

"There you are." Miranda messed with her hair as she uttered an awkward laugh. "Was that oil man interested in investing in our firm?"

Parker eyed her cautiously, but picked up the ruse without a second's hesitation. "He's considering it. In the meantime, we have work to do. If you'll excuse us, Mr. Keegan." He reached for her arm to lead her away.

"Good night, Sam," she called over her shoulder, hoping he'd catch the accusation in her voice.

Sam looked so bewildered, he didn't even reply.

As they headed up one of the deserted aisles she pulled out of Parker's grasp, temper flaring.

"Knock it off, Parker," she grunted under her breath. "There's no reason to be so upset."

"Oh, there isn't?" The quiet fury in his voice made her shudder.

But she stood her ground. "I was doing my job. I had to distract Tenbrook before he left the tent."

"By kissing Keegan?"

She stopped short, shot her arm out to halt his rapid gait and make him face her. "By doing the motorcycle act. It worked. Tenbrook would have left otherwise. It gave you time to get back."

His expression was hard granite. It sliced her heart in two. "And kissing him was some sort of encore?"

She felt her face flush crimson a messy mix of anger and embarrassment. "That was an accident. I couldn't stop him before he—"

"You couldn't stop him?"

She shook her hands in the air in frustration. "No, I couldn't."

His laugh was part disgust, part pain. "This from a woman who regularly uses her martial arts skills to knock men on their asses."

She folded her arms, gritting her teeth. Why wasn't he listening? "I don't do that to clients."

"I've seen you put down a client," he snapped back darkly.

Okay. That was true. But Sam was different. "He's a friend. I don't know what to do with him. I don't want to hurt him."

"Friend? That man is a player. Not the type to care too much that you're married. I don't understand why you don't see that."

She stared at him. Is that what he thought of Sam? What he'd thought all along? Suddenly she felt drained. And angry. And most of all…disappointed.

Tears began to well up in her eyes. Where the hell were they coming from?

Okay, maybe she hadn't handled things right. Maybe she'd let things go too far. Maybe that was because she'd had some feelings left for Sam. But tonight she'd dealt with them. They were over and done with. So why was it all her fault? Why had Parker let her go off to dinner with Sam? Why had he stood by as if waiting for her to screw up?

She bared her teeth at him. If she were a wild animal, she might tear him apart. "If you feel so certain of that, Parker, why don't you do something about it?"

Parker stared at her, shoved his hands in his pockets as if taken aback. A rare experience for him. "I'm trying to be civil."

He was making her insane. "Is that what you think? You think I want you to be civil?"

He turned around slowly, deliberately, his dark gray eyes smoldering.

Parker gritted his teeth against the pain and rage he'd been holding back since they'd arrived in this town. Suddenly a wall of emotion broke forth like a bursting dam.

Miranda was right.

Why should he hold back? Why should he force himself to be a gentleman, to be courteous and well-bred when the woman he loved beyond all reason was at stake?

Why the hell should he be civil?

He turned and marched back toward the ring, his fury mounting with each stride.

When he reached the spot where the cage from the last act still stood, he fixed his gaze on the focus of his ire. The cowboy was bent over, attending to his damned motorcycle. How dare that carnival performer think Miranda was so fickle she could be swayed by a mere toy?

"Keegan," he said. And his voice was so dark and thunderous, it surprised him. But it matched what was burning inside him.

"What?" The man in the cowboy hat turned to face him, a defensive look on his face.

Parker didn't answer. Didn't give the man a chance to say another word. He took two quick steps, drew back a fist, and with all his might cold-cocked him square on the jaw.

Keegan flew back like a roped steer, just missing the cycle, and landed in the dirt on his ass.

He sat up, rubbing his jaw and glared at Parker.

"If you don't want more of that, from now on keep your hands off my wife."

Heart racing Miranda trotted over to the two men, shock rolling over her.

What the hell had Parker done? She wanted to be furious with him. She wanted to scream and yell and have a hissy fit right here in front of the crew.

But she couldn't.

Not with this quivering thrill titillating her insides. Not with this wild sensation that felt like some sort of victory racing around in her heart faster than those motorcycles in the cage. And besides, she was grinning so hard, she thought any minute her face might split.

But the moment didn't last long.

The sound of pounding footsteps pulled her out of the giddiness.

Someone was running toward them. One of the motorcycle riders still dressed in his purple fringed vest and cowboy hat. Miranda recognized the frame and youthful face.

It was Danny Ackerman. Sam's friend.

"Keegan!" he shouted, then he frowned down at Sam when he spotted him on the floor. "Get up. You've got to come quick."

Sam drug himself to his feet, cradling his jaw. "What's the matter?"

Danny glared at his friend, his chest heaving. There was terror on his face as he struggled to sputter out the words.

He batted a hand toward the exit. "I was just down the lane. Over near Harvey's place. I thought I'd stop by and tell him he did good tonight. And I...but I...oh, God." He put his hands over his eyes.

Sam reached out for him. "What's wrong, Danny? What's the matter?"

"It's Harvey. Oh, God."

"What about Harvey?"

Miranda's stomach began to twitch as she watched the man start to cry in earnest.

His chest heaving, Danny shook his head. "You've got to come. All of you. You've all got to get over there now. Harvey is...oh, God, Sam...Harvey's dead."

CHAPTER THIRTY-FOUR

Miranda ran out of the tent and down the lane to Harvey Hackett's trailer as fast as she could go. She was vaguely aware Sam and Danny were just behind her, but all she cared about was getting there. And that Parker was at her side.

She reached the place in a few minutes and found all the lights on. Several performers, still in costume, stood around as if they didn't know what to do.

"Has anyone gone inside?" Miranda barked at them when she reached the lane where she'd first met the old clown, despairing that the crime scene evidence would be impossible to get now.

The group looked at each other and shook their heads.

"I called 911 as soon as I found him," Danny offered. "Then I ran to tell you."

"Okay." She lowered her voice and turned to Parker. "You got any more of those—"

But Parker had already retrieved two pairs of gloves from his secret stash and was holding one out to her.

She took it, eyeing his handsome face. His expression was set and grim. He seemed stronger, bolder, wiser than she'd ever seen him. Her heart filled with emotion for him. This wasn't the time or place to get mushy, and yet, a situation like this was when she felt most connected to him.

Now more than ever.

Turning her attention to the work, she slipped on the gloves, pushed through the crowd and stepped inside the trailer.

The first thing that hit her was the smell of booze. Wine, in particular.

Next was the soft circus music coming from the TV speakers. Once again Layla's image flickered on the big screen. And finally the pungent odor that mingled in the air with the wine.

The nasty smell of recent death.

Harvey sat stretched out in his ratty recliner, an open bottle at his side.

She crossed the room and put two gloved fingers to his neck. "No pulse."

"Look at the label on the bottle." Parker sounded even grimmer than he looked.

She cocked her head to view the side of the wine bottle. "Barefoot Merlot. Awfully convenient."

"Awfully coincidental."

"I'll bet my paycheck Underwood's lab is going to find cyanide in that wine bottle."

"And in Harvey."

"Yeah." She let out a sigh. "Poor old clown."

She turned to the TV and stared at the beautiful aerialist wrapping herself in her silken strands. Everything looked like Harvey had been overpowered with guilt over killing Tupper. That he'd done it because of his uncontrollable crush on Layla.

Sam and Danny were going to get the third degree from the police, but the cops would most likely rule this a suicide.

Her gut told her they'd be wrong. Harvey hadn't seemed like he was contemplating killing himself when they talked to him at the police station that morning.

To her the scene screamed, "Set up!"

"Miranda?"

She nearly jumped at the sound of Sam's voice. Glaring over her shoulder she found him standing in the trailer's doorway.

"Get out of here, Sam," she snapped.

He ignored her and took a step inside. "Danny told me there was a bottle— there it is. Oh, my God. Harvey." His voice broke with emotion.

His eyes filled, making his face even more intense than his makeup. He was still in his sparkly cowboy costume from his act.

"Don't come in here, Sam. Don't touch anything."

He held up his hands defensively. "No, I won't. I wasn't going to. It's just that…" He took a minute to steady himself. "It's just that I saw Harvey right before the show. He told me after what he'd been through, he was through drinkin'. He was takin' his wine bottles out to the dumpster."

That was interesting. "You need to tell that to the police when they get here."

"Okay."

In the meantime, she had a suspect in mind.

She glanced over at Parker, watched his jaw tighten with anger. He gave her a brief nod. They had to keep their client busy.

"Sam," she said, her voice softer now. "Do you think you and Danny can keep everyone out of the trailer until the police get here?"

He blinked at her, bewildered. "Sure. What are you gonna do?"

"Run a quick errand."

And without any further explanation she brushed past him, Parker at her side, and out the door.

CHAPTER THIRTY-FIVE

They took the back way, wending through the trucks and cars and smaller trailers scattered along the neighboring row, and Miranda could see how easy it would be to sneak around this lot unnoticed, even when a lot of people were out.

The killer must know every nook and cranny of the layout.

After a few minutes they reached the Vargas's place.

Miranda hurried around the corner and found the picnic table under the awning just as it had been the other day, except with no laundry on the line, no kids and no parents.

"Their truck is gone," she observed.

Parker strode over to one of the windows. "The lights in the RV are off."

Miranda stared down the grassy lane they'd traversed their first day here. "Yuri could have taken the family out for dinner." Not that she believed that.

She turned back at the sharp rap of Parker's knock and saw him at the top of the steps to the door.

When there was no answer, he turned the knob. Good thing they both still had their gloves on.

"It's open," he told her.

No time for manners or police protocol. "Let's see if somebody's inside."

She scaled the front stoop and stepped inside as he flipped on a light switch.

This was definitely a family dwelling. Kids' drawings on the fridge, big worn couch against the wall of the living room with the cushions awry, toys strewn on the carpet.

Without a word Parker disappeared behind a small opening in the back. Miranda followed him and found a tight, narrow bedroom decorated in an adult style. The parents slept here.

Parker was already in the closet. "Only a few things in here beside costumes."

"Any suitcases?" She asked.

135

"None."

Miranda spotted some tissue covered with makeup on a small desk-like dressing table built into the wall. "Looks like they took off their makeup and got out of here."

She took a quick glance in the compartment under the bed, but it was empty.

"This looks a lot like Layla's place. Like they packed their bags and vamoosed."

Parker nodded, his face a study of unease.

Miranda went back into the living room, scratching at her hair. "Where could they have gone?"

"And why?"

She frowned at him. Wasn't it obvious why? They'd set up Harvey to take the fall for Tupper's death—by killing him, too. But escaping now made them seem guilty. Maybe they panicked.

She plodded into the kitchen, glanced around. The dishes were put away, the dish towel hanging from a knob was dry. A cheery blue bowl of white daises sat in the middle of a tiny table.

She hunted through the cabinets and found baking flour, cookies, chips, lots of boxes of sugary breakfast cereals. She shut the last door, ready to give up when she spied something on the counter.

She stared down at it.

It was a yellow sticky pad, hardly used. But there was an impression on the top paper. "Hey, look at this, Parker."

He came around the counter and saw the same thing she had.

"What was that trick I saw you do once?"

"With the pencil?"

"Yeah."

He hunted through a few drawers and found a pencil nestled in with kitchen utensils and a couple of screwdrivers. "Lightly shade the paper with the side of the lead."

She grabbed the pencil out of his hand. "Let me try."

"Don't press too hard or you'll lose the impression."

"Got it."

She steadied the pad with one hand and gently ran the pencil over the paper. It took a while. Too long for her taste, but at last vague letters began to appear.

She picked up the pad and held it under the kitchen light, squinting at it. "Looks like an address. A hotel. And a room number? One twenty-four. Green Valley Inn. Norman, Oklahoma?"

Parker was already busy Googling it on his phone. "It's a hotel outside Oklahoma City. About a three-hour drive from here."

The Vargas were making a run for it all right. The whole family.

She looked at her watch. "Yuri's act was in the middle part of the show. If they left right after that, they've got at least an hour's head start."

"Then there's no time to lose."

They hurried out the door and rushed to the rental car, barely dodging the police, who had just arrived at Harvey's trailer.

They hopped inside, and the engine growled as Parker pulled out and headed for the main road.

Miranda twisted around to peer out the back. "No cops," she told him with a deep sigh of relief.

But as they raced through a light and swung out onto the ramp to the four-lane, she had a sinking feeling they were already too late.

CHAPTER THIRTY-SIX

They sped past the brightly lit downtown area of Dallas, past their hotel and the ball-shaped observation deck in the sky, and spun around to I-35, heading west and then northward.

As he raced alongside a big eighteen wheeler, Parker dug in his pocket. He handed Miranda his cell. "Have a look."

"At what?" she said, taking it. He'd already told what he'd Googled about their destination.

"The photos."

She sat up straight. "From your little side trip to Tenbrook's office earlier?"

He nodded.

They hadn't even had time for him to tell her the results. Maybe they would have if she hadn't let Sam…She didn't want to think about that now.

She poked at the icons on Parker's phone until something came into view and squinted at the image. It was a copy of an employment authorization card. Had all the pertinent data. Sex. Date of birth. Country, listed as Bulgaria.

She read the given and surname aloud. "Yuri Dolgorukiy Varga."

"Yuri Dolgorukiy was the founder of Moscow," Parker said.

"Oh yeah?" Maybe old Yuri had royal blood, she thought, studying the blurry photo of his thick black brows and bald, scarred head. The dates on the card were for the current year. Sam hadn't said when Yuri'd had the accident that caused those scars.

"However," Parker continued, "the middle name doesn't follow the typical Slavic patronymic form."

She wrinkled her nose. "Huh?"

"It should be the father's given name followed by 'ovich' as the suffix."

Miranda's brow rose in amazement at Parker's knowledge banks. "Where'd you find this card?"

"In a locked drawer in the side of Tenbrook's desk."

She didn't ask how he'd gotten into the drawer. Or how he made it look as if it hadn't been broken into before he left. Parker knew how to cover his tracks.

"There's more."

She swiped to the next photo. This one was of the small, brown-haired Dashia. She looked fearful and mousey just as she had when Miranda questioned her alongside her trailer.

Her name was listed simply as Dashia Varga. Her country was also Bulgaria. Her date of birth was exactly one year after Yuri's. Miranda would have thought she was a little older with two kids. And her husband older than that. But Yuri's DOB put him at twenty-three. Dashia's at twenty-two.

Yuri looked ten years older than his wife. Guess it aged you to get shot out of a cannon all the time. But there was something else that bothered her.

"Something seems off about these cards," she said.

"Yes." Parker tapped the phone. "Look at the next photo."

She swiped to the next image, increased the photo size and squinted down at the corner of the back of Dashia's card. She blinked at the form number, hoping she was misremembering her facts from her studies last year. "That number doesn't look right."

"Good catch. It should read I-766."

"But it's I-736," Miranda said.

"A common mistake of forgers to miss the number."

She slowly turned her head to look at him. "You think Tenbrook forged these documents?"

"I think someone did. Go to the next one."

Her head starting to spin, she did. And got an even bigger shock.

There was a third EAD card. Layla's pretty face stared up at her. She wasn't smiling in this photo as she had been in all the other images Miranda had seen of the woman. She looked sad and frightened.

And then Miranda's gaze went to the name and her heart nearly stopped. Was she seeing the characters right? *Layla Varga.* "Varga? Layla is related to Yuri?"

"So her EAD card says."

What the heck did that mean? Was it some sort of cover up? Of what? Had she and Parker run into some kind of Eastern European crime ring?

Miranda pressed her palm against her forehead, feeling a little sick. This case was getting more bizarre by the minute.

Parker's voice was soft in her ears. "Go to the next one."

She glared at him. "There's more?"

He didn't answer so she simply did another swipe. This time the photo showed a list of names with numbers beside them. There were companies. She recognized some of the names. Big oil and tech companies headquartered in Dallas.

She thought of the crowd who'd come to watch the dress rehearsal tonight by invitation. "What are these? Tenbrook's contributors?"

"They appear to be. Along with records of their donations."

She moved her finger back and forth to see who gave what, feeling like she was prying into something she shouldn't be. Most were nice chunks of change, but probably not enough to fund the operation like the one she'd seen tonight for any length of time.

Then she slid the photo down and caught sight of a huge number. She let out a low whistle. "This one's Tenbrook's sugar daddy."

"So to speak. His largest contributor by far."

"Someone without which, he wouldn't be in business?"

"So it appears. Revenues from ticket sales are brisk but not enough to support the entire operation."

"Not even with the other contributors?"

"Not in my opinion."

And Parker knew how to run a profitable business. He'd been doing it for years before she met him.

She scrolled to the other side of the document and squinted at the sugar daddy's name. "GenaPulse? I don't recognize the company."

"I've never heard of it either."

He hadn't had time to research it but with his family background, Parker was a walking encyclopedia of business names. "Is it some sort of front?"

"Perhaps."

She thought of Yuri and Dashia and Layla and their doctored EAD cards. Her mind raced. "The Russian mob?"

"There's the occasional CIA agent who uses a job with the circus as a cover. But they usually aren't performers."

Right. Too much limelight if you're trying to go undetected. The mob would want the exposure even less. She was grasping at straws.

"So what are they covering up?"

"To be determined," Parker said, his gaze steady on the road.

Miranda swiped back to Layla's photo and her sad face. A chill went through her. A cold wind blowing up her arms that made the hair on the back of her neck stand up and salute.

She'd felt the sensation before. She knew what it meant.

Whatever they were heading for, it would be no good.

A horn screeched out behind her and Miranda whirled around to glare out the back window, her heart hammering in her chest.

"Police?" Parker said easing his foot off the accelerator.

The horn blared again and Miranda saw an arm shoot out of the driver's side window. The hand attached to the arm held a cowboy hat and was frantically waving for them to pull over.

Then she caught a glimpse of the rusty grill of the cherry red pickup in the taillight.

Good grief. She groaned out loud. "We've got to pull over, Parker. It's Sam."

CHAPTER THIRTY-SEVEN

Miranda slammed the door of the rental car and stomped over to Sam as he climbed out of his ratty truck.

Her blood boiling, her hair blown back from the blast of eighteen wheelers and SUVs whizzing by, she sucked their exhaust fumes into her lungs and leered at him.

She wanted to push him into the traffic.

"What the hell do you think you're doing, Sam?" she barked at him. "Why did you follow us?"

He came around the grill, his lanky frame outlined in the headlights, set his hat on his head and leaned against the truck's front fender. Arms folded he glared back at her with a look of belligerent defiance. She could see his jaw was dark and swollen where Parker had socked him.

"It's a free country, ain't it?" he sneered with a hard glance in Parker's direction. "Where are you two goin' is what I want to know."

"You were supposed to be talking to the police."

Sam let out a low hiss. He'd taken off his spangled vest, but he was still in his circus costume, though his makeup was nearly rubbed off by now.

He took his hat off again and ran a hand through his blond hair. "Just after the police got there and started lookin' at Harvey's place. I got a call. I slipped away to take it."

Despite the dusty heat, icy fingers ran down Miranda's back. "A call from who?"

"Layla."

She took a step back. For a moment she felt like she couldn't breathe. "Layla?"

Sam's expression turned sober. "She wants my help. She's in trouble."

That was an understatement.

Miranda looked at Parker. He shook his head just a bit.

She agreed. Wouldn't do to tell Sam they were after the Vargas. Not yet, anyway. Her gaze shifted around to the rear window of Sam's truck. In the headlights of the oncoming vehicles in the opposite lane, she spotted the outline of a gun rack. It wasn't empty.

Her stomach tensed. "What's the rifle for?"

"Like I said, Layla's in trouble. Around these parts, a man defends a woman in trouble."

Good Lord. That was all they needed now. A shootout at the O.K. Corral. "Do you even know how to use that thing?"

His lip curled. "Please."

Parker stepped forward. He was doing his best to appear calm, but Miranda could see he was fuming underneath the surface. "Mr. Keegan, it's very unwise to barge into an unknown situation like a…damned cowboy."

Sam's green eyes blazed. "Mr. Parker," he spat, his accent thick with sarcasm. "I know Layla and I know how to handle myself. And I don't need your permission to do it."

This could get ugly fast.

Miranda laid a hand on Sam's arm to calm him down. "Sam, we don't know what Layla's role was in Tupper's death. In any of this. You have to let us talk to her first."

He pushed her away. "Why? So you can accuse her of murder?"

"So we can find out what she's running from."

"I don't need you two to find that out. She'll tell me herself. Is that where yer goin'? How'd you find out where she is?"

Again Miranda glanced over at Parker. Neither of them said anything.

"You won't tell me? That's just fine and dandy, since you're supposed to be workin' for me. Hell, I'm firing ya'll." He started to turn back to the truck.

Miranda grabbed his arm, her temper blazing. "Sam, are you in cahoots with the Vargas?"

He spun back around. "What?"

"You heard me."

"The Vargas? What in the hell are you talkin' about, Miranda?"

She grunted in frustration, saw a threatening glare in Parker's eyes. "Where exactly are you going?"

"None of your business."

"We can track you, Sam," Miranda warned.

"Like a couple of damn spies?"

"No, like the PIs we are. What did you really want from us, Sam? From me? To find out who killed your friend Tupper? Or to find Layla?"

"I wanted both."

"Then we ought to be on the same side. Where is she, Sam?"

His jaw clenched, he stared down at his hat for a long moment. She could see him thinking it over, realizing he might be in over his head. And that he truly needed their help.

His shoulders sagged as he gave in. "She's at a hotel near Oklahoma City. That's where I'm headed."

"Green Valley Inn?"

Once more his eyes blazed. "How did you know that?"

"That isn't important. What's important is that the Vargas are headed there, too."

He stared at her as if she were clairvoyant, shook his head. "I don't understand why they'd be going there."

"How well did they know Layla? Really?"

He waved his hat in the air. "Same as everybody. They hung around some. I guess Layla and Dashia talked some. It was just girl talk. You know." He looked at Miranda hard, then at Parker. What she'd been trying to tell him finally started to sink in. "What are you thinkin'? You think Yuri planned Tupper's murder?" His voice broke as he said it.

"We don't know what to think."

"We don't know what sort of situation we'll be going into, Sam," Parker said quietly with an almost fatherly tone. He took a deep breath and Miranda knew his next words would be hard to get out. "But it would be wise if we went in together."

Sam blinked hard at Parker as if he'd suddenly appeared out of thin air from behind a magician's cape. Five or six cars zipped by.

At last he nodded slowly. "Okay. You two know your business. Guess I'm convinced of that by now."

Thanks for the vote of confidence, Miranda thought.

"We'll go together. Though I can't believe Yuri would…" Sam's voice trailed off. His expression told her he finally understood he might not be able to trust the people he thought were his friends.

He looked over his shoulder at the truck, set his jaw. "Do you need any fire power? I don't expect you brought any with you on the plane."

Miranda's brows shot up. "What did you bring with you?"

"Just my twelve gauge and a couple of .22s." He strolled over to the passenger side of the truck, opened the door then the glove compartment.

Miranda peeked in and saw two Taurus pistols inside the space. One with a pearl handle, the other a wood grain. Sam was locked and loaded. What in the world was he expecting to find when he got to Layla?

"What do you think?" she said to Parker.

He gave her a short nod.

She took the pearl, left him the wood grip.

"Let me lead the way," Sam told them as he climbed back inside the pickup. "I know where the smokies are."

"Very well."

Without speaking Miranda and Parker got back into the sedan. This was it, she thought, as Parker waited for Sam to spin around then hit the accelerator.

As they sped off into the night, heading for the Oklahoma border, she wondered exactly who the mysterious Layla would turn out to be.

CHAPTER THIRTY-EIGHT

He stepped out of the shower, dried off and sank onto his bed naked.

He was bone weary. Worn out from all the terrible events happening around him. How could things have gotten so out of hand?

He didn't have control any more. That was the problem. He never should have agreed to this plan. He never should have gone through with it. He never should have let—before he could finish the thought his cell rang.

Good God. What now? He snatched it off the nightstand. "What do you want?" he hissed in anger as he flopped back down on the mattress.

There was a pause, then the quiet familiar voice. "Have you found her?"

He scowled up at the ceiling. "Not yet. I'm trying."

"Not hard enough." The voice had a jeer in it. Just like when they were kids.

"I'm doing what I can. Leave me alone. I've got problems of my own." He started to hang up.

"What about the detectives?"

He groaned inside himself, wishing he'd never mentioned them to her. But he'd had to. It proved he was taking some action. "What about them?"

"Do I have to spell it out? What progress are they making?"

"I think they're close." He didn't know that, but it sounded good.

"We want her as soon as they find her."

"Understood." Of course they did. A part of him hoped she wouldn't be found. But another part of him didn't. He just wanted this over.

There was a long pause before the voice spoke again. "And what will you do with the detectives?"

He stiffened. "What do you mean, do with them?"

"You know perfectly well what I mean."

Yeah, he knew. Just like he knew the other two times. He wanted to tell her to go to hell. He hated being manipulated like this. Hated being forced to do things that could put him in prison or worse. But he'd been promised protection.

"I'll need your help on that," he said.

"We can't send you any more pills. It's too risky."

Like it wasn't already? Or maybe it was just risky for them. But he had no choice. He was in too deep. So what could he do this time? He glanced around the room and his gaze landed on his closet. He thought of the Mossberg shotgun he kept there. He hadn't used it in years. But he'd been a good shot. It would do. And he was getting pretty good at creating a set up.

"I'll take care of them," he said into the phone.

"Do it now. Tonight."

Silently he snarled at the phone, baring his teeth. He couldn't stand being bossed around like this. "I said I'd take care of them."

"Make sure you do."

"Don't I always do as I'm told?" He clicked off, more irritated at the situation than ever. He was a rat trapped in a damn maze.

Despite his anger, he yawned. He was dead tired. He'd hardly had any sleep since this whole business started, and it had been a long day.

He had to get some rest. Just a little. He'd catch a few hours of shuteye then track down the detectives. They had to have found Layla by then, and even if they hadn't, they knew too much. He'd do what he was told. He'd take care of business. Just like he'd promised. He hoped that would satisfy them. With any luck the whole damn thing would be done by morning.

His mind already buzzing with a plan to carry out his new assignment, he rolled over and began to snore.

CHAPTER THIRTY-NINE

It was nearly one a.m. and the clear night sky was twinkling with stars when Parker pulled off the highway and made his way down side streets to Green Valley Inn, the tail lights of Sam's truck leading the way.

Miranda scanned the establishment.

The place was like a thousand other hotels in a thousand other towns across the country. A long, two-story brick structure with whitewashed arches along the walkways bordering the building. Rows of well-kept shrubbery completed the homespun look.

The vacancy sign was on, and there weren't many vehicles in the lot. No guests were roaming around. Probably for the best.

Through the glass doors of the check-in area she could see a set of not-too-shabby couches and chairs scattered about a well-lighted space. Behind a wide desk a clerk sat reading a magazine. He looked profoundly bored.

Not a dump, but it definitely wasn't the Ritz.

As the two vehicles curved around the building and room one-twenty-four came into view, Miranda caught sight of the Vargas's truck two doors down. Her stomach lurched.

Sam took the spot in front of the room. Parker pulled in two spaces away from him.

The gang was all here.

She opened the glove compartment and took out the pistols Sam had given them. She handed one to Parker, hoping they wouldn't have to use them.

"What's your plan?" he asked, giving her hand a tender squeeze after he took the gun.

His touch made her long for the comfort of his arms. She was hoping he had some thoughts on how to handle the situation.

But no, she was supposed to be in charge.

She thought a moment. "We should let Sam go in first. Layla knows him." She just hoped there wouldn't be any bloodshed.

Sam must have had the same idea. He was already getting out of his pickup, leaving his rifle behind. He was a trusting sort.

Parker let out a low murmur that sounded like a growl. "As usual, he isn't waiting for instruction."

So much for her plan. Miranda reached for her door handle. "We'd better go. In case he needs backup."

"Agreed."

She jumped out of the rental, but before she reached the sidewalk, the door to one-twenty-four opened and Layla appeared.

In the dim light Miranda could just make out her form, but saw clearly when the young woman threw her arms around Sam's neck and pulled him into the room.

"Doesn't look like he's in danger," she whispered to Parker.

"Not from here. Let's knock and find out."

"Good idea."

Miranda shot ahead of Parker and reached the door first. She gave it three sharp, police-like raps.

Inside there was a moment of shuffling and the door opened.

The towering frame of the human cannonball, dressed all in black, stood before her as his hamhock arms crossed over his big chest. "What do you want?" He sounded like a Russian spy.

"They're with me, Yuri," she heard Sam say from inside.

But she wasn't about to let this bruiser get the better of her. She drew her Taurus and pointed it at his chest. "Get your hands up, Varga. Step inside the room."

Two female screams came from the interior.

"What are you doing?" Sam cried out.

Yuri's face went from defensive to shock, but he raised his hands and stepped back.

Miranda followed him with Parker right behind her. He'd drawn his weapon as well. When they were all inside, he closed the door without looking behind him, using his foot.

Dashia and Layla sat on the single bed, hugging each other, terror on their faces. Sam stood near the door to the bathroom, looking angry. Yuri eyed her cautiously as he backed up to one of the cheap framed pictures on the wall, his big hands atop his bald head, half covering the long scar on top of it.

Miranda had had enough. She was through clowning around. "Tell us why you killed Tupper Magnuson and Harvey Hackett, Yuri," she barked.

"He did not kill them!" Dashia screeched the words.

"I'll handle this, my love," Yuri said to her gently. "Is that why you two are here? Are you going to take us back to the circus?"

"Like hell they are," Sam said.

Miranda forced herself not to let Sam distract her. She could have a killer here.

And yet…he hadn't said, "Are you going to arrest us?" or "Are you turning us in to the police?" He'd said, "Are you going to take us back to the circus?"

"What are you so afraid of at the circus?" she asked.

"Isn't it obvious?" Dashia's voice was hysterical. "They killed Tupper. They killed Harvey. Now they will kill us."

"How do we know you two didn't do it?"

Sam started to take a step toward her then thought better of it. "For God's sake, Miranda. Are you out of your mind? Yuri couldn't hurt a fly."

"He's big enough to hurt several flies." And kill several men.

But if he did, he'd do it with his bare hands or with a weapon. Maybe in a fit of rage if he was the volatile type. Like Sam, he didn't strike her as the type to plan a meticulous murder with cyanide.

Still Miranda kept her eyes on the cannonball. She couldn't take chances. Not with so many in this little room. It would only take one misstep for things to get out of hand big-time.

"I'm waiting for an explanation," Miranda said again, her words coming out like hammer blows.

There was a long span of silence then a single voice spoke. Soft, musical, thick with the exotic accent, the voice trembled with an undertone of dread.

"I can explain." It was Layla. She put her hands to her face. "This is all because of me. Please don't hurt them. I couldn't stand it if anyone else died."

At her words Miranda melted.

"You are the detectives Sam hired?" Layla asked gently.

Miranda glanced over at Parker. He gave her a look that assured her she was doing the right thing. And that he could handle Yuri if she was wrong.

"Yes." She narrowed her eyes at the cannonball but slowly lowered her weapon and stuffed it into the waistband at the small of her back.

Parker lowered his as well but kept it at his side.

She took a deep breath and turned to face the women on the end of the bed.

"Okay," she said to Layla. "Let's hear what you have to say."

CHAPTER FORTY

Miranda watched the young aerial artist gather her thoughts as she stared down at her bare feet and her teal-painted toes.

She wore dark jeans and a plain gray halter top with a modest neckline. Her blond hair, pulled back with a simple dark band, lay flat against her head. Her skin looked pale, her eyes shadowed and weary, like she hadn't slept in a few days.

She probably hadn't.

She took a deep breath and began to speak. "Three days ago, I went over to Tupper's trailer. It was just after the evening show. The performance had gone especially well and I wanted to celebrate with him."

"You'd been fighting with him," Miranda said flatly.

She looked up at her, eyes wide. But she nodded. "Yes, we'd had an argument. I wanted to make up with him." She took another breath. "So I went over to his place. I knocked on the door but there was no answer. It was open so I went inside. And that was when I…found him."

She put her face in her hands.

Dashia slipped an arm around her. "You poor thing," she murmured. "You poor, poor thing."

"He was…dead." Layla's voice trembled as she said the word. "I knew it as soon as I saw him. It was what we had been afraid of. What I knew would happen. I was so frightened. I didn't know what to do. Then I remembered Tupper had told me if anything happened to him, I should leave town. He gave me money for it. He made me pack my things so I would be ready. I never thought I could leave him, leave the circus, but I did. I had to."

Her pretty dark eyes began to fill. Tears spilled down her pale cheeks. "Tupper said I should get as far away as I could. But I only got to here. I'm nearly out of money already. Oh, my poor Tupper." She laid her face against Dashia's neck and sobbed.

Miranda's heart went out to her. But her sympathy was overshadowed by a strange tingling slinking over her skin. Layla had known her fiancé was going to be killed? How?

"Why were you and Tupper so afraid?" she asked, hoping not to upset her any more.

Layla wiped her cheek. "I...I don't know how to explain. There's too much to tell."

"Give it a shot," Miranda said.

That only made the young woman cry harder.

Dashia began to stroke Layla's hair and apparently decided to attempt an answer. "We are not from Bulgaria."

So the Vargas weren't what they pretended to be. The Russian mob idea flashed through Miranda's head again. Was that who they were running from?

"You have fake IDs," Parker said.

Dashia blinked at him as if she had forgotten he was in the room. "Yes, Mr. Parker. They are fakes. But we did not make them. They were given to us."

"Who gave them to you?" Miranda wanted to know. "Tenbrook?" And how did he play into this?

Dashia let out a breath as if she'd never felt more defeated. "We came from a lab."

Miranda glanced at Parker and saw the rare look of confusion on his face.

She thought her hearing must be going bad. Or maybe she'd fallen asleep on the drive and was dreaming. "A lab?"

"An experimental lab," Yuri said.

Oh, well that explained it.

Layla wiped her face again and caught her breath. "We didn't know it was a lab. I didn't. I thought everyone grew up that way."

"What way?" Miranda asked slowly, not sure she wanted to hear the answer.

"We were always inside the building. Only once a week could we go into the yard and play. We had to study. We had to keep to the schedule. We had to exercise." She stopped talking and stared at her toes again.

"What sort of exercise?" Parker prompted. He was going along with the story, humoring her.

Without looking up Layla shrugged. "Gymnastics, strength training, rope climbing. I was very good at that. They said I had amazing dexterity. That was when they got the idea to train me as an aerial silk artist."

"At the lab," Miranda clarified.

She rubbed her bare arms. "At the place where we lived. It was a large place with so many rooms. Big white rooms with no windows. Not at all like the trailers we've been living in at the circus. There was a dining room and a training room and a schoolroom. All connected by long halls."

There was a slipping sound. Sam slid down the wall and landed on the floor with a bump. He sat staring at Layla.

"Go on," Miranda told her.

"The doctors, they gave us numbers, but our mothers gave us our names. Dashia and Yuri and I, our mother was Nurse Varga. She was the one from Bulgaria. She raised us. I suppose that is why we all have her accent."

Miranda walked over to a chair near the door and sat down. She put a hand to her head. Either they were stalling for time with this bizarre narrative or she was still asleep in the car.

"Wait a minute," she said to Yuri. "You're married to your sister?"

"She's not our real mother," Dashia said as if that explained it. "She only carried us. We came from different sets of genes."

As in implantation?

"Okay." Miranda glanced over at Parker. His face was grim, his jaw set. He was obviously getting more out of this than she was.

"There were nine of us at first," Layla continued. "Matthew and Andrew and Lauren, they belonged to Nurse Williams."

"Yes. They were all so good in math," Dashia said smiling nostalgically. "They could do advanced calculus at eight."

Layla smiled at the memory. "They had clefts in their lips all the way to their noses. But they loved to talk. The teacher was always telling them to be quiet. And Chelsea. She had to walk on her hands. She had no legs. But she always made me laugh. And then one day they said Chelsea couldn't come to school anymore because she was sick. I never saw her after that."

"Silvio and Manuel," Dashia said. "They were twins. Their mother was Nurse Martínez."

"They had the bumps."

Dashia nodded. "All over their faces. But they could remember everything they read."

Layla's smile faded to sorrow again. "They were twelve when they took them away."

Now it was Miranda's turn to stare down at her feet. What in the world were these people talking about? Genius children with birth defects? Some kind of wacky baby farm? She had to be asleep in the rental car. She had to be dreaming.

Dashia rose and went over to her husband. His cheeks were wet. These were his memories, too.

She brushed his tears away and stroked his face. "We almost lost Yuri. He used to have such big knots on his head. They said he was disfigured, but he was always beautiful to me."

"As you are to me, my Dashia. Though you are so little."

"But after you begged them," Layla said, "they agreed to try the surgery and it worked. They said he was ready for the Great Experiment."

"Great Experiment?" Miranda put a hand to her stomach. She was starting to feel queasy.

Layla nodded. "They were ready to let us go out into the world. They wanted to see how we would do. They said they were going to send us to a circus. They wanted Dashia and Yuri to go first."

"Everything was ready. Except for his scars." Dashia ran her hand tenderly over her husband's head.

Miranda shook herself. "Wait a minute. Are you saying your husband didn't get his scars from being shot out of a cannon?"

Dashia turned to her. "When they sent us to Under the Big Top, they made up the story about Yuri's accident. They told us we could never tell anyone the truth. Not about his scars. Not about where we came from. Not about anything."

Miranda looked at Parker again. He was a little pale.

No, she thought. These people were professional circus performers. They could make you believe in whole worlds that didn't really exist. This had to be some kind of illusion. A magic trick.

She got to her feet, moved over to Layla. "Okay. This is a nice story, but what has it got to do with Tupper Magnuson?"

Layla bit her lip. "Tupper knew all about it. All about me. I didn't want to tell him, but—"

"But what?"

Layla's cheeks turned pink then she looked up at Miranda with her big watery dark eyes. "Tupper and I were so much in love. We were going to get married. He wanted to make love to me. And one night...I shouldn't have gone so far with him. I couldn't help it."

"What did you do?" She was pretty sure she didn't want to hear this.

"I let him touch me. And he found...my secret place. And then he knew. I had to tell him. They told us not to tell anyone, but I told him. And he was so angry. He said he was going to go to the police, to the media, to anyone who would listen. I told him no, he couldn't. That's what we were fighting about."

Miranda suddenly remembered the books in Tupper's trailer. Cloning. Genetics. Biotechnology. Her lungs constricted in sudden horror.

Layla was telling the truth.

Tears spilled from the young woman's eyes and ran down her cheeks like raindrops. "It's all my fault. If only I hadn't been so weak. If only I hadn't said anything. If only he hadn't seen my secret place."

Secret place? Miranda was pretty sure she didn't mean what young girls usually thought of as their secret place.

By now her head was splitting. Despite her revulsion, she had to know. "Layla, what are you talking about?"

Layla looked up at her, eyes wide. "Do you want me to show you? Show you my secret place?"

"I...well...not really."

"I am not embarrassed. Not if it will help you prove who killed Tupper and Harvey." She got to her feet, put her arms around her waist and lifted her halter top above her waist.

She turned around and there it was.

Two short claw-like fingers about three inches long each grew out of the young woman's back near the spine, just under her ribcage. As she closed and opened them, retracting them into her flesh then extending them again, Miranda could see they were strong as a vice grip.

Secret place and secret weapon. Biata Ito was right. That was how Layla did her act. How she hung onto her silk strands without falling.

Miranda didn't gross out easily, but as she stared at the moving claw fingers, she'd never felt so sick in her life.

Hand over her mouth, she ran for the door. "I need some air."

CHAPTER FORTY-ONE

Miranda had just finished depositing her stomach contents behind the hotel's nicely manicured bushes when she felt Parker's steady hand on her back.

He held out a handkerchief to her.

She took it and wiped her face. "Talk about embarrassing." She tried to laugh, but it wasn't working.

"I feel like joining you," he said darkly.

Her brain was still spinning from the things she'd just heard.

"Did you hear the same thing I did in there? All three of them were generated in some lab? A nurse was fertilized with them and carried them to term? Gave them her name? Cared for them?"

"That's what I heard."

"Can they really be telling the truth, Parker?"

He stared off into the distance. "There have been experiments with test tube babies for decades. Cloning and genetic research has been ongoing for years. But I've never heard of anything like this. The ethical implications are enormous."

They were enormous all right. "And some of those kids were 'taken away'?" She made quote marks in the air with her fingers. "Even the ones who could do calculus at eight? This place, whatever it is, gets rid of little kids with birth defects like...cleft palates and...bumps?"

"Tumors of some sort. Perhaps elephantitis."

"Experiments that had gone wrong? That lab is run by monsters." An icy shudder went through her as if it had swept down from the North Pole. She wanted to stick her head in the bushes again. She felt her eyes sting with tears. "There couldn't have been just nine of them. What happened to the others?"

Parker stood in silence, the frame of his body rock hard. She knew he wanted to do something. Anything. She did, too. But they didn't even know where this so-called lab was.

Suddenly she gasped in air as the answer snapped in place in her head. She stared at him, almost unable to speak.

And then they spoke at the same time. "GenaPulse."

She snatched her cell out of her pocket and began to search. "C'mon, c'mon."

The connection speed here sucked, but she had a feeling she wouldn't find anything. Not a website or listing of any kind. A place like that didn't make itself known.

She looked up and saw Parker had his own phone out.

She peered over his shoulder and watched him swipe through the photos he'd taken in Tenbrook's office. When he got to the accounting records and the line item for the company in question, there was an address. Tenbrook might be the only outsider who had it.

"They're north of Dallas. Plano."

"Okay." She stared down at his screen. And sucked in another breath as a new wave of revelation hit her. "Was that what the big donation was for? To take on three...experiments and keep your mouth shut?"

"So it appears."

She stared off across the parking lot at the highway beyond and rubbed her arms, though the air was warm. What kind of a man had Sam been working for?

She turned back to Parker. "We need to tell Underwood. She has to shut that place down."

Parker considered it a moment. "The police would need a search warrant for the lab itself. I'm not sure we've got enough for one."

He was right. The cops wouldn't buy what they'd just heard in that hotel room. They needed proof. And a warrant would take time. Too much time. "So what do we do now?"

Before Parker could reply, the door to one-twenty-four opened and Yuri stepped out onto the lighted walkway.

There was fear in the big man's eyes as he lumbered toward them. "Mr. Parker, Ms. Steele. We've woken our boys."

"Your kids?" Miranda hadn't seen them.

He nodded. "They were asleep in the adjoining room. Dashia is getting them ready. We've decided we can't stay here. If you found us, whoever killed Tupper and Harvey will find us, too."

They couldn't just run away. Not now. Miranda folded her arms and glared at the cannonball. "What happened to the others, Yuri?"

"What?"

"There had to be more than nine of you."

He winced, stared down at the sidewalk and finally took a long, deep breath. "Dashia, Layla don't know. I never told them. They may have figured it out. I don't know. But yes, there were others. Many others."

"How do you know?"

"I've seen them."

"At the lab?"

"In another part of it. A part we weren't allowed into. Before the surgery to remove my growths, I thought they would take me away like Silvio and Manuel. I tried to escape. I found a lower floor. A tunnel, a long hall. And several large rooms where others were being kept. There were so many of them. Oh, they were in worse condition than we were. Then two workers came down the hall and I hid in a closet to avoid being seen. But the workers stopped outside the closet door and began to talk. I was so afraid they were going to find me. I stood there, shaking while I listened to their conversation." He rubbed his eyes with his big hands as if trying to wipe out the memory.

"What did you hear, Yuri?" Parker asked gently. He had more of a stomach for this than she did at the moment.

"One of the workers said what a shame it was that so many of the batches had failed. That is what she called us. Batches." His shoulders jerked as he fought his own emotions.

Parker laid a hand on his arm. "Go on."

"The other worker sounded more experienced. She explained that when an experiment fails, it is no longer cost effective to keep the subject alive. And so the subject must be recycled."

Her breath growing shallow, Miranda eyed the bushes again. "Recycled?"

"The experienced worker began to describe the process. I didn't want to hear any more, but I couldn't move." He put his hands to his face, his chest heaving with distress.

"What did she say?"

Yuri caught his breath. "She said that the subject is put under anesthesia and the cells, the organs, and useful body parts are harvested for the next experiment. The good parts are kept, the defective ones discarded."

Like taking out the trash. "Then what?"

"Then they put the subject to sleep."

There was a catch in Miranda's throat. "Permanently?"

He nodded. "The experienced worker was certain the process caused minimal pain and distress."

Parker's face was hard as flint. "Involuntary euthanasia is murder, Yuri."

Miranda's heart beat kicked up as something else struck her. "And I bet when they put those kids to sleep, they use cyanide."

Parker nodded as Yuri's eyes went wide with understanding.

She had another thought. "That information would be enough for Underwood to get a warrant."

"If we can prove it."

"They keep documents," Yuri said. "Records."

"What sort of records?"

"Everything is documented by hand and on computer. I saw that, too. They are stored in a special room."

The hotel room door opened again and Sam came running out. He grabbed Yuri by the arm. "Yuri, you can't be on the run for the rest of your lives. You have to let the detectives help you. I've talked to Layla and she agrees with me." He turned to Miranda. "You can do something, can't you?"

Miranda looked at Parker.

She could see the wheels in his head turning. "If we could get inside GenaPulse unnoticed and get copies of those records, it would give us solid evidence."

And Underwood could easily get a warrant. Except for the B&E part, but Underwood wouldn't be responsible for that. She and Parker weren't connected with the police.

"We've got to stop them, Parker."

"They're called GenaPulse?" Yuri said. "We did not know that. We do not even know where the lab is located."

"We do," Miranda told him. "And we're going there."

Suddenly it was as if the fearless human cannonball came back to life. "I will help you. I can get you inside. I can show you where the records are stored." He looked back at the hotel room. "But my family…"

Sam thought a moment. "My brother's got a ranch in Atoka. It's just a couple hours southeast of here. They'd be safe there. I'll take them. Dashia, the kids, and Layla."

"You're sure your brother won't mind?" Miranda asked.

"He's a good guy. Got a family of his own. They'd like the company. And I'll chip in with expenses. I won't tell him anything…about all this."

Slowly Yuri nodded. He turned back to Parker. "When do we leave?"

"As soon as possible."

CHAPTER FORTY-TWO

After Yuri told the others the plan and said a tearful goodbye to his family, they watched Sam and his new charges take off in the pickup. Then he, Miranda and Parker piled into the rental and raced back down the interstate with the human cannonball in the backseat.

When they got close to a cell tower Miranda dialed Underwood and woke the police detective up. She explained, vaguely, what they were doing and what their suspicions were about the mysterious research company hidden in plain sight in Plano. She added she was convinced the lab was the source of the cyanide that had killed Tupper Magnuson and Harvey Hackett, whose COD Underwood confirmed.

Miranda could tell Underwood didn't believe her.

She listened to the woman hem and haw about going through proper legal channels, having to wake up a judge, too little evidence for the DA, yada yada—all while Parker was ironically breaking every speed limit on the highway.

But being a good cop, Underwood had to follow the lead and agreed to work on getting a warrant.

Wouldn't be much help on their current venture, Miranda thought as she hung up. The legal process would take too damn long.

As she relayed the information to Parker, she stared at the asphalt rushing toward her in the headlights.

Right now, they were pretty much on their own.

She glanced over at him. His face was hard and set. He was thinking of those kids.

Turning her head she saw Yuri staring out the side window. His thoughts must be burdened with all sorts of painful memories.

Sighing she settled back in her seat and closed her eyes. Might be a good idea to get a little shuteye before they got to their destination. Something told her she'd need all the strength she could muster.

As she drifted off, images of trapeze artists and jugglers came to life in her head. The colors, the music, the applause. She saw clowns scamper out and chase each other around the ring with their silly buckets of confetti. The images blurred and she saw Harvey Hackett sitting dead in his recliner, the lethal bottle of Barefoot Merlot beside him. Even though he'd just taken all his bottles to the dumpster.

She saw Tupper Magnuson, the once happy clown, lying stretched out on the couch in his living room, a glass of Barefoot Merlot on the coffee table before him. He had loved entertaining kids. He'd fallen for a beautiful woman and was about to be married. He'd had his whole life in front of him.

But he'd made the mistake of telling someone what he knew about Layla and that he was going public with it. And that person said, "No, you're not."

With a jolt she sat up, eyes wide open, heart pounding wildly.

That was it. She knew who the killer was.

"Are you all right?"

"Yeah." She took a quick look at Parker.

He gave her a telling glance in return, reading her thoughts, as she read his. He knew who the killer was, too.

CHAPTER FORTY-THREE

Parker made record time.

It was a little before four a.m. when they reached Plano. The motor purred steadily, as it had for the last two hundred miles, while they pressed on, heading northeast through the darkness. Beyond the tech offices and well-heeled suburbs of the city they drove, until at last the car rolled into a rural section.

Here there were farms and brick homes with acres between them, their outdoor lights scarcely exposing their presence.

Parker slowed, made a turn and drove down about fifty feet. At the end of the paved road in a wide, flat field of prairie grass surrounded by trees stood a sprawling three story building.

He turned into the lot and cruised around the few rows of vehicles, finally pulling into a spot.

"A lot of cars here for this hour," Miranda commented as he turned off the ignition.

Yuri roused in the backseat. "Most of the staff lives here."

Cozy.

She gazed at the dark structure, its outline illuminated by the security lights. Flat, plain, rectangular. Several rows of raw molded concrete formed jagged, uninviting walls. As Layla had described it, there were few windows. Just a row or two down the middle. Probably for staff only.

It looked like a prison camp.

"How do you suggest we get in?" Parker said to the cannonball.

Yuri was silent a long moment, staring through the windshield at the frightening building that used to be his home. "There's a back way," he said at last. "It leads to the office where the records are kept. It would be better if we went on foot from here."

She and Parker did a weapons check and the three of them climbed out of the car as noiselessly as they could and made their way along the edge of the lot, hunching down beside the tall grass so as not to be seen.

160

Miranda squinted at the building. She didn't see any security cameras mounted on the walls or the flat roof, but it was dark enough and they were far enough away to miss them.

"Are there guards?" she whispered.

"Inside. Mostly to keep us in," Yuri said, as if he'd forgotten he was on the outside now.

"If we run into any, we'll take care of them," Parker said as casually as if he were accepting an invitation to a social event.

Still, she wished they'd had a pistol or a knife for Yuri. Sam didn't have another spare and everyone had agreed his shotgun might come in handy and he should keep it. Still, the cannonball's large hands might be weapons in themselves.

They reached the far side of the building, made a turn and scooted along in the shadows until they were facing the back.

Yuri stopped and peered into the darkness. "Is it still here?"

Miranda didn't know what to make of that question. Before she could ask what he meant, he let out a breath of relief.

"Yes. Over there. See it?" He pointed toward the lower part of the building's side

In the dim light she could make out a ramp and a concrete platform with a garage-like door above it. Loading dock.

"Is that where they receive supplies?"

"Yes, I think that's what they use it for. There is a door there. It leads to the lower floor of the building. The part I told you about."

Where the records were kept.

She squinted into the shadows. To the left of the bay was a metal barrier that looked like double doors. No one was around. They could make it there.

"The coast looks clear," she whispered.

"We should be able to get in."

"Let's go then."

Beside her Parker nodded.

Crouching down, they scurried across the pavement, up the incline of the walkway to the platform. In a few seconds they reached the double doors.

Miranda spun around, half expecting to see a guard. But there was no one.

She turned back to the barrier in time to see Parker slowly place his fingers around the handle.

He gave it a jerk. And it opened.

She could feel her pulse in her ears. None of them had any idea what might be beyond that door.

Trap?

"Ready?" Parker said, his voice steady and low.

She had no idea what they'd face inside but from what Layla and the Vargas had told them, it wouldn't be pretty. She thought of the six kids who'd been "taken away" never to be seen again. She thought of what Yuri had told them about the "batches" and the failures and the organ harvesting process.

Only way to go, she thought. Only way to stop these killers before they murdered more innocent children.

She straightened her shoulders and nodded. "Ready."

Parker nodded back, stepped through the door and she followed him into darkness.

CHAPTER FORTY-FOUR

Okay, he was up and taking care of it. Just like he promised.

His head pounded from a fatigue headache and he craved a large dose of Jim Beam, but he'd get that later. After he'd taken care of business.

Except his assignment was turning out to be harder than he'd thought.

He'd forced himself awake after only a few hours sleep, cleaned his shotgun and gone in search of Sam Keegan to find out where those two prying detectives were.

But Keegan was gone.

And so were the Vargas. The whole damn family.

He wanted to wake everyone up and find out what the hell was going on. But he didn't dare let anyone know he was looking for Keegan or his detectives. That would be a detail the police would pick up on later. Too risky.

Did that mean the Vargas knew? And if so, how much? Were they going to hook up with Layla? She had to know everything. She must have seen Tupper's body the night he died. That had to be why she took off. She must have thought she'd be next.

And she was supposed to be. Except he couldn't find her.

Why had he let himself get sucked into this? But he knew all too well. He'd wanted the money. Needed it for his project. He had dreams. Big dreams. And dreams like that cost a bundle.

His dreams deserved to come to fruition. That could still happen. He'd make it happen. And she would help. She owed him that much.

So now he was executing Plan B. Cruising up US-75 in his silver Camaro convertible on his way to Plano. He patted the Mossberg at his side.

She was going to help him find everyone. Together, they'd take care of all of them one by one. And then it would all be done. Except for the fallout. But he'd take care of that, too.

It was only a matter of time before that cop Underwood or those two PIs figured everything out.

And when they did, she was taking the fall for it, not him.

CHAPTER FORTY-FIVE

As Miranda's eyes adjusted to the lack of light in the spacious warehouse-like room adjacent to the loading dock, she could make out stacks of bulky cardboard boxes piled against one wall. More on the other side.

Storage area.

It was quiet and smelled clean. And it was empty of people.

That was a relief, but how did they get to that records office from here?

She felt Yuri's nudge.

"There's another door at the far end," he said in a hoarse whisper.

She could hear fear in his voice. Already the place was getting to him.

Parker took out a pocket light and swept it along the floor. Following the light they inched their way across the platform hoping not to bump into any boxes or trip over any equipment or unexpected rises in the concrete. As they reached the wall on the opposite side, he shined it over the cinder blocks until he found the opening.

Miranda heard him grunt under his breath at the same time his light illuminated their next obstacle.

A keypad.

Parker could beat any mechanical lock, but a digital one was a different story.

Scowling he studied it. "If I had the right equipment, I could rewire it."

"That would take too long." Her heart was pounding so hard she was sure somebody inside the building could hear it. "We could try to guess the code."

"And what would happen if it's incorrect?"

He was right. If the thing had a warning system, an army of nurses or orderlies or guards could come barreling through that door and put them all in strait jackets.

"Wait," Yuri extended a finger toward the pad.

Parker grabbed his hand before he could touch it. "Don't guess, Yuri. If you're wrong, it could set off alarms."

"I am not wrong." He sounded so sure, Parker released him.

Yuri gave Miranda a questioning look.

She thought a moment. What choice did they have? The only other thing she could think of was using their weapons to shoot the device. She was sure that would only backfire.

"Okay," she said at last. "Give it a try."

She held her breath as the big man poked at the numbers. As his forefinger hit the last digit, she braced herself for the ear shattering clang of alarms.

Instead—there was only a quiet click.

Miranda didn't wait for an invitation. She pushed the door open, stepped across the threshold and found herself in a dimly lit stairwell.

They were at the top. A raw concrete ceiling loomed overhead. Below was a flight of concrete stairs.

"C'mon," she hissed over her shoulder and led the way down.

"How did you know the code?" Parker whispered to Yuri behind her.

"Layla's birthday. I saw the nurses use it on the doors inside."

And they hadn't changed it since he'd left? Must feel pretty sure of themselves.

It was two flights down. Another door met them at the bottom. With another keypad.

She turned to the cannonball. "Are you saying they use the same code with every lock?"

"Only in this area."

This area. The lower level he'd described to them back at the hotel. No telling what they'd find on the other side of this door. But they had to find out.

She stepped aside. "Work your magic."

Once more he punched in the code and again the door clicked open.

Now was the time for the army of nurses and orderlies, right? And they'd all be armed with syringes filled with something deadly. Did they have even a fraction of a chance of pulling this off?

Maybe, maybe not. But it didn't matter. They had to try.

Gritting her teeth, she pushed the door open.

CHAPTER FORTY-SIX

They were in.

Miranda stood blinking under the harsh fluorescent light of a long, L-shaped hallway.

The sound of a generator somewhere hummed in her ears. The walls were painted in a pale blue, like a hospital floor, with no decorations on them at all. The air was cool. Too cool, as if it were almost refrigerated. And it smelled sterile, like disinfectant.

Beneath their feet stretched yards and yards of shiny beige linoleum. They were in the corner of the L so there were two ways to go.

She gave Yuri a where-to? look.

He peered down one path then the other. His face strained with the effort of accessing old memory banks. Finally, he nodded toward the right and started down the hall.

Noiselessly she followed, Parker at her side.

As if by instinct, she pulled the Taurus from the small of her back and held it up and at the ready. She glanced at Parker and saw he had his weapon drawn as well.

But just now they didn't need them. The place seemed pretty deserted.

The halls were lined with small doors, all unlocked. One by one they opened them as they went, discovering utility closets filled with cleaning supplies, uniforms, medical stuff.

"Reagents of various sorts, solvents, ethanol," Parker murmured scrutinizing the shelves of one space.

But no records of the residents or anything else they could base an arrest and prosecution on. They closed the door and moved on.

The lower floor was a crisscrossing maze of intersecting passageways. Yuri led them down one corridor, turned down another, turned the other way and took them down a third. They continued to open every door they encountered.

Some of rooms were empty. Others held a desk and chair, but none had filing cabinets or even a computer.

They continued this way and that, turned another corner, headed down a long, wide hall. Miranda studied the door at the end of it. Its shape looked awfully familiar. Good grief. It was the one leading to the loading dock where they'd come in.

They were going in circles. Damn.

"Are you sure those records are down here?" she hissed to Yuri.

"Yes. I am sure."

"They didn't rearrange things, did they?"

"No. This is the most secret place in the building." He covered his head with both hands, his big fingers pressing into his scars as if he were trying to squeeze out what was stored in his brain. After a moment, he stifled a cry of distress. "I am sorry. I simply do not remember where the office is."

Parker seemed perturbed.

Tapping her foot, she peered down the artery they'd just come through. The place was huge. They had covered maybe a quarter of it, if that much. It was only a matter of time before they were discovered.

They had to get those records and get out of here.

"We need to split up," she said.

Parker didn't like that idea at all. "We can't split up, Miranda. How will we know when one of us finds the record office?"

"We've got our cells. We'll text."

He shook his head. "Not the best plan."

"The longer we stay down here, the more likely someone will find us."

He let out a breath. She knew he didn't want to let her out of his sight, but he saw her point. "Five minutes."

"What?"

"We check in every five minutes. And I say when to cut our losses."

She met his gaze, wanting to stare him down, but she knew he was right. They'd blow everything if they stayed in here too long and risked getting caught.

She gave in. "Okay. Make sure everyone's cells are on vibrate."

"Already done."

Right. Before they got here. She was losing her cool. Pull yourself together, she thought.

She took a deep breath. "You go that way," she said to Parker indicating the direction they'd just come from, "and try going straight at the T. Yuri, you turn and go for the middle. I'll head off this way." Going back over the path where they'd started.

"Agreed," Parker said, sounding as if he really didn't. "Remember. Five minutes."

"Five minutes."

And she turned and headed down the corridor.

CHAPTER FORTY-SEVEN

Miranda hustled across the polished linoleum wondering when Parker was going to call time. She shouldn't have given into his demand, but what was she supposed to do? Stand there and argue with him until somebody heard them? The man could be infuriating at the worst possible times. But she couldn't think about Parker now. She had to concentrate on finding those records.

They'd already checked the closed doors on either side, so this time she didn't bother. She went straight for the area where they hadn't been yet, turning left then right, then left again, burrowing into the center. The heart of the place.

Her instincts played out.

Around the next corner she discovered a set of double doors that made her suddenly feel like she was in a hospital.

The décor here was different. The lights were more muted, the walls pale green with a waist high beige and brown strip running in a horizontal pattern.

A logo about the size of a pie pan had been painted in the center of the doors.

A dark green circle with two twisting bands inside. What was that called? Double...helix? DNA, right? The first indicator of what this place really was.

Whatever that symbol was, the sight of it made her blood feel like ice.

On the wall beside the door sat a fat round metal plate. Access. But what would she find inside?

No choice, she thought for the hundredth time. She reached out and gave the thing a push.

The doors opened and the helix in the logo split apart.

That was symbolic, she thought as she stepped inside.

She looked around and found herself in a wide open space. This one even more hospital like. A long stainless sink stood in a niche off to one side. Several rolling carts were parked along the wall across from it. The lighting seemed surgical, even though the air was less medicinal smelling here. The floor was a homey oak laminate, the doors along the walls were painted a friendly blue. But Miranda had a feeling this spot was anything but friendly.

The rooms—or whatever was behind those affable doors—seemed to be large, since their portals were spaced far apart. Time to have a look.

She moved to the first door. It had a window, though the glass was covered with a mesh barrier and too opaque to see through. No way to tell what she was walking into.

She put her hand on the knob and turned. It opened.

Hand on her weapon she peeked inside. Nobody here. But there had been.

Tables with clean white surfaces lined two sides of the large room. Matching white cabinets hung on the walls overhead, along with several shelves stacked with tube racks and colorful long-nosed bottles holding mysterious liquids. In the middle of the table sat a microscope and several odd-looking machines that did God knew what.

A lab of some sort.

She heard a hum on her left and noticed a refrigeration unit with digital numbers on the outside. It had a glass door. She inched over to it and peered inside. There were stacks and stacks of small round receptacles. The kind of container she remembered from some long ago science class in high school. The kind of container you grew things in. And each of these containers held an unidentifiable substance.

Her stomach began to churn. She felt dizzy.

Was this what she thought it was? The beginning of life for GenaPulse's "experiments." What else could it be?

This was how Yuri and Dashia and Layla started out? In…Petri dishes?

Struggling to keep her head, she stuffed her gun into her waistband and dug for her phone. She began snapping pictures. The microscope, the tubes, the machines, the unit with the organisms growing in them. Or at least that's what she thought they must be.

This wasn't the written documentation they were looking for, and a defense lawyer would argue it was just a regular lab, but these photos were proof of something. Especially with all that Layla and the Vargas had to say.

Done. She put her phone back in her pocket and drew her weapon again.

Fighting down the powerful urge to hurl yet again, she pushed open the door and got out of the room.

CHAPTER FORTY-EIGHT

"Not that way, Yuri."

Parker watched the large man come to a stop at the bend in the hall and turn around.

"Why not?" he said. "Ms. Steele said to separate."

"It's too risky. You don't have a weapon."

His thick Bulgarian brows rose to the top of his hairless head. "You disagree with her?"

Disagree? That was certainly an understatement.

He should have taken over the reins as soon as they left the hotel. Miranda was vigilant and determined, but she was inexperienced in an operation like this. In fact, he would have insisted on taking the lead when they found Harvey Hackett dead in his trailer if it hadn't been for that stupid agreement he'd made with her on their first case.

Back then he'd imagined they'd take on a few surveillance jobs, a cold case or two. Nothing very risky. Nothing that would put her in so much danger.

He'd never been more wrong.

He never should have let her separate them in this God-forsaken labyrinth. But he knew what her reaction would have been if he had challenged her. And right now, they couldn't afford a loud argument in these halls. He had a feeling they were being watched.

"Let's go this way." Parker said to Yuri and pointed down a passage they hadn't tried.

Yuri seemed apprehensive. "Mr. Parker. What if I cannot find it?"

There was no room for nerves on this expedition. And as Miranda had said, they were running out of time.

He put on his most confident smile and gave Yuri a pat on his muscular arm. "You're doing fine. It's been a long time. I'm quite sure it will come to you in bit."

The giant still seemed doubtful, but he nodded and turned in the direction Parker had indicated.

As they hurried along Parker tightened the grip on his weapon. In a place like this, you never knew what might be around the next corner.

CHAPTER FORTY-NINE

The open, hospital like space was still empty when Miranda stepped back into it from the lab room. Still fighting the gag reflex from what she'd seen in the refrigeration unit, she followed the curve of the wall around to a small alcove with a sign marked "Elevator."

Uh oh.

This was probably where the staff would come in to work. When that would be she had no idea, but she'd better get going.

She hurried along the wide passage and the wall began to curve the other way. She continued to follow it, wondering if she was heading for a dead end. But at last it recessed, revealing another set of doors.

Without stopping to think about how hard she was shivering, she pushed them open.

Gazing at the large circular space, she rubbed her arms, her fingers running over her own goose bumps. The temperature seemed to be ten degrees cooler in here. The air smelled very pure.

Dark screens hung along the walls. Beneath them monitoring machines stood idle. Narrow counters lined the room. Portable tables with tiny drawers were scattered about and covered with sharp-looking surgical tools. Overhead big pie-shaped lights were suspended from moveable pipes for easy adjustment. The piping was a twisted mass of white that must be terrifying to wake up to. Or fall asleep to.

The lights were positioned to aim at the single bed in the middle of the room.

The operating table.

This must be where they performed surgeries like the one they'd done on Yuri to remove his growths. It also had to be where they harvested the organs before putting their "experiments" to sleep for good.

Then she noticed the straps on the bed to hold the patient down. And the tubes hanging from the ceiling. IVs. Take the organs then pump the subject full of cyanide, and that was that.

Stretching out a hand Miranda leaned against one of the counters and sucked in air. She felt like she was about to heave again.

Keep it together, keep it together.

As she struggled to force in several deep breaths to clear her head, she spotted another door on the opposite side of the room. Summoning all her strength, she sucked up her nerves and hurried toward it.

Behind the door she discovered a long narrow room.

An equally long table stood against one side of it. Oblong cardboard boxes and particleboard containers had been piled atop the table. Against the wall hung masks and protective caps and aprons.

At the far end of the room was yet another set of double doors. This pair was made of menacing-looking metal. She moved over to them, shivering. She had a feeling she knew what she'd find behind them.

She pushed them open anyway and stood blinking in an unlit space.

She waited for her eyes to adjust to the dim light. This area was much warmer than the operating room. And the darkness was a stark contrast. Had they changed interior decorators here?

No, something told her this space had just the atmosphere they intended.

At last she could make out the single bulb that hung over a large gray metal chamber in the middle of the room. A conveyor belt, as wide as a human body, ran into a door recessed in the chamber. A door just big enough for a small casket. One of those particleboard containers. The chamber ran all the way to the ceiling like a chimney.

Controls blinked along the side of the unit and there was an odd smell in the room. Like…ash. From behind the closed door came a low rumble.

She stepped over to the chamber and dared to put her hand against it. Hot. There was a fire burning in there.

Long handled shovels leaned against the opposite wall. On the floor at her feet was something hard. She bent down to examine it and her stomach turned to lead. Somebody had missed a bit during cleanup. It was a bone fragment. This was where they got rid of the bodies.

The cremation chamber.

She picked up the bone and put it in her pocket, then her gaze followed the length of the space to another door. Where did that one lead? Outside? To the yard? Where they buried the remains?

Her hands shook as she reached for her phone and took shots of as much of the place as she could. These would make a defense attorney turn to jelly.

But after another minute she couldn't take it anymore. She was shaking and sweating bullets like she had a fever.

She had to get out of here.

She turned back and headed through the hall, now relishing the icy cool air. She thought she was retracing her steps through the lab, but she must have taken a wrong turn.

Before her stretched a curving peach painted wall she hadn't seen before. She followed it around and found a long partition made of frosted glass and etched with the double-helix logo she'd seen before.

Behind the glass she could hear soft moaning, whimpering.

Heart pounding, she put her hands against the surface and found another access button. She pushed it and the glass door opened.

She stepped inside and immediately knew what it was.

A hospital ward of sorts. There must have been more than two dozen beds. But what lay in those beds broke her heart in two.

Kids. Various ages. Some maybe only two. Others five, ten? She couldn't tell. But each one of them had some sort of horrible disfigurement.

One little dark haired boy lay sucking the end of an arm with no fingers that was almost too short to reach his mouth. His other arm was twisted around his back.

The blond girl in the bed next to him was as skinny as a doll. The next child had grotesque looking bumps all over his face and arms. That was the condition Yuri had had.

A red-headed girl lay in the next bed, breathing through a machine. Her stomach looked like it was outside of her body. The boy beside her had no legs and no lips.

They were all asleep. Or kept asleep by drugs. The whimpering came from the sounds they made as they slept. The muted subconscious cries of the weak and helpless. They were all so lost and alone. Abandoned by their creators. About to be destroyed.

Miranda had been angry plenty of times in her life. She'd seen more injustice than most. But just now a rage more powerful than any she'd felt before began to well up in her, billowing and seething like an ocean geyser.

She stood, fighting back tears as her gaze went from bed to bed.

If it was the last thing she ever did, she was going to save these kids and get them out of here.

But to do that she had to keep her head. She forced down a deep breath and once more she took out her phone. She took photos of the patients. The boy with no lips. The girl with the thin limbs. The child with the bumps. She turned the recorder on and stood letting the machine take in their soft cries.

Her heart ached for them. She wanted to gather them all up in her arms and carry them far away. To some place safe. Some place that would help them. But she couldn't. Not just yet. She had to finish this job first.

Not wanting to leave, she made herself turn away, forced her feet through the door. She found her way back into the main area, the hospital-like open space near the lab.

As soon as she stepped inside she felt her phone buzz. She was still holding it. She blinked at the screen. Text from Parker.

Where are you? Five minutes!

Good Lord. She glanced at the time.

It had been way longer than five minutes since she'd left him. Slow transmission. And she'd forgotten to text him as she'd said she would. No time to fuss about that now.

Her thumbs worked the keys.

Found the lab. And more. Coming to find you.

Just as she hit the send button she heard a muted bell from somewhere. She remembered the sign she'd seen before.

Elevator.

Her mind raced. They'd been there for hours. It must be morning now. Time for work.

Her heart began to bang painfully against her chest as she hunted around for a hiding place. There was none. She ran for one of the utility rooms, but before she could reach it, the double doors with the helix on the far end of the room swept open.

She froze as a tall, imposing looking woman in a flowing white lab coat stepped inside. She spotted her right away.

"Who are you," the woman boomed and Miranda thought she recognized the voice. "What are you doing in here?"

The woman came closer and Miranda made out her name tag. She did a double take. No wonder she knew that voice. Now she got it. Now it all made sense.

When Miranda didn't answer, the woman dug in her pocket. "I'm calling Security."

No choice, she thought again, drew her weapon and pointed at the woman. "I wouldn't do that if I were you, Dr. Tenbrook."

CHAPTER FIFTY

The layout of this building was getting on Parker's nerves.

They had been down half a dozen passageways and found nothing. Security must be the motive for the esoteric design. Even if you could get into the place, you couldn't find anything incriminating. To the designer's credit, the scheme was rather ingenious.

But like Miranda, he was beginning to think the records office had been moved. Or had never existed at all.

He would tell her so, but she hadn't replied to his text. He forced down irritation at the reminder as they passed a small alcove with an elevator.

His suspicions roused. She wouldn't have taken that elevator to another floor, would she? Or had someone come down that elevator and caught her? He couldn't let himself think those thoughts. Miranda might be headstrong, but she was highly competent. She might have discovered something, he told himself. She was focused on her task. There was no reason to believe she was in trouble.

Yet.

He glanced up at his volunteer guide and saw a flash of recognition on his face.

"Do you see it, Yuri?"

Yuri nodded slowly and kept walking. "This area looks familiar. Here?" He hurried ahead and disappeared around a corner. "Yes!"

"Shh," Parker hissed as he rounded the turn and followed him into a room.

He stared at the contents, which were partially illuminated from the hall. Yuri had been right. This was a records office.

But it was huge.

A room full of shelving units, seven racks deep, each shelf crowded with color coded manila folders like a doctor's office.

"There are so many of them," Yuri whispered, awe in his tone. "We cannot photograph them all."

"No." Parker murmured. And where were all the "patients" that corresponded to these files? The thought made him cringe.

He turned his head. Behind them stretched a low wall-mounted shelf that served as a desk for several workers. There were more papers there. Folders, labels, and other office paraphernalia.

Parker eyed the computers. They most certainly held important data. No doubt they'd be password protected.

They didn't have time to hack the units. And he hadn't heard from Miranda. They had to get the information quickly, find her, and get out of here before they were discovered.

He took out his penlight and studied the colored tabs on the files closest to him, trying to decipher their code. It appeared the files near the front were the most recent.

He pulled one down and scanned it.

The title page was marked with the name GenaPulse and a handwritten case number. What must be the organization's logo was stamped in the center. A DNA molecule in a circle. The logo alone was incriminating but certainly not enough to make a firm case.

He turned the page and began to read the abstract.

It described the cultivation of a particular cell culture, the various microbes and tissues and eukaryotes used. The temperature, humidity and other conditions. The growth and implantation of the subject.

The following pages were details of the subject's progress. Height, weight, length. The description ended at six months old. The paper was dated last week.

Too recent. "Let's try to find the names of the people you told us about."

"You mean Matthew and Andrew and the rest?"

"Yes. That was at least eight years ago?"

"I think so," Yuri said.

Hoping the records went back that far, Parker examined the codes on the opposite shelf for a moment then pointed toward the far corner. "They might be over there. Let's see what we can find."

The cannonball squeezed through the narrow aisle and began opening files. "I cannot read these. There are no names. Only numbers."

Parker reached below him and took a file from the lowest shelf. He opened it.

The first page, the one with the GenaPulse name, logo and case number was stamped in big bold letters with a single word.

"Terminated."

Quickly Parker opened the file and read, deciphering the medical terminology as best he could. The cultivation, growth and implantation details were similar to the other file, but variations in the process were highlighted. And then came the negative findings.

Chromosomal defects, this or that possible syndrome postulated. There were x-rays and test results. The right and left femurs were misshapen and had to be measured at various intervals. After six months, no growth was detected. A portion of the subject's intestines were missing. There were liver issues. A battery of tests was administered regularly, including cognitive, which was high, and muscular strength, which was average.

There were several pages detailing lack of growth, disappointing surgical results, and general degeneration. Parker's insides chilled as he read the last page. The decision to terminate had been reached unanimously by the director and two scientists.

The subject had been six years old.

He turned to Yuri, wondering how the man had managed to survive such a place. He held up the file. "This one is a good start."

He pointed out the pages that were relevant then began snapping photos of them with his phone while Yuri hunted for more.

They found dozens of similar files in these shelves, took photo after photo as they moved toward the back of the room. They were so far into the stacks Parker barely heard the elevator ping outside.

"Stop, Yuri," he whispered when the sound finally registered in his ears.

He slid the last file back in place and crouched down. Yuri did the same.

A woman stood in the doorway, feeling for the light switch. She found it and the room flooded with light.

She had on a teal scrub uniform with soft white shoes and a stethoscope around her neck. Her straight dark hair was pulled back into a severe bun.

"Who is there?" she demanded in an Eastern European accent.

Parker flinched.

"Mama." Yuri started to get to his feet.

"Stay down," Parker hissed.

But the giant pushed his way around Parker and hurried out of the shelter of the stacks. "Mama," he said again when he saw her.

She put a hand to her breast in shock. "Yuri! What are you doing here?"

Parker watched the woman put her arms around the giant's neck in a motherly embrace. Her face was lined, her hair tinged with gray. Tears shimmered in her eyes. She might have been forty or sixty. It was hard to tell. But despite the bizarre circumstances of her long ago pregnancy her feelings for the child she'd borne were apparently real.

She ran her hand gently over Yuri's face. "They sent you away. You and Dashia."

"I came back."

"What are you doing in the records room? And who is that man?" She turned her head and looked at Parker warily as he stepped out from the aisle, then back at her son. Duty warred with maternal instinct. "I...I...have to get a guard."

There was a fire extinguisher on the wall and a red alarm next to it. The nurse spun and made a move for it.

Parker lunged forward and grabbed her wrist just before she reached it. "You can't do that Ms. Varga."

"Why not? Who are you?"

He studied her face. Her brown eyes were kind, but her features were sharp and birdlike, lined with the grief of the terrible facts she had been forced to keep secret for so many years. She looked nothing like Yuri or Dashia.

He decided to try persuasion. "I'm here to help."

"Help with what? What were you doing back there in the files?"

"I'm a private investigator. There have been two murders. We need your help to solve them."

Her eyes went wide then filled with confusion. The woman did not seem to have evil intentions, but she had to be considerably brainwashed to live and work in this place with the knowledge of what went on here. And God only knew how many offspring she had carried to term for GenaPulse.

She began to shake her head. "No. You must be the enemy."

"No, I'm a friend. I've come to help."

"You are come to destroy us and you have involved my son." Her voice was rising with hysteria.

"Calm down, Ms. Varga," Parker said softly. "If you'll listen, I'll explain everything."

But she kept shaking her head back and forth. "No. No. You are going to destroy us. They told us about people like you." Suddenly she turned and ran down the hall. "Help!" she cried. "Robbers in the building. Someone help."

Yuri shot after her. "Mama, come back."

Parker cursed under his breath, his gut wrenching inside him. How could everything have gone so wrong so fast? He couldn't let either of them get away.

Drawing his gun, he ran after the pair through the circuitous maze as fast as he could go.

CHAPTER FIFTY-ONE

The tall woman towering before Miranda was on the husky side.

She seemed to be in her mid-fifties with thick gray brows and gray-brown hair parted in the middle and done in a severely straight bob cut that hit her at her square jaw line.

Her thick lips were painted a ruby red, matching a dress that peeped out from beneath her white lab coat. A single strand of pearls hung around her neck. She even had on high heels.

Everything about her said Power with a capital P.

"Who are you?" she said again in just as demanding a tone, even though Miranda was the one with the .22 aimed at the woman's heart.

"The better question is who are you? And what the hell do you think you're doing here?"

Her eyes blazed but there wasn't a shred of shame in them as she narrowed them at her. "I know who you are now. You've got to be one of those detectives my brother hired."

"Your brother?" Sam? He didn't have a sister. "Oh, wait. You mean the circus owner."

No doubt he'd been in contact with her, keeping her informed on the progress of their investigation. He must have lied to her about hiring them. Though why, she couldn't imagine. Wait. That was their relationship? Brother and sister?

Miranda let out a smirk. "And here I thought you were his mother."

"You impertinent snip. We'll see how smart you are when they take you to jail for breaking into a research lab."

Miranda let out a laugh. "Research lab? Is that was you call murdering little kids? Research?"

Now the woman's features contorted like a scary Halloween mask. She made a jerky move toward the gun.

"Stand back, Tenbrook. This thing fires real bullets, you know."

Miranda watched the woman's chest heave up and down as she fumed. She was obviously used to giving orders, not taking them.

"My staff will be in any moment. You'll be arrested."

"No, I don't think I'm the one who's going to be arrested."

"Don't be ridiculous."

Miranda wanted to drop the gun and just choke this bitch. Who did she think she was? Then she remembered the recorder on her phone was still on.

Keep her talking. "I think it's ridiculous to think you could get away with what you're doing here. What is it exactly? Test tube babies?"

The woman inhaled dramatically and rolled her eyes. "It's an ingenious process we've developed over decades. It combines genetic engineering, stem cells, and in vitro fertilization. Far too complex for non-scientists to understand."

She could understand murder.

Miranda was about to ask for details when the door opened and a dark-haired woman in scrubs ran in screaming hysterically. "Dr. Tenbrook, Dr. Tenbrook. There are robbers on the floor." That accent.

Yuri barreled in just behind her. "Mama, please don't do this."

The woman saw Miranda's gun and started screaming.

It was enough to distract her. Tenbrook lunged for Miranda, locked onto her wrist like a vice and twisted the weapon away from her until it fell to the floor. Her red lips parted in a vulture like grin.

"Let her go!" It was Parker. With his gun drawn, replacing hers.

"You cannot hurt my mother, Mr. Parker." Yuri grabbed the nurse and the two of them huddled behind a cart.

Tenbrook did as she was told and released Miranda's arm, but her face was as red as her dress with rage. "Parker. You're the other detective my brother hired, I presume. You'll never get away with this. How dare you threaten the chief scientist of a respected research lab?"

Parker laughed just the way Miranda had at the woman's hollow claims. "You're not a research lab. You're a slaughterhouse run by lunatics."

"We do important work. Some of the most important work in our field. We're government funded."

Miranda's jaw dropped. "The government sanctions what you're doing here?"

The doctor parted with a thin, condescending smile. "What the government doesn't know won't hurt them. Our grant writers are very talented. Besides once we have solid success, they'll be throwing funds at us, begging us to supply their armies."

What did she just say?

The nurse, who must have been Yuri's mother, was crying hysterically. "What are you going to do? What is going to happen to us?"

Good question.

Miranda bent down and picked up her gun. "I'll tell you what's going to happen. We're going to call the police. We're going to show them what you have down here. The lab with the Petri dishes, the operating room for organ harvesting, the cremation chamber."

"I have no idea what you're talking about. We're a highly respected research facility. Our work here is profound."

"Profoundly disgusting. Profoundly illegal," Parker said.

Miranda couldn't resist waving her weapon at this arrogant excuse for a scientist. "You're going down, doctor. All of you."

She still wasn't convinced. "You don't know who you're going up against. Our legal staff will destroy you."

"I don't think so."

They had won. It was over. Miranda reached into her pocket for her phone to call Underwood. The sooner this bitch and her staff were arrested and they got those kids out of here, the better.

But just as her fingers touched her cell she heard the doors sweep open once more.

"Drop your weapons," boomed the big, familiar voice.

CHAPTER FIFTY-TWO

Miranda spun around to see the big man in the black UBT shirt with his vest, jeans and cowboy boots. His curly gray hair was disheveled and the nostrils of his wide crooked nose were flared like a charging rhino.

He stood there brandishing a big, black pump-action shotgun. It looked like a Mossberg.

So here was little brother to the rescue. She wished she could have seen through this game earlier.

"I said drop it!" he boomed again.

Far cry from, "the most exciting, the most titillating entertainment experience of your life."

Though she was seething inside Miranda opened her hand and let her gun drop. Beside her she heard Parker's weapon hit the floor and her heart sank.

"Turn around. Put your hands on that wall."

She did as he said. Raised her arms, moved to the nearby wall, pressed her hands on it over her head. She shot Parker a quick look.

His face told her, "Keep your head."

How? she wondered.

"You too, Cannonball."

From the corner of her eye, Miranda watched Yuri raise his big hands and move to the other side of Parker. She also saw the wicked gleam in big sister's eye.

"That's right, Paxton. Now you're going to shoot them one by one."

Mommy has to tell you what to do, doesn't she? Can't think for yourself, can you, Paxton?

The nurse began to shriek. "Do not kill my boy, Dr. Tenbrook. You created him. You saved him."

"Shut up!" The circus owner shouted and the nurse forced herself to muffle her sobs.

Miranda dared to peek over her shoulder again and saw Tenbrook the circus owner glaring at Tenbrook the doctor.

"Why me?" he said to her.

The doctor frowned. "What do you mean, Paxton?"

"Why do I have to do the killing?"

Do we have some sibling rivalry here? Miranda risked a quick glimpse at Parker.

He saw it, too.

Dr. Tenbrook blinked at her brother as if astonished. "It's our agreement, Paxton. Your payment for our generosity."

His thick lip curled. "You never cared about UBT or what I wanted to do with it, did you?"

"Of…of course I cared."

"Lies. It was all lies. You only did it for yourself. You used me, Gloria."

Right on. If he could see through her shenanigans and mind games, maybe there was a chance they'd get out of this alive.

"Paxton, we have to stay focused on the task at hand."

"To hell with your tasks. First you send me cyanide pills so I can take care of the clown who told me he was going to the media about UBT and whatever it is you're doing here."

She knew it, Miranda thought. Tenbrook killed Tupper Magnuson to shut him up. Good time to play dumb. "You killed Tupper?" she dared to ask over her shoulder, as if she were totally astonished. "How?"

The pride beaming on Tenbrook's face was just what she was looking for. "I went over to his trailer with a bottle of wine and offered him a glass. I said it was a toast to reconcile our differences. That was supposed to be the end of it. But then you two detectives showed up. The police thought it was suicide, but you had to keep digging and asking questions."

He raised his shotgun and Miranda's heart began to clamor. The guy was almost as crazy as his sister. Set him off and this scene could turn into the Saint Valentine's Day massacre.

"You should have taken care of them then," Dr. Tenbrook hissed.

"I had to cover my ass since you wouldn't do it," he yelled at her. "I had to use my backup plan."

The doctor's eyes narrowed.

"That's right. I thought ahead. I planted the bottle in Harvey Hackett's rose bushes so it would be discovered. That was why I used the brand he drank. It almost worked. But I didn't know Harvey's brother was a top defense lawyer. He was going to go free, and the police and the detectives were going to figure out everything. So I had to make it look like he committed suicide. The damn drunkard wouldn't take a glass from me. I had to force a mouthful down his ungrateful throat."

A full confession. Good for Harvey for seeing through Tenbrook's lie and trying to fight him off.

Miranda hoped the recorder in her pocket was still going. And that the police would find it if they all ended up a bloody heap on the shiny floor.

There was a long pause. The scientist was recalibrating. She took a step toward her brother and her voice was serene and calm when she spoke. "We've always helped each other, haven't we, Paxton?"

She seemed to have a hypnotic effect on him. Miranda could see he was falling back under her spell.

"Keep your head, Paxton." Parker said calmly, sounding like a therapist treating a volatile patient.

Dr. Tenbrook ignored him. "We have one more task to accomplish."

"What task?" Paxton asked warily.

"Where's the girl?"

The circus owner groaned in frustration. "Dammit, Gloria. I don't know."

"She's out there Paxton. She'll destroy us if we don't find her."

Yuri let out an agonized laugh. "Are you talking about Layla? She is far away and safe from you."

Miranda winced. The cannonball was a loose cannon. She wished he'd kept his mouth shut. Especially when she saw the doctor's red lips twist into a grotesque smile.

"Make them tell us, Paxton. Make them tell us where she is. Shoot one of them."

This time he didn't argue. He wanted Layla as much as his sister. The performer knew what he'd done to Tupper.

"You." He wagged his gun at Miranda. "Turn around."

She did as he said, keeping her hands in the air.

"Where is she?"

"I don't know." She tried to sound convincing, though the tremor in her voice was real. Not that that would buy them much. It didn't.

"You like this detective, Yuri?"

"Do not hurt her, Mr. Tenbrook," the giant whimpered, sounding like one of the kids in the ward.

"If you don't tell me where Layla is, I'm going to shoot her."

"No, Mr. Tenbrook." Yuri began to cry. He'd break any minute.

She took a step in Paxton's direction. Just a step. If she could just get to that Mossberg.

He saw her move and aimed the gun at her chest. "I'm going to do it now, Yuri. One, two…"

Parker turned around, making Miranda's heart constrict with pain. "I'll show you where she is, Tenbrook," he said.

Tenbrook's lip twitched. "Show me?"

"I'll take you there."

The doctor began to pace back and forth, infuriated at her sudden loss of control. "We're not going anywhere. We'll shoot you one by one, if we have to. You'll all end up dead."

"We can't do that, Gloria," Paxton said.

Was he starting to grow a conscious? Or lose his nerve?

"Of course we can," the doctor told him. "We can dispose of the bodies. No one will know."

In the incinerator in the back.

Miranda risked another step toward the circus owner. "Like you dispose of the little kids who don't meet your criteria?"

"What?" Paxton's face twisted with genuine surprise.

Miranda raised a brow. "You don't know what big sis is doing here?"

"She's a scientist. She does important experiments." He glared at her. "What is she talking about, Gloria?"

From the corner of her eye, Miranda watched Parker take a cautious step toward the circus owner while he was distracted. It made her nervous, but she kept her focus on the doctor.

"She doesn't understand, Paxton."

"What is she talking about?" he screeched it this time, demanding an explanation.

The doctor drew in a breath, raised her hands as if that would calm him. "Imagine a world populated with geniuses. People five times as intelligent as anyone now living, five times as strong, with astounding physical dexterity and vibrant health. Think of it, Paxton. People like that could end war, poverty, disease. Every problem that plagues mankind. It's a future almost beyond our comprehension."

"Pretty ironic what you have to do to get there," Miranda muttered.

Paxton pivoted to her, swaying to one side. The side Parker was closing in on. "What do they have to do?"

Might as well spill it all. It was the only chance of breaking the spell his sister had over him.

"They have to manufacture kids in Petri dishes in that lab over there." She pointed to the room at the side. "But the experiments don't work. Layla and Yuri and Dashia were the lucky ones. Most of them end up with horrible defects." She gestured the other way. "Back there are about two dozen kids waiting to be put to sleep because they just didn't make the cut."

Tenbrook's eyes began to glaze over with disbelief. "To…sleep?"

Miranda pressed on as Parker inched closer. "Put to sleep before their organs get harvested and the rest of them goes into the incinerator." She watched Paxton's ruddy face turn pale. "It's right back there. Wanna see it?"

"What?" His glazed eyes went from his sister to Miranda and back again. "I didn't know. I swear to God, I didn't know."

The doctor fisted her hands at her side. Her face turned as red as her dress. "Paxton, you're making too much of this. This woman doesn't know what she's talking about. I'll wager she barely finished high school. She can't understand our work."

"Your work?" He stared at her as if he'd never seen her before. "What exactly is your work? Was this what Tupper Magnuson knew? You're killing kids? No wonder you didn't care about what I had to do to him or to Harvey.

No wonder you don't care if I kill these detectives. When does it stop, Gloria? When?"

"It can't stop, Paxton. Not until we prove what we're doing. We're helping mankind. We're about to produce a strain of the human race far superior to any before it."

"You're crazy."

"Crazy, am I? I'll show you crazy." She began to crouch down. "If you won't do as I say, I'll do it myself." She reached for the pearl handled pistol Miranda had left on the floor.

"You," Paxton boomed in agony. "This is all because of you!" He raised his rifle.

The next few minutes seemed to pass in slow motion.

Miranda saw something flash beside her. And Parker going for Paxton. She crouched and lunged for the doctor.

But she was too late.

"Look out," someone screamed. Maybe the nurse. It sounded like she was underwater.

A loud white blast, a spray of gunshot, rang in her ears like a sonic boom. She felt pain ripple through her body. For a moment she couldn't see anything, couldn't feel anything. Then she heard a muffled sound. Like crying.

Her head buzzing, she raised herself on her hands and looked around.

She was on the floor. Her fingers were bloody. She craned her neck and saw Parker on the floor on top of the whimpering Tenbrook, the Mossberg at his side, staring across the room in horror.

She turned back. Beside her on the floor in a pool of blood lay Tenbrook's sister, lifeless, her face gone. Beyond them Yuri and his mother were holding each other, both of them sobbing in shock.

"You're hurt." Parker was trying to get to her.

She felt a throbbing. She looked down and saw the gunshot spray had grazed her upper arm. Some of the blood on the floor was her own.

Miranda's phone buzzed. Groggily she groped in her pocket with her bloody hand to answer it. The recorder was still running.

"Hello?" she said in a voice that didn't sound like her own.

It was Underwood. "We're at GenaPulse. In the lobby talking to a guard. We saw your car outside, Ms. Steele. What the hell's going on here?"

She sat up, her head clearing, and brushed the hair out of her eyes. "Have them take you to the basement," she said. "There's a mess to clean up here."

"Drop your weapons," boomed the big, familiar voice.

CHAPTER FIFTY-THREE

Miranda stood in her bloody clothes on the front steps of GenaPulse with the piece of cloth Parker had torn off a bed sheet bound around her arm.

As she raised a hand to shield her eyes from the bright morning sun, the first thing she saw was a horde of reporters.

They swarmed around her and Parker and Underwood like flies.

They wanted a story.

Under other circumstances Miranda would have told them all to go to hell and walked off. But this time she took the opportunity to tell them about the children she'd found inside the facility. The ones who now were being put into ambulances and taken to nearby hospitals for treatment.

She described some of the conditions she'd seen, her voice quivering as she watched the expressions on the reporters' faces turn grim.

"These kids need your help," she said into the camera. "The police are setting up a hotline where you can call and pledge donations for the care they'll need."

She swept a glance at Underwood, who looked stunned at her impromptu offer. But the sergeant gave her a nod and told the press they'd release the number to call soon.

"You were magnificent back there," Parker murmured in her ear, as they made their way back to the rental car.

"You mean my speech to the press?"

"I mean everything."

He stopped and turned to her. Then took her in his arms and kissed her as hard as he dared.

She melted into his kiss, grateful for his courage. And that they were all still alive.

They were exhausted, but they swung by the hotel to change, and after Parker gassed up the rental they made the two-hour trek up to Atoka and Sam's brother's ranch.

They needed to bring their client up to speed and to get Yuri back to his family. The police were detaining his mother, but there was talk of an immunity deal if she corroborated all the evidence Miranda and Parker had gathered against GenaPulse. After that, who knew?

As they headed for Oklahoma again, Underwood called to tell them a unit had just found the Director of GenaPulse at home and arrested him. Miranda hoped they'd put him in the cell next to Paxton Tenbrook.

Right now the police were busy shutting the place down, questioning the workers and moving the children to nearby hospitals, some of which Tupper had visited.

Miranda liked to think that would have made him smile.

Underwood also said donations had already started pouring in on the hotline. One of the doctors had told her with treatment, he felt all the rescued children had a shot at a normal life. There had even been enquiries about adoption.

That made Miranda smile even bigger. And think of Mackenzie. She hoped all of these kids would go to a home as good as her own daughter had.

Maybe Texas wasn't so bad after all.

It was nearly noon when they reached the ranch in Atoka.

Sam greeted them at the door with smiles and ushered them inside for lunch. Everyone gathered around a big oak table in a rustic dining room for a hearty country meal of fried chicken, corn on the cob, and homemade biscuits provided by Sam's sister-in-law.

While they ate, Parker explained what had happened, emphasizing Miranda's courage until she wanted to blush. She had to add what Parker did had not been too shabby, either. And they couldn't have even gotten inside if it hadn't been for Yuri.

"You saved them," Layla said to Miranda, reaching across the table to squeeze her hand. "You saved all those children and you stopped the experiments. You gave us our lives back. How can we thank you?"

Miranda didn't know what to say. She looked down at her empty plate, then the spread on the table. "Maybe pass me a piece of that cherry pie?"

When the meal was over, Miranda rose from the table and leaned over to whisper to Parker that she had some things to settle. He gave her an understanding nod and she went for a walk alone with Sam.

CHAPTER FIFTY-FOUR

Miranda strolled silently next to Sam along a dirt path with a quaint hewn fence and a clear narrow creek running beside it. She breathed in the clean country air, glad to be alive. Glad they were all alive.

Sam walked with his head down, hands in his back pockets, the brim of his Stetson hiding his features.

At last he spoke. "Miranda, I had no idea—"

She cut him off. "I know you didn't, Sam."

He grimaced with repulsion. "That horrible lab? All the horrible things they were doing in there? I never would have gotten you involved if I'd known."

"I know. It turned out okay."

"I'm glad. I knew you could take care of things. Just didn't know how bad it would get." The corner of his mouth turned up in a half grin. "Guess you're still ole Kick-Ass Steele."

"Yeah." She had to laugh at that.

They strolled a little farther and Sam took a deep breath. "I'm sorry I put the moves on you, Miranda."

She stopped walking. She didn't know what to say to that.

He turned to her, hands still in his pockets. "Layla threw me over for Tupper. I guess I was on the rebound. I meant what I said. We were good together once."

"Yeah, we were." Breathing in the smell of hay, she stared out at the gently rolling field that stretched beyond the homey ranch house all the way to the horizon where a row of deep green trees stood guard over the land.

She turned her focus back to Sam and studied his expression. She had to tell him what she was thinking. "You knew all along it was Tenbrook who killed Tupper. Didn't you, Sam?"

His cheeks turned a little pink. Avoiding her gaze, he looked down and kicked at the dirt with the toe of his boot. "You are a good detective."

"Yeah, I am."

He raised his palms. "I couldn't prove it. I couldn't even say it out loud. What if I was wrong? I had to have somebody prove it for me. Somebody who knew what they were doing." He dared to look at her. "Somebody like you, Miranda."

"And like Parker," she said firmly.

He tipped his hat back on his head. "Yeah, and like Parker. You two make a hell of a team."

"Thanks."

"And I have to admit…"

"What?"

"You two are pretty much made for each other."

That made her smile. Guess they were.

He put his foot on the rung of the fence and was silent a long moment, staring back at a spot near the barn. Layla and the Vargas had gone out to the paddock with the boys. They were getting two horses ready for them to ride.

He smiled at the scene, longing in his eyes.

"You're in love with her, aren't you?"

His grin grew deeper. "Does it show that much?"

"You are pretty transparent when it comes to your feelings, Sam."

"Guess so."

She had a feeling this time the young performer would love him right back. "What will you do now?"

Sam drew in a slow breath. "Yuri said he'd like to stay on here a few more days. The kids like the horses, and he needs some time for it all to sink in."

"Your brother's good to let them."

He chuckled. "He'll put Yuri to work as a hand, with all his muscles."

"Good idea." But she couldn't see Sam as a full-time rancher. "What then?"

"We'll have to see how Yuri feels about it, but Layla and I have been talking about taking over the circus."

"Under the Big Top?"

His forest green eyes twinkled as he grinned his boyish grin. "We want to form a corporation and run it ourselves."

Her mouth opened in surprise. "That will take some doing."

"We're thinking of asking Harvey's brother to draw up the papers and help us with the details."

She looked at him, feeling a surge of admiration. "Big plans."

"I know. But we all love the life so much, I know we can make it work. We're going to organize as a charity and do shows for the children in the local hospitals, the way Tupper did. Hey, wouldn't it be great if we could do some of his bits for the kids you rescued?"

She had to smile at the idea that ole Yosemite Sam had gone from reckless cowboy to businessman. A little hard to believe, but she had a feeling he'd make it. After all, he had a heart of gold.

"I think that would be downright wonderful."

After watching the kids ride a couple more hours they said goodbye to Sam and Layla and the Vargas, thanked Sam's brother and sister-in-law for the hospitality and headed back to Dallas in the rental car.

As they drove through the miles of vast, flat green and brown Texas fields, Miranda reached over and took Parker's hand. "I want to say something."

She felt him tense. "Oh?"

Time for some more truth.

"I hate what you had to go through on this case, Parker. I mean, the things I let Sam get away with." She'd caused him pain and she was angry with herself for it.

He didn't reply, only nodded, his eyes on the road.

"I guess I was sucked in by the memory of what I once felt. It was the only good thing that happened to me, relationship-wise—until you came along. That means something. I guess it always will."

"Of course."

She turned to face him in her seat. "But it doesn't mean it's real. Those feelings are just memories. Days gone by that will never come again. They might be pretty and enticing, but in reality they're as fleeting as a circus act."

He nodded again.

She looked down at his strong hand. Traced a line over his knuckles with her finger. "What you and I have together, Parker, our lives, our work. It's not a fantasy world and it's not always pretty. But it's the life I want."

At last he broke a smile. But he remained silent.

She could see from the lines on his face he was taking in her words, processing them in his heart.

She eyed the strong muscular frame that had been beside her through so many cases. The hands that had saved her life any number of times. The ruggedly handsome face she'd been waking up to for almost a year now, and her heart constricted with unbelievable emotion. No one meant to her what Parker did. No one could ever come close.

"It's you I want, Parker. It's you I love." Her next words came out in a whisper. "I chose you. And I will always choose you."

Finally he lifted her hand to his lips and kissed her fingers. "I'm so glad you did, Miranda. So very glad."

CHAPTER FIFTY-FIVE

They made it back home in time for the Atlanta Open.

After a long flight and a good night's rest, the next morning Miranda sat beside Parker under the high-domed skating center in the front row seats Fanuzzi had gotten them.

In a fairylike silver outfit, her dark ponytail flowing behind her, Wendy Van Aarle slid gracefully across the ice in time to the classy music she'd chosen. Miranda's heart swelled as she realized how well the girl she'd once thought was her daughter was performing. Her jumps were high and flawless, her crossovers and sit spins were perfect.

Miranda felt a squeeze on her hand and her heart swelled again.

Mackenzie Chatham, her real daughter, sat beside her all smiles. "Isn't she great? She's going to win." Mackenzie had had a big part in Wendy's training.

Miranda nodded. "I think she just might." She was so proud of both her girls.

As she watched Wendy execute another perfect leap, Miranda spotted a young man standing beside the rink. He had longish, curly dark hair and his plaid shirt hung over a pair of worn jeans and sneakers in a typical teen look. As everyone applauded, he turned his head and shot Mackenzie a flirty grin.

She acknowledged him but turned her head to concentrate on Wendy with a casual air.

Miranda blinked. Was this the boy from biology class Mackenzie had told her about? Was she getting serious about him? And what would Miranda do if Mackenzie wanted to introduce them later? Deciding she'd figure it out when the time came, Miranda focused on the conversation around her.

Parker was chatting with the Van Aarles and the Chathams who were seated beside him.

Behind Miranda, Fanuzzi's Brooklyn accent crackled in her ears while she, their bubbly blond friend Coco, and Parker's daughter Gen chatted over plans for the anniversary party. At the end of the row Becker sat fiddling with his e-pad thingy, thick brows knitted, his big nose buried in the screen. He was really into that stuff, wasn't he?

But her coworker wasn't completely oblivious to his surroundings. He managed to keep his eye on what was going on in the rink and when they announced the winners, he cheered louder than anyone.

Wendy placed first.

They were standing around near the boards, waiting for the winner to appear and making celebration plans. The boy who'd smiled at Mackenzie seemed to have disappeared. As she was enjoying the relief of that realization, Miranda felt her cell buzz.

She pulled the phone out of her pocket and stepped away from the group to take the call, wondering who it was.

It was a text message. She looked down at the screen and her blood froze in her veins.

I know what you are.

Her throat constricted. For a long moment she couldn't breathe. This was the third message she'd gotten like this. Anonymous. No email address. She'd dismissed the other two as pranks. But three?

I know who you are.

I know where you are.

And now, *I know what you are.*

And they always came at the same time. Right after getting home from a case. After being on the news.

She glanced over at Parker who was having an intense discussion with Mackenzie, no doubt about the fine art of training skaters.

Things were so good right now. His wounds were healing. Wendy had just won this tournament. They were closer than ever. If she told him about these messages he'd worry himself sick. There was still a chance they could be nothing.

She scanned the group of her friends and family and her gaze landed on Becker. The newly hatched computer geek.

She strolled over to him, gave him a punch on the arm.

"Hey, watch it, Steele," he teased.

"I need a word with you." She nodded to the glass doors that led outside.

When they were on the sidewalk, he turned to her, frowning. "What's up?"

"I need a favor."

"Okay."

She held out her phone, showed him the message.

His brow furrowed in a deep frown of concern. "What's this, Steele?"

"I don't know. I've been getting texts like this lately. Every time I come home from a case." She explained the details, what little she had. "Can you find out who this is?"

"Who's sending them?"

"Yeah." She'd figure out the next step once she knew that information.

He scratched his head. "Maybe. I can give it my best shot."

She let out a breath of relief. Becker was good. He'd figure it out. "Thanks."

He put the phone in his pocket. "I'll get you a replacement first thing Monday."

"Thanks," she said again as she reached for the door to go back inside. "Oh, and Becker."

"Yeah?"

"Don't let anyone know about this little project."

He squinted at her. "Not even Parker?"

"Especially not Parker."

He seemed a little apprehensive but friendship was friendship. "Whatever you say, Steele. Mum's the word." And he made the locking his lips gesture.

They stepped back inside and found that Wendy had emerged from the dressing room and everyone was applauding and cheering and hugging her. It looked like the party had already started.

Miranda worked her way over to Parker's side. He beamed at her as he slipped one arm around her and the other around Wendy and declared them both winners.

She smiled up at his handsome face, her heart full of love for him.

They had just closed down a secret lab and saved the lives of over two dozen kids. She had family and friends and people who loved her. Life, as they say, was good.

She returned Parker's hug. There was nothing to worry about. Nothing at all.

Deep in her heart she knew everything was going to be just fine.

THE END

ABOUT THE AUTHOR

Writing fiction for over fifteen years, Linsey Lanier has authored more than two dozen novels and short stories, including the popular Miranda's Rights Mystery series. She writes romantic suspense, mysteries, and thrillers with a dash of sass.

She is a member of Romance Writers of America, the Kiss of Death chapter, and Private Eye Writers of America. Her books have been nominated in several RWA-sponsored contests.

In her spare time, Linsey enjoys watching crime shows with her husband and trying to figure out "who-dun-it." But her favorite activity is writing and creating entertaining new stories for her readers.

She's always working on a new book, currently books in the new Miranda and Parker Mystery series (a continuation of the Miranda's Rights Mystery series). For alerts on her latest releases join Linsey's mailing list at linseylanier.com.

For more of Linsey's books, visit **www.felicitybooks.com** or check out her website at **www.linseylanier.com**

Edited by

Editing for You

Donna Rich

Gilly Wright
www.gillywright.com